# *Truth or Dare*

Ethan quickly scanned the night shadows again. Was Gil bluffing? Could he be alone, and just *saying* he had partners out there in the darkness, just itching to kill him and make away with the gold shipment? One thing had always been certain about Gil Stark—he was never wedded to the truth.

"What's it going to be?" asked Gil.

Ethan swung the scattergun around and pulled one trigger, blasting a load of buckshot into the ground at Gil's feet. He was close enough to blow a hole clean through Gil, even in the dark, but in spite of everything he simply couldn't bring himself to kill someone who had been his only friend for so many years.

Gil let out a yelp of surprise and jumped backward, twisting his body away instinctively. The muzzle flash was blinding, the discharge of the scattergun deafening — and a quick flurry of gunfire from the woods suddenly added to the din.

When the shooting started, Ethan knew that Gil was telling the truth about having partners. He threw himself onto the ground as bullets began to fly.

St. Martin's Paperbacks Titles
by Jason Manning

# GUNMASTER

# GUN JUSTICE

# THE OUTLAW TRAIL

# FRONTIER ROAD

## JASON MANNING

St. Martin's Paperbacks

FRONTIER ROAD

Copyright © 2002 by Jason Manning.

ISBN: 0-312-98202-X

Printed in the United States of America

St. Martin's Paperbacks edition / May 2002

St. Martin's Paperbacks are published by St. Martin's Press, 175 Fifth Avenue, New York, NY 10010.

10  9  8  7  6  5  4  3  2  1

# PART I

# CHAPTER ONE

"How do you think she'll take the bad news, Ethan?"

Ethan Payne shot a look of surprise in Gil Stark's direction. His friend's comment, coming as it did after a long stretch of silence, was startling. Ethan had been deep in thought, as he supposed Gil had been, and for the last mile or so not a word had passed between them; the only sound being the shuffling of their feet—Ethan's bare and Gil's booted—in the yellow dust of the old wagon trace that followed the Rock River. That, and the whir of grasshoppers in the tall brown grass on either side of the trace and, of course, the ever-present murmur of the rowdy river, all sounds so commonplace that Ethan would not have paid them any heed even if he *hadn't* been so pensive and pre-occupied. In fact, he'd almost forgotten that Gil was at his side. Usually he came alone to his Sunday rendezvous with Lilah Webster.

"She'll take it just like a woman, I guess," replied Ethan with a shrug of feigned indifference. He tried to sound as though he didn't care all that much *how* Lilah took the news he was bringing her, but he wasn't sure how well he succeeded. In fact, he did care. He wasn't indifferent at all. He had been worrying about how he would tell Lilah and how she would react ever since he and Gil had made up their minds. That had been a couple of days ago. A couple of days so filled with anxiety, accompanied by nights of constant tossing and turning, that it seemed to Ethan like a month of Sundays had passed since the big decision had been made.

"Yeah," said Gil, nodding. "Women are like the weather. If you know what to look for you can tell what's coming, pretty much all the time."

As he nodded too, Ethan threw a sidelong glance at his friend. Gil lived in town, and for over a year now he'd worked diligently to convince Ethan that he had made love to Becky Shriver, and even before this had (allegedly) happened, Gil had acted like he was experienced in the ways of the gentler sex. But Ethan didn't believe Gil had done *that* with Becky. He wasn't sure why he didn't believe it. Rumor was that Becky had done it with a good many of Roan's Prairie's boys. Ethan was willing to admit, if only to himself, that maybe he just didn't *want* to believe that Gil had done *that* with a girl before Ethan had. Whatever the case, he was fairly certain that Gil didn't know any more about what women thought, or why they acted in the peculiar ways that they did, than he himself knew. And he knew next to nothing, even though he'd spent so much time with Lilah these past few years. Why, he had known her since way back—back when his mother and father had first come to this part of Illinois. He'd been ten years old at the time, and steadfast in his conviction that all girls were just nuisances.

Ethan still marveled at how abruptly his opinion of girls—and Lilah in particular—had changed only a couple of years ago. But ever since that changing time he and Lilah had spent just about all their free time together. He was sixteen now, she a year younger, less a month, and most of the people in and around Roan's Prairie assumed that one day Ethan Payne and Lilah Webster would be married. Ethan had always thought so, too. Now, though, he wasn't quite so sure. That all depended on how Lilah would react to the news he was carrying with him today. And, in spite of his pretense of worldly wisdom where women were concerned, he had absolutely no idea what her reaction would be.

"There she is," said Gil, stopping suddenly.

Ethan stopped, too. He saw the old oak tree, the one that marked the rendezvous point. The one with the big limb shaped likc a sideways S extending out over the river. The tree had been struck by lightning many years ago, before Ethan had ever laid eyes on it, maybe even before he'd been born, so that it grew now to the sides rather than upward. A bolt of lightning was enough to kill most trees but the old oak was made of stern stuff. It was hard to kill a tree like that. Lilah had once told him that she thought their love for each other was like the oak—that nothing could destroy it. Ethan found himself at this moment hoping fervently that she was right.

He did not see her at first, but then Gil asked what she was doing in the river, and then Ethan spotted her. She was wading in the shallows. He could see only her shoulders and head, because the tall reeds growing profusely along the bank blocked the rest of her from his view. She was looking down into the water and had not yet seen him or Gil. Ethan thought he knew what she was looking for. A heart-shaped stone, worked smooth by the river. It was something she'd been in search of for quite some time now. Why did women put so much stock in such things? Ethan shrugged.

"Now that's foolish, if you ask me," said Gil.

"What is?" For an instant Ethan thought his friend was referring to Lilah's hunt for the heart-shaped stone, but then realized there was no way Gil could know about that.

"That's a dangerous river," replied Gil, frowning. "Lots of folks have drowned in it. Why, don't you remember, Ethan? Ike's little sister died in that river just last summer. Remember?"

"Lilah is a good swimmer. She won't drown."

"She is?" Gil peered at Ethan—and a wicked, lopsided grin curved his lips. "Hey, have you and her been skinny-dipping here? Is that why you come out here every Sunday, rain or shine?"

"Shut up, Gil." Ethan was dismayed to feel his cheeks getting hot.

Gil laughed. "You're blushing like a schoolgirl after a first kiss. So it must be true! You've been skinny-dipping with Lilah Webster. I bet that isn't all you've been doing with her, either." He nudged Ethan with a bony elbow, and winked.

"I said shut up," snapped Ethan. It was true that he and Lilah had gone skinny-dipping a time or two, but he wasn't about to admit it, because he knew that such an admission would inevitably lead to more questions, and maybe more assumptions on Gil's part. It was only natural for Gil to think that skinny-dipping had been a mere prelude to something else. This wasn't the case, but it would be an uphill battle trying to convince him otherwise. Besides, Ethan knew that even if he could convince Gil that he and Lilah had never done it, he would then be faced with the equally daunting—and embarrassing—task of explaining why no lovemaking had taken place. Far better to put a halt to the entire business before it progressed any further.

Gil was grinning at him, a speck of devilry dancing in his dark eyes. "Well, all I know is, if I'm ever lucky enough to go skinny-dipping with Lilah Webster, swimming isn't all we'd do."

Ethan turned on him, fists clenched, anger flaring. When he got mad he tended to get tongue-tied. "Damn it, Gil, you better not . . . I ought to . . . If you don't . . ." Completely disgusted with himself, Ethan gave up trying to articulate a warning. "God, just shut your trap, Gil!"

Gil stifled a laugh, and opted for practicing mercy. "Hey, I didn't mean anything by it. I'm just saying if I was you, I'd—"

"You're not me."

"Oh, I know that," said Gil sublimely. "I'm much better looking than you, for one thing. And I'm much better with words, and the right words make all the difference where women are concerned."

He was making a joke of it, trying to improve Ethan's frame of mind. But Ethan wasn't amused. Gil *was* better looking than him. Where Ethan was tall and lanky and graceless in his movements, Gil was broad-shouldered, strong, and prone to a confident swagger. Ethan's features included high, prominent cheekbones, gaunt cheeks, a jutting chin, rebellious black hair, and eyes that were swamp-mud brown. Gil, on the other hand, had very even features and wavy brown hair that (he said) the girls loved to run their fingers through. And then there was that crooked buccaneer's smile. Gil was more articulate, too, and a good bit smarter, as he'd read a lot more books. Ethan's schooling had been hit and miss—and more the latter than the former, especially since his mother's death two years before. His father had never put much stock in book-learning, even in the best of times, and these days he didn't seem to care if Ethan got an education or not, just as he didn't seem to care about anything. Ethan didn't care that much, either—except that by going to school he'd been able to spend a lot of time gazing across the schoolhouse at Lilah. But there was always a lot of work that needed doing on the farm, so his attendance had been sporadic. Now, at sixteen, he was almost too old for schooling, anyway.

"I know how you talk about Becky and some of the other girls in town," said Ethan curtly. "And you . . . you just better be careful what you say about Lilah, unless you want to get into a scrape with me."

"I don't want to fight you, Ethan, especially over a girl."

"No, you sure don't."

They'd fought before—even best friends would fight on occasion, and Ethan always prevailed. It was his nature to fight with a ruthless detachment, fearlessly, seemingly oblivious to pain, indifferent to the damage he sustained. Some boys—and men, too—fought defensively, their first priority self-protection; Ethan fought with one objective in mind—to deliver the maximum amount of suffering to his adversary. Though lanky and on the thin side, his body was whipcord tough, honed by a lifetime behind a plow. However hurt he came out of a scrape, he knew he would heal. As for the pain—he also knew how to live through physical pain. It always faded, given enough time.

He wasn't so sure about living through the pain that inhabited his heart at this moment, however. It was caused by the sudden realization that this could be the last time he would meet Lilah here, at their rendezvous point.

"Well, go on," urged Gil. "Go tell her. I'll wait right here. What are you waiting for? Don't beat around the bush, now. Just tell her straight out. That's always the best way."

"The best way," said Ethan crossly. "How would you know?"

There was that disarming, crooked grin again, the one that made it difficult to tell if Gil Stark was serious in what he'd said, or was about to say. "Why, I know because I've already said my farewells to all the pretty girls of Roan's Prairie. I don't need to tell you how heartbroken they were, either."

Ethan shook his head. Looking in the direction of the river, he realized that Lilah was still unaware of their presence, so consumed was she in her search for the heart-shaped river stone. He was nearly overcome by the cowardly urge to turn and run. It would be easier just to leave without telling her. He could write her a letter instead. He'd never actually written a letter before, but he could manage it somehow. Yet leaving without saying goodbye would hurt her, and just the leaving in and of itself would hurt her badly enough. So, much as he might want to take the easy way out, he just couldn't.

"Oh, Lord," sighed Gil. "You've got a bad case of cold feet. I was afraid this might happen. That's why I came along. Look, you can't just run out on her, Ethan. It just isn't a fitting thing to do. And besides, you'd regret it all the rest of your days."

Gil *was* smarter. It wasn't that Ethan didn't know in his heart everything that Gil had just told him. But his friend had a knack for effortlessly putting into words the jumble of emotions that he experienced.

"I'm going already," said Ethan, with the exasperated tone of someone being prodded, needlessly, to do what he had every intention of doing anyway.

He proceeded down the trace for a spell, then cut through the tall, summer-dry grass to the river's edge, and as he came to the rim of the embankment Lilah looked up and saw him for the first time. She smiled, that smile that so often before had warmed his heart. But now for some reason it *broke* his heart instead. For an instant time stood still, and his mind's eye captured the image of her, standing there knee-deep in the river, holding up her plain blue cotton dress to keep it as dry as possible, so that he could see her wet thighs glisten, her copper-colored hair windswept into a veil for her bright blue eyes, and all this set against the backdrop of the high hot sun's light scintillating off the lively surface of the river. He knew this was an image that would stay with him forever, no matter what the fates held in store for him. It would never fade. And it was an image that made Ethan wonder if he wasn't a lunatic for even thinking about leaving. Nauseated by a fresh dose of indecision, he stood there with a stricken look on his face.

"What is it, Ethan?" she asked with that soft, melodic, throaty voice that was too mature for a mere fifteen-year-old girl, but that suited her perfectly nonetheless, since in many ways Lilah Webster was wiser than her years. "What's the matter?" The smile began to disintegrate, but she rescued it, bravely kept it flying at half mast.

He had rehearsed his speech fifty times if he'd done it once since reaching the decision to go, but here, now, abruptly, he couldn't recall a single word of what he had planned to say.

"Gil and I," he said, with trepidation. "Well, we've been talking it over and, well, he . . . I mean we . . . we've decided . . . decided to . . ."

"Decided to go to California," she said, very calmly.

"Yes." He had to look away from her steady, disapproving gaze and the distinctly disappointed look on her face. "But I'll be back, Lilah. Soon as I strike it rich I'll be back."

"What makes you so sure you'll strike it rich in California? Not everyone who goes there finds gold, you know. Remember Joseph Griggs? He owned the farm up the road from our place. He left his wife and children and went to California a year and a half ago. He told my father that he was going to come back a wealthy man. But when he came back a month ago he wasn't wealthy. He was broke. Mr. Felder at the bank had been obliged to take Mr. Griggs's farm because Mr. Griggs couldn't repay the money he had borrowed so that he could supply his trip, and provide for his family while he was gone. And his wife took their children and went back to California, where her folks live. Just this morning, after Sunday service, my father told Mr. Felder that he was afraid Mr. Griggs might take his own life he was so despondent. Mr. Felder said he hoped that wouldn't happen, but there was nothing much anyone could do if it did, and that Mr. Griggs had been a fool for going to California."

"Your father agreed with that, I reckon. You think I'm a fool, Lilah?"

Her expression softened and she gave her head a little shake, pushing tendrils of copper hair away from her eyes. "No. No, I do not think you're a fool, Ethan. I think Gil Stark is a fool, though. In fact, I always have thought so. And he's always getting you into trouble. But nothing to match this."

"Gil isn't twisting my arm. I'm going of my own free will. I'm going for you, too, Lilah. Well, for you and me. For us. I don't know Mr. Griggs's story, but Gil says that ever since they found gold at Sutter's Mill two years ago, plenty of men have gotten rich."

"One day you'll find out that a lot of things Gil says aren't true." She shuddered. Even though the sun was hot on her shoulders, she'd been chilled by standing too long in the river. Wading across the shallows, she held out her hand and Ethan took it and pulled her up onto the embankment.

"Didn't find your stone?" he asked, thinking he might be able to change the subject.

She shook her head. "I guess now I can stop looking."

For a reason he could not fully comprehend, Ethan was particularly hurt by that comment. "How come?" he asked, even though he had a hunch this was a question he would have been a lot better off not asking.

"Because I didn't want it for myself, Ethan. I wanted to give it to you as a symbol of my . . . Oh, never mind. Here. Help me up into the tree."

He put his big strong hands around her slender waist and lifted her, effortlessly, into the curve of the limb that reached out across the river. Sitting there, Lilah could slide her feet through the tops of the riverside cattails.

"I really am coming back, Lilah," he said in words as earnestly spoken as any that had passed his lips. "And I *am* going to strike it rich. And then . . . And then I'll ask your father for your hand in marriage, when I have enough money to take care of you the way you deserve."

Lilah sighed. "You don't need money to take care of me. You have strong hands and a good and faithful heart. Those, and your love for me, that's all it will take."

Ethan shook his head adamantly. "No, I want nice things for you. A big house. A carriage to ride around in. A servant to wait on you, just like the Queen of Egypt got waited on. You won't ever want for anything if I have my way."

"I'll be wanting you all the time you're gone. Oh, Ethan." Suddenly she was close to tears, and the sight both shocked and pained him. "You might be gone for years.

You might *never* come back. Then what will I do?"

"Just say you'll wait two years for me, Lilah." He took her hand in his, held it tightly. "That's all I ask. Two years. I'll try to write—but even if you don't hear from me, please just wait that long."

"I'll wait forever if I have to," she said, and it was hardly more than a whisper.

"Promise me."

She wrapped her long legs around him, her knees tucked under his arms, her ankles crossed in the small of his back, and she bent low to kiss him firmly on the lips, and her red hair, smelling like flowers and sunlight, fell across his face.

"I promise," she said as their lips parted.

Ethan put a hand on her thigh. "Lilah, I . . ."

"No, you'd better get going." She released him. "Gil is waiting on you." She was looking beyond him now, toward the spot along the old wagon trace where he had left Gil Stark. "When are you leaving?"

"Tonight, I reckon."

Lilah nodded. She'd rediscovered that valiant smile, but a tear escaped and put the lie to it. She wiped furiously at her cheek with the back of a hand. "The sooner you go, the sooner you'll be able to come back to me."

"I wish you'd sound like you really believed I *will* come back."

She picked her words carefully. "I believe you mean to," she said at last.

# CHAPTER TWO

Ethan and Gil planned to leave at night, to steal away like thieves for the simple reason that they *knew* their parents would try to stop them. Gil's mother would stand opposed to their venture because, ever since her oldest son had died of some never-diagnosed malady several years ago, she had begun to cling even more tightly to Gil as her only surviving child than she had in the past. This motherly smothering was a secondary reason behind Gil's desire to go to California—the primary motivation being to get rich, of course. Gil's father would disapprove because he loved his wife and was solicitous of her happiness—and Gil's leaving would break her heart. And also because his lifelong dream had been to start a thriving business that he could hand down to his progeny when the time for the handing-down came along.

Gabriel Stark's mercantile was *the* store in Roan's Prairie. He carried everything the thirty-odd families that lived in the area could possibly want. It wasn't the first store he had started—there had been one back in Kentucky, but that one had failed because Stark made the mistake of entering into a partnership with a man who turned out to be as crooked as a dog's hind leg. But the Roan's Prairie store was a success, and Stark was proud of his accomplishment.

Gil, though, didn't want to be a shopkeeper. In fact, he'd told Ethan—told him once if he'd told him a hundred times—that he couldn't think of any fate worse than being an apron-wearing store clerk peddling calico and crackers. Where was the adventure in that? Well, maybe there was one thing worse, Gil would add, always donning that disarmingly crooked smile. Being a farmer. "No offense, Ethan," he would say, even after he learned that Ethan wasn't going to be offended by a sentiment he shared wholeheartedly.

Ethan had to steal away because not only would his father forbid him to go, but also would go to almost any length, including violence, to detain him. Abner Payne was prone to violence, being an angry, bitter, and disappointed man who felt as though life had been unfair to him ever since he was old enough to dwell on the inequities inherent in human existence. He would not try to stop Ethan from going because he loved his son, but rather because he needed someone to do the work on the farm that he no longer had the heart to do, now that his wife had been taken from him. Ethan thought there was another reason too— because Abner did not want to be alone. Misery loved company, after all.

Parting company with Gil—they agreed to meet at midnight where the road to Fulton crossed Blood Creek— Ethan headed home with the afternoon sun behind him, so that it cast his gangly shadow in front of him. He was bemused by the fact that he was following his own shadow, as though the shadow was going home of its own volition, dragging him along, with him less than willing to go but powerless not to. Ever since the death of his mother he had hated going home, had often given serious consideration to running away, and probably would have, he thought, but for his desire to be near Lilah. For some months this desire had prompted him to turn a deaf ear to Gil's entreaties regarding the fame and fortune that waited them in California. Until, that is, Gil had shown him how his going to California would be the best thing he could do for Lilah. "You don't want her to end up like your momma, Ethan," Gil had said. "Working her fingers to the bone, breaking her back, breaking her *health* too, just to scratch out a living on that patch of poor ground."

No, he didn't want that. The farm wasn't "poor ground," really. That Abner Payne was an indifferent farmer was closer to the truth. Some people were doomed to have bad luck their whole lives, and Abner Payne seemed to be one of them. He couldn't make anything work for him, even when by rights it should have. After a while, you just stopped trying, stopped caring whether an enterprise panned out or not. Regardless of this, though, Ethan had figured Gil was right—if he truly loved Lilah and wanted to demonstrate his commitment to her happiness, he couldn't very well doom her to the life of hardship and misfortune that, as far as he could tell, was the fate of most farmers' wives. The cruel irony of it all, that to do right by Lilah he had to leave her for a year, or maybe two, was not lost on him. But he took it in stride. Abner Payne's son would know all about life's cruel ironies.

It was a four-mile walk east from the riverside rendezvous to the Payne farm, which lay almost due south of town, across prairie untouched by plow and stands of timber—usually in the low places close by running water—untouched by the axe. In 1850 this was still frontier. In Ethan's lifetime there had been Indian wars in this part of the country. The Black Hawk uprising was recent history, and not too long ago the Sioux had been contesting the white man's relentless westward progress in their lands to the north. The Mississippi River was a day's wagon ride to the west, and beyond the river lay a frontier even wilder. There were some homesteads scattered along the Rock River, but Ethan avoided them. He wished he could avoid his father's farm.

Abner Payne had never wanted to be a farmer, though his father had been, and his father's father before him, too. So the notion that the farm was something of value that he could proudly wish to pass down to his son had not, as far as Ethan knew, ever crossed his mind. But Abner had never seen a way out of farming. He lacked that love of the land most good farmers possessed; he did not derive an iota of satisfaction from making things grow by the sweat of his brow. He had tried, but his heart had never been in it. And nowadays he didn't even try, relying on his son to do what had to be done so that they could at least survive, all the while seeking solace in corn liquor he bought from a hundred-year-old runaway slave who had a still a few miles away.

As he drew near his destination, Ethan could no longer avoid thinking about his father and the farm and the details of escaping both, as he had tried to do all the way from the rendezvous place with musings on shadows and such. It was the middle of the afternoon, and that meant Abner Payne was, in all likelihood, well and truly steeped in corn liquor. Ethan was of half a mind to settle down in the timber that bordered the forty acres of spring-planted corn and wait for nightfall, confident that by dark his father would probably be deep in a likkered-up stupor. But he decided he didn't have the patience to wait for several hours in the woods. Not today. So he steeled himself and proceeded, hoping he would be clever enough to conceal from his father that something very momentous was afoot—hoping, too, that in the event he wasn't clever enough that Abner Payne would be just too drunk to notice.

He passed through the strip of timber and crossed the cornfield, the stalks at shoulder height, and he figured that since he would not be here to harvest the corn it would not be harvested at all. Not much of anything would get done here after he was gone. And then what would become of his father? Ethan tried to block that train of thought from entering his mind. He was burdened with enough guilt already because he knew he had hurt Lilah with the news of his plans.

The cabin was in view now. From a distance it did not look as derelict as Ethan knew it to be. Last winter's blustery winds had dislodged some of the roof shingles, so that now, when a hard rain came, the roof leaked in several places. The door was coming off its hinges. The walls needed re-chinking. A number of planks on the porch were rotting away, and one had broken in two under Abner's weight just last week. Ethan recalled how his father had cursed the house as though it were a living thing that was conspiring against him, when in fact it had been his own fault for letting the cabin fall into such disrepair. Only as one got closer did the accumulative effect of all these structural shortcomings become apparent. Eventually one would be able to tell from a greater distance that the cabin was a derelict—just like the dreams of its owner.

Ethan slowed as he drew nearer the cabin. When his father was drunk there was no telling what he might do. Once he had staggered out of the cabin and fired his shotgun, both barrels, shouting incoherently. Later he explained that he'd gotten hold of some bad whiskey and it had made him loco, so that he'd thought the cabin was under attack by a host of scarlet, fork-tailed demons. Fortunately, the recoil from a double-barreled blast of buckshot had thrown him backward, and he had fallen, striking his head against the wall of the cabin, which rendered him unconscious. When he came to forty-eight hours or so later, he swore he would murder the old black man who had sold him the bad whiskey, but Ethan hadn't taken the threat seriously. Abner Payne had an arrangement with the old black; he got three jugs of corn liquor every fortnight in exchange for his entire corn crop. It was a good deal for the old black, and for a drunkard like Abner, too—but it meant that nearly all the farm's livestock had to be sold, over time, so that staples like coffee and sugar and flour could be purchased at Gabriel Stark's store in Roan's Prairie, Gabriel being too astute a businessman these days to extend credit to a man like Abner Payne. These days the only stock left in the place were some chickens, a milk cow, and a plow mare. Abner wasn't about to kill the old runaway slave, Ethan figured, since if he did, and got away with it (which wasn't that hard to do if you killed a black man) he'd be faced with the prospect of having to pay hard money for his liquor from then on. That wasn't easy to do when all you had in your pockets was dust.

Napoleon, the old one-eyed hound, was sprawled on the porch, and scarcely lifted his head at the sound of Ethan's approach. His big black nose twitched, and then his heavy tail began to thump lethargically against the rotting planks. Napoleon had lost his eye to a cougar years ago. In the old days Abner had gone hunting several times a week with Napoleon, usually returning with something for the cook pot. Nowadays, though, he seldom went hunting. Napoleon was old and stiff and that encounter with the cougar had taken the spirit right out of him. And Abner wasn't usually sober enough to make a shot count. Hunting was Ethan's responsibility now. He didn't mind, as it meant he could get away from the farm more often. He was a good shot, too—nine times out of ten he came back with fresh meat for the table.

Ethan paused to bend down and scratch Napoleon's belly. The old hound groaned with pleasure. Stepping over the prostrate dog, Ethan went to the door, pulled the rope latch, and lifted at the same time that he opened the door, so that it would not make too much noise on its loose hinges. Sticking his head in, he saw his father sitting at the table with his head down, chin on chest, an arm curled around a jug of corn liquor on the table, the other dangling, blunt dirty fingers nearly brushing the puncheon floor. He was snoring. Ethan breathed a sigh of relief. With any luck his father would sleep right through the night.

He slipped outside, closing the door as quietly as possible. Going to the ramshackle barn, he gave the plow mare some fodder. He fed the chickens, too. He milked the cow. For once he didn't mind doing these chores, and, strangely, he felt sad doing them for what would be the last time. He wondered what would happen to the old cow, and to the mare. It all depended, he supposed, on what happened to his father. This was a consideration he could no longer ignore.

Abner Payne had always been a stern father, strict and unforgiving. His treatment of Ethan would have been harsh all along but for the fact that his wife had tempered it with her gentle nature. Since her passing, though, Abner's attitude toward his son varied from seeming indifference to a kind of gruff civility. And sometimes Ethan got the impression that his father resented him, though he couldn't figure out why that would be so. Ethan supposed he would never know now that he was leaving, for he did not expect to see his father ever again.

And yet, in spite of the way his father often treated him, Ethan felt stabbing remorse for what he was about to do. Without his sweat and toil the farm would fall into complete ruin. And when that happened, how would Abner Payne survive? He had few friends, having lived in self-imposed isolation these past few years. He had no family that Ethan knew of—at least he had never spoken of any, and none had ever come visiting, so that these days Ethan assumed he had no other relatives, distant or otherwise, left alive.

"Your pa can take care of himself if he has to," Gil had said. "Thing is, he doesn't have to, long as you're around to do everything for him. Shoot, Ethan, you leaving might be the best thing for him. Might force him to sober up a little and start fending for himself again. And if not, well, the sooner you get to California the sooner you can send him a poke full of gold nuggets the size of walnuts. At least then he could afford a better grade of whiskey."

Ethan hadn't liked the way Gil talked about his father, but it was the general consensus around Roan's Prairie that Abner Payne was a worthless, drunken wreck of a man, shattered on the rocks of his grief, inexorably dismantled over time by corn liquor. And Ethan couldn't deny any of that.

Returning to the cabin, Ethan sat down beside Napoleon

on the rotting porch and watched the sun set. Right before it got dark he cat-footed inside and lit a tallow candle. By its uncertain light he stuffed his one extra shirt and his only pair of shoes into a burlap sack. A bar of lye soap and some dried venison wrapped in a scrap of oilskin went into the sack as well. He moved to the old bureau that had once been his mother's. Though scarred and with a drawer out of kilter, it was the only piece of decent furniture they'd ever had. And in its top drawer was a bowie knife in a leather sheath. His mother had given it to him for his fourteenth birthday—just a month before she got sick. It was his prized possession, and he paused to pull the knife partially from the sheath to admire the way the sharp, heavy, perfectly balanced blade gleamed in the candle's anemic glow.

"What're you doing with that pig sticker, boy?"

His father's gravelly, whiskey-thickened voice made Ethan jump. He whirled to see Abner Payne laboriously lifting his head from the table, squinting as he tried to focus his vision.

"Answer me," growled Abner, his words slurred. "Maybe you're coming to murder your old man so's you can claim your inheritance." His lips twisted into a bitter grin, and he began to chuckle, and the chuckle quickly deteriorated into a hacking cough, and Abner groped for the jug and drowned the cough with corn liquor, gulping it down like water.

"No," said Ethan gravely. His heart seemed to be hammering wildly against his rib cage. "I'm just taking it with me."

"Taking it with you." Abner nodded absently. "Taking it with you." His bushy eyebrows came together, setting deep furrows into his brow as he tried to plumb the meaning of those words. "Taking it with you where?"

"To California."

Abner stared at the jug of corn liquor, not moving—and after a full minute had passed Ethan began to wonder if his father was still conscious. His eyes were open, but he seemed petrified, as inanimate as a statue carved from stone.

"Gil and me, we're going together," said Ethan. "We aim to strike it rich out there, like everybody else is."

Abner Payne moved then, so suddenly that Ethan was startled, and so clumsily that he got his feet tangled up and toppled over the split log bench he'd been sitting on. He fell heavily as a result, flat on his back, and lay there for a moment, wheezing. Ethan took a step forward to help him, but didn't take a second. He wasn't sure what to expect, and until he did know he wasn't inclined to venture too close to his father.

"Well," muttered Abner, laying still on the floor, one leg draped across the overturned bench beside him, "maybe you will strike it rich. But I doubt it. You're a Payne, after all. And Paynes never have that kind of luck."

Ethan didn't know what to say to that. Could it be true? Was his father going to let him leave without a fight?

"I'll send you some of the gold I find," he said. "Enough so you won't want for nothing."

"Not nothing. Anything. So I won't want for anything. Didn't your ma teach you better than that?"

Ethan went to him then, profferred a helping hand. But Abner just lay there, unmoving, gazing at the shadows moving against the cabin ceiling, shadows in a dance choreographed by the lively flame at the tip of the tallow candle, a flame that seemed to have a life of its own—but that was illusion, because it was being manipulated by a breath of air unseen like a ghost. Abner was wearing a funny smile, and had a faraway look on his stubble-darkened face, and Ethan caught himself glancing overhead in hopes of seeing what his father saw. All he saw were shadows.

"Leave me be," said Abner. "This is where I belong. Go on, get moving. California is a long way from here."

Ethan put the bowie knife in the burlap sack and started for the door. Suddenly he felt like weeping. That surprised him. He hadn't cried since the day they had put his mother in her grave, over at the Roan's Prairie cemetery. There had been a lot of people there to pay their last respects, as Mary Payne had been well liked in the community, and some of them, as Ethan recalled, had been weeping, too.

"I'll be back," he said, fighting to keep the tears in check.

"What for?" asked Abner, without rancor, without sadness, without any emotion whatsoever in his voice. "There isn't anything here for you to come back to."

Stepping out of the cabin, Ethan realized that *that* was why he felt like crying. He stepped carefully over the snoring Napoleon and hurried into the darkness.

It took him a couple of hours to reach the rendezvous with Gil, and Gil was there waiting for him, holding the reins to a tall bay saddle horse.

"Have any trouble?" asked Gil.

"No." Ethan glanced at the sky. The position of the half moon in relation to the summer constellations confirmed his belief that he'd made it to the rendezvous before the appointed time. Then he glanced at the bay. "Where did you get her?" He knew Gil didn't own a horse.

"I bought her this evening. She's a beauty, isn't she?"

"You bought her? How could you afford a horse like that?"

"Well, I didn't actually buy her with my own money." Gil grinned, and the grin was enough to warn Ethan that his friend had done something underhanded, if not downright dishonest. "The livery man had put her up for sale. He said some gentleman from Tennessee boarded her and then couldn't pay his bill, so the livery man kept her as payment for services rendered."

"What would a gentleman from Tennessee be doing in Roan's Prairie?" wondered Ethan.

Gil shrugged. "He didn't say and I didn't ask. Anyway, I gave him a note with my father's signature, redeemable at the bank for the sum of a hundred dollars, the price of the horse. And before you ask me why my father would sign such a note, he didn't. I signed his name to it. But at least I struck a hard bargain. Made the livery man come down on his price some, and throw in a saddle and bridle to boot." Gil laughed and added, with a strong dose of acrimony: "Father would be so proud."

Ethan just stared at his friend. Gil had pulled some audacious stunts in the past, but nothing to compare with this bold piece of larceny. "I don't think he'll be proud, Gil. I think he'll be furious."

"All the more reason to get started. On this mare we can be in Fulton by late morning, if we ride straight through. By this time tomorrow night we'll be on our way down the Mississippi River."

"What are you going to do with her once we get to Fulton?"

"Sell her, of course. We'll need a grubstake, Ethan, once we get to California. Not to mention funds for the journey there."

"We agreed we'd work to pay for our passage. Besides, whatever you get for her in Fulton wouldn't possibly pay our way to California."

Exasperated, Gil shook his head. "You worry too damned much, Ethan. When the money runs out we'll just get some more."

"You talk like it grows on trees or something," said Ethan, dubious.

"No, I know it doesn't grow on trees," sighed Gil. "It's in people's pockets. And if you use your head"—he tapped a finger against his temple—"you can find a way to get it out of their pockets and into yours. Now, are we going to get started for Fulton, or do you aim to stand here and chew the fat all night?"

Ethan didn't cotton to the business with the horse. Once Gil's trick was discovered there would be hell to pay. Gabriel Stark would not hesitate to brand his son a thief—and

Ethan would be tarred with the same brush once the good people of Roan's Prairie heard, as they eventually would, that he had disappeared just like Gil, and at the same time. Hardly an auspicious beginning to the adventure. Gil had gotten him into trouble—and it wasn't the first time, either. Ethan occasionally wished that he had a less rakish and trouble-prone friend. But he didn't have any other friends at all, and beggars couldn't be choosers. Besides, Gil was the only boy in Roan's Prairie who didn't look down his nose at the son of Abner Payne.

Climbing into the saddle, Gil offered Ethan a hand up. Ethan put foot into stirrup, grabbed the profferred hand, and settled in behind Gil in the saddle.

"So," said Gil grandly. "Here we are, bound for gold and glory. No more clerking and plow-pushing for us. And that's another thing—I figure my father owes me this horse for all the clerking I've done for him, for free." He half-turned his head. "What do you say, Ethan? Any last words for Roan's Prairie?"

"Nope."

"Any regrets?"

"No," lied Ethan. "No regrets."

"That's the spirit!" Gil turned the horse around. They clattered across the narrow wooden bridge that spanned Blood Creek and headed west.

# CHAPTER THREE

Gil had said they would find a riverboat at Fulton, and he was right. He sold the horse and saddle for fifty dollars more than he—or rather, his unsuspecting father—had paid for it less than twelve hours earlier. That, mused Ethan, was just like Gil, being able to profit from wrongdoing. And he had to admit, when Gil asked him, that he was glad he hadn't been forced to walk all the way from Roan's Prairie.

There was a stern-wheeler tied up to a dock, the *Drusilla* by name, taking on a few passengers, a load of hogs, and some produce bound, Ethan supposed, for New Orleans or Natchez. As he understood river commerce, the boats took livestock and produce down the river to the cities along the route, and brought manufactured goods carried into New Orleans on ocean-going vessels back up the river to the farms.

Having never been on a steamboat, Ethan felt a moment's trepidation as he surveyed the majestic sweep of the mighty Mississippi. The river was at least a half-mile wide here, by his calculation. He'd seen it once before, many years ago, but back then he hadn't been confronted with the prospect of spending a fortnight or more on a boat at the mercy of a river that swallowed up boats, passengers and all, on a regular basis. It seemed that once or twice a year, at least, word would reach Roan's Prairie of some terrible disaster on the river, attended by great loss of life.

A boat would catch fire, or its boilers would explode, or it would break open on a bluff reed, and dozens would end up dying. Gazing at the untamed river, rolling vigorously by, Ethan wondered how many human lives it had claimed. He could swim, but he wasn't sure if he could swim the Mississippi. The Rock River had challenged him a time or two, and the Rock wasn't anywhere near as big and powerful as this.

The stern-wheeler's captain was a craggy, robust man named O'Rourke, who had big wooly whiskers covering most of his cheeks, the hint of an Irish brogue in his voice, and a decided limp. He wore a white slicker—the day was overcast and the wind blustered, threatening rain—and a battered cap with a visor pulled down low over eyes that were a washed-out blue. Ethan and Gil went up the gangplank, only to be detained by a brawny crewman who demanded to know their business. When they answered, the crewman took them to O'Rourke, who stood on the texas deck in front of the pilothouse, watching the river, glancing frequently at the sky, and consulting his key-winder watch every few minutes.

"Cap'n, these lads say they got to have a word with you," said the crewman.

"Do they, now." O'Rourke gave Ethan and Gil a stern perusal. "And why is that?"

"We want to go down the river, sir," said Gil.

"We'll gladly work for our passage," added Ethan. "Any kind of work you have, we'll do."

"Is that right. Let me see your hands, the both of you."

Ethan glanced at Gil, who shrugged, and they both stuck out their hands, palms up.

"A farmer's boy, I'd guess," said O'Rourke after a quick examination of Ethan's hands. "We need a few more men on the woodcutting crew. You'll do well enough for that, I suppose. Not so sure about you, though," he said, fastening a piercing gaze on Gil. "You're no farmer. You have soft hands. Nary a callus."

Gil turned red. "Maybe not, but I'm not afraid of work."

O'Rourke nodded. "We'll see about that. Where are you boys bound?"

"California," replied Gil. "We aim to get our share of the gold. They say you can pick the nuggets up right off the ground."

"Is that what they say. Well, I warrant that by the time we reach New Orleans the majority of the passengers aboard this ship will be gold seekers, just like the two of you. Mr. Louden, show them where to stow their gear. We must be under way before too much longer."

And they were, within the hour. Ethan and Gil left their meager belongings in the crew's quarters, located on the hurricane deck aft of the captain's cabin, and were put immediately to work, with Gil dropped off at the galley and Ethan escorted to the engine room by Mr. Louden, who identified himself, without hubris, as the *Drusilla*'s first mate. He handed Ethan over to a burly, soot-blackened man named Ed Smiley. In time Ethan would come to speculate as to just how whimsical Fate could be, that it would conspire to give that name to a man like the *Drusilla*'s engineer—a man who scowled all the way down the river, so that Ethan was pretty well convinced that Smiley's facial muscles were unequipped to accommodate a smile, had the man ever wanted to adorn his features with one. For all that, though, Smiley turned out to be a fair-minded individual. He expected his crew to work hard, and Ethan did just that, earning the engineer's respect in the process.

As Ethan quickly learned, the *Drusilla*'s propulsion system was a simple affair. Wood was fed into the steam engine's boilers, which sat securely upon a thick iron bottom plate protecting the wooden hull of the ship. The water contained in the boilers, replenished by means of a pump, was heated by a wood fire, creating steam that passed through supply pipes and oscillating cylinders, which moved a series of pistons and struts, which turned a main crank, which in turn revolved the paddle shaft. From his platform, Smiley handled the ahead and astern controls, obeying orders transmitted from the pilothouse at the top of the boat through a speaking tube. What amazed Ethan most of all was how steam could move all the heavy machinery, and how the packet used the water from the river to conquer the river itself.

To keep the water in the boilers heated to a temperature sufficient to produce enough steam required a lot of wood; Ethan was informed that the woodcutting crew, of which he was a member, would go ashore four or five times in the course of the journey downriver to replenish the *Drusilla*'s store of fuel. While aboard, he would spell the stokers—the brawny men whose task it was to keep the fire in the bellies of the boilers burning hot enough to maintain the water at the right temperature. It was hard labor, particularly in the hot, close confines of the engine room, but Ethan didn't mind. Every piece of wood he cut or fed into the boilers got him that much closer to California. Besides, while he worked he didn't seem to dwell quite so much on Lilah and his father.

The *Drusilla* was not a grand packet by any stretch of the imagination. Before they got to St. Louis he would see one of the so-called "floating palaces" that plied the Mississippi, and the *Drusilla*—the *Dru* as the roustabouts called her—paled in comparison. Still, she seemed plenty grand to Ethan. She was one hundred and eighty feet in length, yet drew less than five feet of water. Her twin smokestacks, set forward of the pilothouse, were adorned with red and green storm lanterns, used during night running to alert other vessels on the river to her presence and direction. The main deck was like a huge warehouse, open but for the engine room housing. The livestock, along with stacks of cordwood, some crates and barrels, and a handful of "deck passengers"—those who could not afford rooms off the boiler deck's dining room—were packed together on the main deck. The rooms themselves had been christened with the names of states in the Union; Ethan would discover that this was a tradition adhered to by nearly all riverboat builders. The roof of the boiler deck was called the hurricane or texas deck, where the captain's and crew's quarters were located. Atop it all stood the pilothouse.

Captain O'Rourke had been eager to put Fulton behind him, and before long the *Dru* was under way, her stern wheel churning at the water, the boat tailed by a host of waterfowl who had learned that the wheel regularly churned up a fish or two. Ethan remained all day in the engine room, venturing out only to fetch wood from the stacks on the main deck. Once, when he left the hot, smoky din of the engine room, he heard the singsong calls of the leadsmen stationed at the bow, one to port and one to starboard, measuring the river's depth and bellowing out their findings loud enough that the pilot atop the vessel could hear over the rhythmic splash of the stern wheel. Fascinated, Ethan paused for a moment to listen to the enigmatic poetry of their words.

"Deep four!" shouted the port leadsman.

"Deep four here," bellowed the starboard leadsman, then quickly amended it to: "Mark three!"

"Quarter less four," countered the man on the port bow, quickly checking his weighted line before hurling it back into the river.

Starboard: "Quarter less three!"

Port: "Mark three!"

Ethan felt the deck shift slightly beneath his feet as the pilot steered the *Drusilla* a few points to port, staying with the deeper water.

Starboard: "Mark three!"

Port: "Quarter less three! Mark twain!"

Starboard: "Mark three!"

Port: "Quarter less three!"

The deck shifted again, and the *Drusilla* altered course again, this time veering to starboard. Ethan wasn't sure what the difference was between a mark three and a quarter less three, but clearly the pilot was relying on the leadsmen to keep track of an elusive stretch of channel. He noticed that they were negotiating a bend in the river, where it seemed to narrow somewhat—and then, a moment later, they were past the bend and the river straightened and the leadsmen called "Deep water!" and Ethan picked up as much wood as he could cradle in his arms and made his way back into the engine room.

By the end of the day Ethan's every muscle ached. He was tired down into the marrow of his bones and it was all he could do to climb up to the hurricane deck. He wondered what Gil had been doing all day, and if his friend had worked as hard as he. Gil was averse to strenuous labor, but Ethan was not of the opinion—shared by so many others—that this aversion was in any way a shortcoming. But Gil wasn't on the hurricane deck, and Ethan was too tired to search the boat for him. All he wanted to do was crawl into the hammock that the mate, Mr. Louden, had said would be his for the duration of the journey down the river.

The crew's quarters had been virtually empty earlier in the day, when Ethan and Gil had deposited their belongings there prior to going to work. Now there were a half dozen men in the small confines, including a couple of the firemen Ethan had worked alongside in the engine room. He heard someone mutter "Who's this?" and one of the firemen vouched for him, and the others went back to what they were doing, no more interested in Ethan than he was in them, at that moment. Several sat at a table playing cards. A fourth sat on a big iron-strapped trunk, playing a plaintive tune on a harmonica, and the other two were in their hammocks. They were river men all—brawny, unkempt, sun-whacked. Living so near the Mississippi, Ethan had heard many of the tall tales told about them, about how they were as rough a lot as one was likely to meet anywhere on the face of the earth, about how they were boisterous and brawling and hard-drinking men who lived hard, violent, adventuresome lives, men who had nothing but contempt for drylanders. But the fireman had vouched for him, so he was accepted, with reservations, and Ethan felt comfortable enough in their presence. Too weary even to worry about tending to the knot of hunger in his belly, he crawled up into the hammock and with a great sigh of relief stretched out his lanky frame. A hatch was open, and an evening breeze cooled by the river washed over him in his canvas cocoon, and he quickly dozed off.

He was awakened by Gil, who shook him urgently. "What's the matter?" he asked, groggy. "Is it morning already?"

"I think we've got a problem," said Gil.

"A problem?" Ethan yawned, tried to knuckle the sleep out of his eyes. "What kind of problem?"

"A *big* problem. See that fellow at the table?"

Ethan rolled over on his side, peered across the cabin at the table where, now, two of the same men he had noticed earlier were still playing cards.

"Which one?" he asked.

"The one," said Gil wryly, "who has your knife in his belt."

Ethan stared at the bone-handled bowie knife stuck, sheath and all, under the man's broad leather belt. His heart skipped a beat. There was no question that it was his knife. Just the same, he rolled out of the hammock and rifled through the burlap sack in which he had carried all of his belongings from Roan's Prairie. The spare shirt, the pair of shoes, the lye soap and the dried venison were all still there. But his knife was gone.

"I already looked," Gil told him. "That's your knife, all right. How many knives like that are there, anyway?"

Ethan turned his attention back to the brawny riverman at the table. The bastard had gone through his things and appropriated the knife and now he sat there bold as brass, paying him no attention, indifferent to Ethan's reaction once the theft was discovered. It was bad enough to be robbed. But for the robber to act so unconcerned was an insult. The man wasn't worried about getting caught, or about the consequences of his larceny, because he didn't think there was anything Ethan could do to him.

Tight-lipped, his fists clenched in anger, Ethan took a step toward the table—but Gil grabbed him by the arm and detained him.

"In case you hadn't noticed, Ethan, that man is twice your size," warned Gil. "And he looks meaner than hell. Maybe you should just cool down and think about this for a minute."

"What's there to think about? He stole my knife and I'm going to get it back."

"Or you might get your neck broken."

Ethan looked sternly at his friend. "You saying I should just let it go? Let him keep the knife?"

"No. I'm just saying that maybe we should tell Mr. Louden what happened, or Captain O'Rourke, and let them handle it."

"Let go of my arm."

Gil let go and shrugged, as though to say, *I tried to talk some sense into him. I tried to save his skin. But he's as stubborn as a mule. He always has to do things the hard way.*

Ethan walked up to the table and stood there until the riverman who had stolen his knife condescended to look up from his card game. He was one of the largest men Ethan had ever seen. The muscles in his arms and thighs threatened to rip the fabric of the muslin shirt and stroud trousers he wore. His black, greasy hair was tied up in a queue in the back, and his face was covered with an unkempt black beard stained brown at the chin by tobacco juice. His eyes were like dollops of a cold, gray sea.

"What do you want?" he sneered.

"You know what. I want my knife back."

"What, this?" The man wrapped his hand around the handle of the knife. "Who says it's yours?"

"I do. You stole it out of my sack. You're a low-down thief."

The man grinned across the table at his opponent at cards. But this roustabout was staring curiously, gravely, at Ethan—wondering, supposed Ethan, how anyone could be so suicidal as to challenge the black-bearded riverman like this.

"Prove it," sneered the thief.

"I can do that. My initials are carved in the bone of the handle."

The man's sneer froze into place. He didn't say anything, just glowered at Ethan, and Ethan returned his gaze without faltering. One of the firemen Ethan had worked with all day swung out of his hammock and approached the table.

"Well, what about it, Claude?" he asked. "Let's see the knife, find out if what he says is true."

"I found it up on deck," said Claude truculently. "Don't matter if his initials are on it or not. Finders keepers. The knife belongs to me now."

"The captain might see things differently," observed the fireman.

"You'll stay out of this," rasped Claude, "if you know what's good for you."

The fireman turned his attention to Ethan. "Come on. We'll go tell the captain. He'll set things straight."

"No," said Ethan firmly. "This man is going to give me back that knife, and then we'll forget that anything happened."

Claude scowled, realizing that suddenly Ethan had gotten the upper hand with an offer that, coming from a victim of theft, was more than generous—realizing, too, that the room had turned against him. The expressions of the other men made it plain that they were on Ethan's side, not only because he was the injured party, but also because of his pluck. By dint of his bulk and his mean streak, Claude had ruled the roost in the crew's quarters ever since he'd signed on with the *Drusilla*, and now his power was being undermined. Worse, it was being undermined by a scrawny farmer's boy! Claude didn't care that Ethan had called him a thief. He *was* a thief, and made no bones about it. But the rest of the crew didn't like him, they feared him, and when they ceased to he was in trouble. If he didn't crush Ethan the rest of the men would turn against him.

"I'll give it to you, all right," he growled, and shot to his feet, reaching out to grab for Ethan and drawing the bowie knife from its sheath at the same time. Eluding his grasp, Ethan grabbed the table by its corner and heaved it over, so that the opposite edge caught Claude in the groin, then struck his thighs and knocked him down. Ethan moved in quickly, hoping to make full use of the advantage he had gained—and which he knew would be fleeting—by taking possession of the knife. But Claude recovered more swiftly than Ethan had expected him to, and with a snarl of the purest rage surged to his feet and lashed out with the bowie knife. The tip of the sixteen-inch blade came so close to disemboweling Ethan that he instinctively clutched at his midsection and looked down, expecting to see blood spewing from a gaping wound. Instead, all he saw was his shirt neatly sliced open. Claude took a step forward, fully prepared to make a second attempt at gutting his adversary—but froze as the fireman placed the business end of a pistol to his head.

"Not with the knife, Claude," said the fireman. "If the lad wants a fight, so be it. But it will be a fair fight or none at all."

"Fine," said Claude coldly. "I don't need a knife. I'll tear him apart with my bare hands." And he drove the tip of the bowie's blade deeply into a nearby vertical beam.

Ethan knew his only hope was to prevent Claude from closing with him, to dart and dodge and get in a quick punch whenever an opening was presented to him—in short, to use his only weapons, superior speed and agility, to full advantage. But this was not easily accomplished in the close confines of the crew's quarters. He managed to elude one roundhouse blow and then a second, but Claude was no fool, and he feinted with a left hook, waited until Ethan dodged to the right, and landed a crushing blow with his right fist that caught Ethan solidly in the face and sent him sprawling. The impact of Claude's huge fist nearly knocked Ethan out cold. Sheer will got him to his feet—he dared not linger on the deck or he'd be finished.

Reeling, he tried to block the next blow, but Claude plowed right through his defenses, hit him in the sternum, which made him double over, wheezing for air, and then brought a knee up into his face. Ethan jackknifed backward, blood slung from his nose and mouth, and he hit the deck again. This time he couldn't get to his feet quickly enough. Claude gathered him up by the front of his shirt, lifted him completely off the deck, and slammed him into a bulkhead. The riverman stepped back, expecting Ethan to topple forward, but pure stubbornness kept Ethan on his feet, even though his knees were uncertain and his head was spinning. Claude hit him with a hard right uppercut, followed by a left to the face—and Ethan collapsed.

But he wouldn't stay down, managing somehow to raise himself up onto hands and knees, drooling more blood—he'd bitten deeply into his own tongue. Dimly, through a loud ringing in his ears, he heard someone say, "Stay down, boy," and then Claude kicked him in the midsection, and Ethan found himself on his back again, heaving desperately to draw air into punished lungs, one eye swollen shut, with the socket of the other a pool of blood from a deep gash above the brow, so he could not see Claude's leer, could only hear it in the brawny riverman's voice.

"That's what happens to any son of a bitch who crosses me."

And then someone else said, with his voice full of awe, "Christ! He's getting up again! Don't he know when to quit?"

Only then did Ethan realize that he was, indeed, struggling to his feet, even though every tortured bone, sinew, and organ in his body screamed in pain at the slightest exertion. It was all he could do to keep his balance; the deck seemed to be tilting first this way and then sharply that way beneath his feet. He blinked the blood out of his good eye so that he could see Claude—and wondered if he was just imagining it, or was that a shading of fear and uncertainty on the riverman's dark and sullen countenance? Ethan sensed that while he could not win this fight, neither could Claude, not as long as he kept getting up for more— and if Claude didn't win then all was lost for the riverman.

"That the best you got?" mumbled Ethan over the blood and swollen tongue that filled his mouth.

An incoherent sound of rage welled up in Claude's throat, and Ethan braced himself as the riverman surged toward him, as elemental and dangerous as a tornado or a flood or some other unstoppable, destructive force of nature, and Ethan stood there in destruction's path, too tired and hurt to run even had he been so inclined, which he wasn't. *Never run away*, his father had told him, on what occasion Ethan could not recall, *because if you do you lose your self-respect, and that's all a man has, sometimes*. This had been before Abner Payne had fled from his grief, seeking the sanctuary of drunken oblivion provided by the old runaway slave's potent corn liquor. Abner had proven by example the truth of his words, an example Ethan had promised himself he would never forget.

Suddenly, a man inserted himself between Ethan and Claude, pushing the latter back, and when he spoke Ethan recognized the voice of Mr. Louden, the mate. All he could see now were shapes and shadows, murky and indistinct, and the voice seemed to be coming from the bottom of a deep well.

"That's enough of that," said Louden sternly. "Fight's over." He turned—just in time to catch Ethan as the latter pitched forward, out on his feet.

# CHAPTER FOUR

Ethan came to lying in a hammock, feeling the pulse of the stern wheel through his body, and hearing the lapping of the river against the *Drusilla*'s hull. There was light coming through the nearby hatch, and he wondered what day it was. He moved, thinking he would shift over onto his side and lift his head and see whether he was in the crew's quarters—he could hear no sound to indicate that another person was in the room. But moving was a monumental mistake; pain shot through his body. In fact, his body no longer seemed to be made of flesh and bone but rather of pain, from skull to shin, solid pain. He gasped, groaned, and lay very still. Aware that someone had come to stand beside the hammock, he was careful not to move his head and he looked out of the corner of an eye at Gil.

"How are you feeling?" asked Gil.

Ethan had to laugh—but cut it short. It hurt too much to laugh. "I feel like . . . like I've been trampled by a herd of wild horses."

"I thought that fellow was going to kill you, Ethan."

"I believe he did his utmost, Gil."

"That's why I slipped away and fetched Mr. Louden. Good thing I did, too, if you ask me."

"I guess so."

Gil laid the bowie knife, sheathed, on Ethan's chest.

"They put Claude in the sounding boat this morning and had him taken to shore. I don't think Captain O'Rourke was sorry to see him go. I know I wasn't. Claude swore he found that knife on deck, but I swore you wouldn't lose anything that meant so much to you, something your mother had worked so hard for so long to afford to buy for you. Claude said she must have slept with a lot of men to afford a knife like that, and that's when Mr. Louden hit him. There would have been another fight right there except the captain had Claude clapped in irons. He wore them until they put him ashore. He swore he'd get you, Ethan. And the captain, and Mr. Louden, and me, and a few others. But I don't think we'll ever see him again."

Ethan had laid his hand on the knife. "Thanks, Gil."

Gil shook his head. "I've known you your whole life, Ethan, and I still don't understand how you think. Maybe I never will. Why did you do it? When you could have just gone to the captain. O'Rourke would have gotten that knife back for you—and you wouldn't be laying there all stoved up the way you are." He shook his head some more for good measure. "You should see yourself. I hardly recognize you myself. Can you see out of that eye at all?"

"Just barely. But I'll heal."

"Sure. But that's not the point, is it. You had to know you couldn't whip a man the size of Claude. You did know that, didn't you?"

"I don't have much to my name, Gil. I never have had much. And I won't let people take what little belongs to me."

Gil was silent a moment, digesting this revelation, trying to make sense of it and, apparently, failing.

"Nothing's worth dying for," he said. "That's my motto." He grinned. "Well, one of them, anyway."

Ethan felt himself drifting off, and he was powerless to stop himself. "I got to . . ." he began, and was asleep before he could form the next word with swollen lips and tongue.


He'd never been so hurt in his life, but he was young and healed quickly, and luckily, amazingly, there were no broken bones, as that would have significantly slowed his recuperation. He missed St. Louis altogether, sleeping straight through the night the *Drusilla* was tied to the wharf at that city. Gil came to tell him they had taken on twenty or more passengers and a lot more cargo, and that some of the passengers were gold seekers, bound for California just like they were. Gil also told him that he didn't mind his job, which consisted primarily of helping the cook in the galley, and delivering food and drink to the stateroom passengers. He liked the second part best, because he sometimes got a gratuity, and often overheard interesting pieces of conversation.

"We don't have to sail all the way around South America to get where we're going, Ethan," he said excitedly. "A lot of men are crossing over to the Pacific at a place called the Republic of Nueva Grenada. Shaves weeks off the journey, and there's always a ship on the Pacific side to take you the rest of the way to California."

"If it's so quick why isn't everybody going that way?"

"Well, there are some risks in the crossing. Bandits and fever, for the most part. One man said he'd heard that the natives were cannibals, but I suspect that's just a tall tale."

"I heard there was a tribe of cannibals down along the Texas coast once," said Ethan.

"Cannibals or not, I say we go by way of Nueva Grenada crossing. We'll get to the gold fields a lot quicker that way."

"Unless we end up in some cannibal's cook pot," said Ethan, smiling. Like Gil, he figured the talk of cannibals was hogwash, pure and simple. And if it meant less time on a ship sailing the high seas, then he was all for making a land crossing.

"Well, you aren't scared of Claude, so you can't be scared of getting eaten," said Gil.

"Oh, you know me. I ain't scared of anything."

"Neither am I. Except of not getting to California before all the gold is discovered."

Ethan was up and around—though not moving all that spryly—by the time the *Drusilla* docked at Memphis. He went to O'Rourke and told the captain that he was ready to go back to work. O'Rourke was skeptical.

"You can barely walk, son. You'll be of no use on the woodcutting crew, for a while yet."

"I wouldn't feel right if I didn't work for my passage."

"I'm not worried about that, so why should you be?"

"I don't feel right taking charity, is all."

O'Rourke smiled. "You're a proud one, aren't you? Nothing wrong with pride, so long as you practice it in moderation, right along with everything else. Otherwise it can get you into trouble."

"Yes, sir. But I just don't feel it's right to take something and not pay for it in some way."

"You're an honest one, too. Well, when you're fit for it I'll put you back to work. In fact, I'm willing to take you on permanently. The river trade needs brave and honest men, God knows. You should consider making your living on the river. You could become a pilot, maybe, or captain of your own packet someday."

"Thank you, sir, but I'm dead set on going to California."

O'Rourke nodded, clearly disappointed. "I hope you find what you're looking for when you get there. I hope you escape the fate of so many who go to California with big dreams of striking it rich."

"What fate is that?"

"Ruination. I've seen many a man go west these past years, ever since James Marshall found a nugget of gold in the millrace of a sawmill he built on the American River—"

"I thought it was Captain Sutter who discovered the gold."

"The find was made on Sutter's land. Sutter had hired Marshall, who was a carpenter, to build the mill. Marshall showed the gold to Sutter and Sutter tried to keep it a secret, but there was no hope of that. When a Navy lieutenant showed up in Washington back in '48 with about two hundred ounces of gold carried in a tea caddy, the rush was on."

"How do you know so much about it, sir?"

"I read the newspapers. I listen to the talk. It's been all about gold for the last two years. Sometimes seems like the whole country has gone gold-crazy. Farmers throw down their plows, doctors and lawyers take down their shingles, sailors jump ship, preachers abandon their flock and teachers their pupils. They've all been infected with gold fever. I heard or read somewhere that these days nearly a hundred ships a month are said to sail into the bay at San Francisco, loaded to the scuppers with gold hunters. Fifty thousand men last year alone. You think they all found the mother lode?"

"No, I guess not all of them." Ethan grimaced. O'Rourke was going to paint a bleak picture, was going to try to talk him out of California, and Ethan didn't want to hear it. All his hopes for the future hinged on his finding gold. He was risking everything on that chance.

"No, they most assuredly do not. Like I said, I've seen them go, their eyes bright with the fever, their talk full of big dreams and big plans. And I've seen just about as many come back, their dreams shattered, their plans come to naught—and they come back to a life that lays in ruin. They come back expecting to pick up where they left off, but you can't forsake something and then expect it to be as it was before when you return." O'Rourke peered at Ethan, aware that his words were having an unsettling effect.

"I know of someone that very thing happened to," admitted Ethan, thinking of the story Lilah Webster had told him about Mr. Griggs.

"What are you leaving behind, son?"

"A girl. She promised to wait for me, though."

"I see." O'Rourke scanned the river, as was his habit while moored to a wharf; he scarcely paid any attention at all to the activity on the gangplanks. The *Drusilla* was taking on a load of cotton and another of tobacco—and quite a few passengers besides.

Ethan longed for a bit more reassurance from O'Rourke that, indeed, Lilah would be there for him when he got back from California. Instead, the *Drusilla*'s captain seemed to be trying to mask a good deal of skepticism. His noncommittal response seemed to do more than just hint at a conviction on O'Rourke's part that Ethan was a fool, in the first place, for leaving and, in the second, for believing that when he got home nothing would have changed—with the exception that his pockets would be filled with gold instead of dust. Ethan was smart enough to know that his desire for reassurance was evidence of his own doubts on that score.

They put Memphis behind them, and a few days later docked at Vicksburg. There they took on more passengers, and still more cotton and tobacco, and now the packet was fairly bulging at the seams with a full load and then some of cargo and humans. As usual, O'Rourke was in a hurry to be off, and no time was wasted in getting all aboard. The order to haul in the gangplanks was just being given as a man came running along the wharf, carrying a single carpetbag, which he used to clear a path through the throng of onlookers. Some were bidding farewell to travelers who were about to embark on the *Drusilla*, and others were merely the usual bystanders who came down to the riverside to watch the goings-on attendant to the arrival or departure of a steamboat. A few of the men in the crowd raised shouts of protest or fists of anger as the man bulled his way past them, and it was these shouts that drew Ethan's attention.

He was up at the pilothouse, having received permission from O'Rourke—and the blessing of the pilot, Mr. Dickerson—to spend some of his recuperation there. Ethan had reached the point where he felt he could not bear to spend one more hour lying about in his hammock, when the walls of the crew's quarters began to close in on him. At least up on the texas deck he could listen to Mr. Dickerson, whom O'Rourke had described as one of the best pilots on the river, talk about his craft, about how the river was like a lady of the evening, cunning and sometimes dangerous, her moods mercurial, who could get you where you wanted to go but would exact a price—sometimes a very steep price—for taking you there. Dickerson had been on the river for as long as Ethan had been drawing breath, and he relished having an audience to regale with his adventurous tales, stories guaranteed to appeal to the boy in Ethan, who enjoyed them so much that Gil started to worry, afraid that his friend might forget all about California and accept O'Rourke's offer to make his living on the Mississippi.

From the texas deck Ethan had a bird's eye view of the turmoil caused by the man racing along the wharf, looking for all the world like he had the law or an irate husband or the hounds of hell after him. The roustabouts manning the *Drusilla*'s gangways were drawing them in, and the mooring lines were being cast off bow and stern, and Ethan calculated that the man wasn't going to make it aboard. But he was wrong. In pure desperation the man dared a great leap from the edge of the wharf, sprawling onto one of the gangplanks, and his weight at the very end caused the entire gangplank to dip toward the river. Shouts of alarm mixed with bursts of laughter came from the onlookers ashore. But the roustabouts were strong men who were able to perform their duty, extra weight or no—with the result that the man, clinging to the plank like a leech on a warm-blooded creature, was hauled aboard the riverboat.

"Ethan! Go tell that fellow I want to see him."

So absorbed was Ethan in the excitement down below that he hadn't noticed O'Rourke at the texas deck's railing only ten feet away.

"Yes, sir!" Ethan scrambled down the guy to the hurricane deck, and thence to the boiler deck, ignoring the complaints from his still aching body at all this exertion. He was curious to know why the man with the carpetbag had risked, at the very least, a dunking in the river, to get aboard the *Drusilla*.

When he reached the boiler deck he found a crowd had already gathered to gawk at the late arrival, and Ethan told them to make way, pushing through until he stood before the man O'Rourke wanted to see. He was of medium height and build, in his mid-twenties, and wore long sideburns along with a mustache and goatee, after the fashion of the day. But all the facial hair could not entirely disguise the fact that he was an altogether ordinary-looking fellow, with a weak chin, a round fleshy face, and small furtive eyes set close together. His hair was black, thinning on top, and brushed back from a pronounced widow's peak. His clothing—a black broadcloth coat and gray vest over a linen shirt, and gray woolen trousers over scuffed halfboots—had all seen better days; the garments were frayed and worn in places. This made the gold chain arching across his vest seem incongruous, as obviously it was attached to an expensive timepiece tucked into the watch pocket—and based on the condition of his attire, an expensive timepiece was something this man could probably ill afford. The man's carpetbag had been mended in several places by someone unskilled in work with a needle and thread. Ethan's initial impression was that this man, clearly a drifter, would likely be hard-pressed to produce the funds for so much as deck passage aboard the *Drusilla*.

"The captain wants to speak to you, sir," said Ethan.

"Does he, indeed," responded the man with a wry smile. "That does not surprise me, sir, considering the somewhat unorthodox manner of my boarding his vessel."

Ethan was surprised by both the man's accent, which he believed to be British, and the refinement of his diction and vocabulary.

"You could have been hurt, or drowned," observed Ethan.

"Not drowned, surely. I can swim like a fish. Hurt, perhaps. But then, I daresay I'd have been hurt far worse had I remained in Vicksburg a moment longer."

He pointed to the wharf, a gesture drawing Ethan's attention to a trio of men running through the crowd that, with the *Drusilla*'s departure, had begun to disperse. They were shouting something that neither Ethan nor anyone else aboard the packet could make out due to the distance involved and the noise made by the stern wheel. One of them waved a fist in impotent rage.

"Are you wanted by the law?" Ethan asked the man.

"No. Not in Vicksburg, at any rate." He chuckled and extended a hand. "Ash Marston at your service."

Ethan hesitated, not thoroughly convinced that Marston wasn't a fugitive from justice. But he shook the hand, and found it to be soft, the grip flaccid. Marston's was the handshake of a man thoroughly unacquainted with manual labor.

"Ethan Payne—and, like I said, Captain O'Rourke is waiting for you. He doesn't like to be kept waiting, either."

"Then lead the way, Mr. Payne. I'll be right behind you."

Ethan guided Marston through the onlookers and up the companionways to the texas deck, where he introduced the Englishman to O'Rourke, whose expression fused suspicion with stern disapproval as he looked Marston over.

"Those men were after *you*, I take it," said O'Rourke.

"Quite right, Captain," replied Marston cheerfully. "I won't bother denying it."

"What did you do to them?"

"I beat them in a game of cards. Fair and square, as you colonials say."

"Fair and square? Then why were they chasing you?"

"I assume they wanted their money back. And, in the case of one gentleman, this gold watch. They were poor losers, who were particularly offended by the fact that a foreigner like me had gotten the best of them."

"So you're a gambler? A cardsharp? I don't allow such on my ship, sir."

"Not at all, Captain." Ash Marston appeared slightly offended by O'Rourke's assumption. "I may be the black sheep of my family, but I am an honest man. Mine is a very respectable family, too, I might add, a long and illustrious roster of lords, admirals, generals, judges, even an archbishop and a chancellor of the exchequer."

"Is that right," said O'Rourke, clearly unimpressed. He gave Marston's shabby attire another pointed perusal.

"I was robbed of my inheritance," said Marston, "by my two elder brothers, who conspired against me following the death of my father, God rest his soul. To avoid imprisonment for debt I fled my homeland and made my way to America. With the money I won—honestly—in Vicksburg, I intend to enter into some sort of enterprise in California. I'm not quite sure of the nature of said enterprise yet, but I do know I do not possess the desire, much less the physical fortitude, to dig gold out of the ground. So I shall let others do that, and take it from them when they're done, by providing a service they will veritably lust after."

"I see," said O'Rourke, overwhelmed by Marston's loquacity. "Very well, then. You're welcome aboard my ship, sir, so long as you can pay for your passage."

Marston thanked him, smiled affably at Ethan as he turned away, and headed aft along the texas deck.

"Ethan," said O'Rourke, watching the Englishman go, "you're to keep an eye on that fellow, you understand?"

"He seems right enough to me, sir."

"Either you're still naïve or I'm too much the cynic. But I want him watched. If I've learned how to do one thing in my forty-six years on this earth, it's to smell trouble. And that's just what our Mr. Marston smells like."

# CHAPTER FIVE

At first Ethan thought Captain O'Rourke was being overly suspicious of Ash Marston—skepticism regarding people and their motives being a deeply engrained element of his nature. He figured it had been the unusual manner of Marston's arrival aboard the *Drusilla* that had served to trigger the captain's doubts.

But as the packet steamed resolutely down the Mississippi for Natchez and thence to New Orleans, Ethan began having second thoughts about Marston, too. Gil Stark and the Englishman seemed to hit it off immediately, and before long Ethan hardly ever saw one without the other, and more often than not they had their heads together, whispering and smirking like conspirators.

At the same time, one and then another and then several more stateroom passengers reported the theft of valuable personal items—a set of pearl-handled dueling pistols made by French craftsmen and carried in a cherry wood box, a battle scene featuring Napoleon Bonaparte on a proud charger and surrounded by fusiliers intricately carved into the lid, a woman's vanity set of brush and comb and mirror made of chased silver, another woman's jewelry, including a pearl necklace and a ring set with a large ruby that (the weeping woman told O'Rourke) had been handed down from generation to generation ever since her great grandmother's time. A roll of notes issued from a St. Louis bank and a pouch filled with hard money also went missing.

Clearly, a thief was at work aboard the *Dru*. It seemed likely that the criminal was one of the passengers, as the thefts had only recently begun to occur; nonetheless, O'Rourke had the crew's quarters thoroughly searched, including the trunks and warbags in which the men kept their personal belongings. The entire ship was gone over with a fine-toothed comb—with the exception of the staterooms, as several of the gentlemen passengers who occupied those quarters made it plain that they would consider having their cabins gone through a personal affront to their honor. Sensitive to their concerns, O'Rourke postponed a search of the staterooms. But he posted notice, prior to the steamboat's arrival in Natchez, that all baggage being taken off the packet was subject to inspection. This caused some turmoil among the ship's well-heeled passengers, too, but O'Rourke stood firm this time. The distinction between searching a man's stateroom and his baggage was too fine for Ethan to make. Either way could, in his opinion, be interpreted as an insult, and he'd noticed that gentlemen were awfully thin-skinned where such things were concerned.

"You're right on that score," O'Rourke told him. "These southern cavaliers in particular are very jealous of their honor, and if you sully it in the slightest they're apt to react violently. I can't just search some of the staterooms and not others, though. That would injure the pride of those whose privacy I choose to intrude upon. They would wonder why they were being singled out and not the others." The *Drusilla's* skipper glumly shook his head. "This is a nasty business, but not the first time I've seen it happen aboard a ship under my command. By threatening to check all baggage leaving the ship, we may persuade the thief to leave the goods he's stolen behind—and in that event we'll recover them, eventually."

"Unless he decides to throw them overboard," said Ethan.

O'Rourke nodded. "There'll be two crewmen patrolling

every deck, port and starboard, day and night, to prevent that very thing from happening. We must all keep our eyes open, Ethan. With any luck we'll catch the culprit before we run out of river."

Later that day Gil found Ethan on guard on the starboard side of the hurricane deck and asked him what he was doing, a disingenuous question in Ethan's opinion, since every crew member was well aware of the captain's determination to apprehend the thief.

"I'm here just in case the man we're after decides to dump the evidence of his crimes into the river," said Ethan. "I don't suppose you've seen anything suspicious, have you, Gil?"

Gil smiled that crooked smile of his. "Not a thing."

"Maybe you should keep a close eye on Marston."

"Ash? Why would I want to do that?"

Ethan shrugged. "He boarded at Vicksburg, and right after that the robberies started."

"That doesn't prove anything. Twenty other people came aboard at Vicksburg. At least twenty. Why do you think Ash has anything to do with this?"

"I don't trust him, and neither does the captain."

"O'Rourke doesn't trust anybody. As for you, you're sure it's that you don't trust him? Or do you just not like him?"

"How come you're so quick to defend someone you've only known for a week?"

"I like him. And I'm not one to judge. You know what the Good Book says. 'He who is without sin,' or something like that."

"Take my advice, Gil, and steer clear of him."

Gil cocked his head to one side and peered inquisitively at Ethan. "If I didn't know better I'd say you were jealous."

"Jealous? Of who?"

"Ash. Because he and I have become friends."

Ethan shook his head incredulously. "I never have had

much luck keeping you out of trouble, Gil, and I don't rightly know why I keep on trying."

"You don't have to go out of your way to look after me. I can fend for myself."

With that Gil walked away—and Ethan was taken aback. It was one of the few times he had seen Gil truly angry. Usually his friend managed to use a glib tongue and that enigmatic half-smile of his to mask his true feelings. For the first time in the history of their long acquaintance, Ethan wondered just how well he knew Gil Stark.

As they approached New Orleans a few days later the thief had not been exposed, though some consolation could be had in the knowledge that no further thefts had occurred. If the man they were looking for had disembarked at Natchez, he had departed the ship without his ill-gotten gains, as everyone had been thoroughly searched prior to leaving the *Drusilla*. By now Captain O'Rourke was fairly convinced that the culprit was himself a stateroom passenger, as the rest of the packet had been gone over not once but several times. Ethan didn't need to point out to the captain that this did not eliminate Ash Marston, as the Englishman had purchased a stateroom upon coming aboard. In fact, O'Rourke had several suspects in mind, and one of them was Marston. But there was no way to resolve this short of conducting a search of the staterooms—even if it meant incurring the wrath of a handful of prideful southern gentlemen.

O'Rourke agonized over this decision, but not for long. Time was running out. The day before the *Drusilla* was due to arrive in New Orleans, the captain requested that all stateroom passengers assemble in the saloon on the hurricane deck, a long chamber filled with tables and chairs and flanked by nine staterooms on either side. O'Rourke announced that all the rooms would be searched in the morning, prior to their arrival in New Orleans. And then he stood there, dauntless and unflinching in the face of a withering storm of protest launched by the southerners. A couple vowed to defend their honor by preventing the searchers from entering the rooms. O'Rourke waited until the fury of outrage had spent itself before speaking again.

"Resistance would be futile," he said coolly. "The state-rooms *will* be searched, with or without your blessings." With that he bid them good day and left the saloon.

Ethan lingered, searching the crowd for Ash Marston—and spotted the Englishman just as the latter slipped into his room. He was about to leave the saloon when he saw Gil, wending his way through the passengers now formed in muttering, discontented cliques. Gil went straight to Marston's door and knocked, gaining immediate entry. Frowning, Ethan considered what he had tried previously not to think about—that Gil was in cahoots with Marston in carrying out the thefts. There could be no denying that Gil was capable of such larceny. This Ethan had known even before Gil stole the horse that carried them from Roan's Prairie to the Mississippi River. Gil had taken items from his own father's store, and had expressed no remorse after the fact. Ethan assumed that, if his suspicions were correct, Marston had devised the scheme and recruited Gil. But he knew it wouldn't matter to Captain O'Rourke which of them had instigated the thievery. Both would be clapped in irons and handed over to the authorities in New Orleans where, no doubt, they would be promptly convicted and sentenced to a long spell in some Louisiana prison. And there would be nothing Ethan could do to save his friend. Sick to his stomach, Ethan left the saloon.

That night he volunteered to take the duty of a crew member posted on the starboard side of the hurricane deck—the side where Marston's stateroom was located. The night was stormy and dark, and for this reason the pilot, Mr. Dickerson, had advised O'Rourke that he should put the *Drusilla* to shore and wait until morning to proceed, especially since news had traveled upriver about new sand-bars forming at a great bend near a plantation called Remairie. The captain nearly always bowed to the judgment of his pilot, and this time was no exception.

Early in his watch, Ethan saw a gentleman emerge from his stateroom and, standing at the rail, fire up a cigar. The man gave Ethan a cursory glance, and then studiously ignored him. Ethan kept a respectful distance. As one of O'Rourke's crew he had come to expect a chilly reception from some of the stateroom passengers, above and beyond the cool superiority adopted by these gentlemen in their dealings with all those relegated to a lower station in life— a category that evidently included riverboat roustabouts.

The gentleman savored his cigar and then returned to the stateroom. An hour later a couple emerged from the aft door of the saloon, intent on a stroll around the deck in spite of the inclement weather. As the rain was slanting in from the east, they eschewed the port promenade and opted for the relatively dry starboard side, where Ethan was on duty. The woman was slender and pretty, and her gloved hand rested delicately on the arm of her escort. Seeing her brought Lilah to mind, and Ethan felt a stab of homesickness. Standing there on the rain-slick promenade, he felt very much alone. Especially since it seemed that his best friend now preferred Ash Marston's company to his own. He wondered if maybe Gil had been right, that he *was* jealous of Marston. If so, was that jealousy clouding his judgment? Was this the reason he suspected the Englishman, to the point that he would be surprised to learn that the thief was someone else?

The couple walked the length of the promenade and back again. The woman smiled pleasantly at Ethan in the first passing, but the man noticed and said something to her that Ethan could not make out because of the tumult of the heavy rain on the river, and when they passed him the second time the lady was careful not to look at him. Apparently the man was yet another of those fellows deeply affronted by the merest suggestion that he might be a thief. This honor business was a funny thing, mused Ethan. Cap-

tain O'Rourke's decision to search the staterooms seemed
a reasonable one, considering the circumstances. Yet reason
flew in the face of honor. Catching the thief was in the best
interests of all the honest folk aboard the *Drusilla*, yet obviously self-interest and honor did not always coincide.
Ethan reflected on his own actions with regard to challeng-
ing Claude for the return of his bowie knife. Taking his
complaint to the captain and letting O'Rourke deal with
Claude would have been the sensible thing to do. Yet he
had opted for handling the situation himself. Had a sense
of honor provoked him to take such risks? Or had it been
foolish pride? Ethan wasn't sure he could make the distinction. All he knew was that some people were willing to
sacrifice everything for what they thought was right, while
others did not care deeply enough about anything to suffer
for its cause.

After the couple returned to the saloon, Ethan spent the
next two hours alone on the starboard promenade. The wind
shifted so that the rain began to slash across the starboard
bow, quickly soaking him to the skin. He moved aft and
sat on his heels against a stateroom door, as sheltered from
the storm as it was possible to be under these circumstances. Louden, the first mate, had loaned him an old
woolen coat and a cap with a broken visor, and Ethan
pulled the cap down over his eyes and tugged the coat more
tightly around him as he huddled there—and found himself
missing the meager comforts of the Payne cabin a thousand
or so miles away. A thousand miles, and still he was weeks,
if not months, away from California. He shook his head,
wondering why he had been born such a fool.

Then he saw two dark shapes at the forward end of the
promenade, silhouetted against the uncertain light of a
storm lantern at the bow. They had, he thought, slipped out
of one of the staterooms, and they were doing something—
Ethan couldn't tell exactly what—near the stanchions that
held the sounding boat suspended beyond the railing.

Keeping to the shadows as much as possible, Ethan crept

closer. For the first time he was grateful for the storm; it concealed his approach until he was no more than twenty feet away from the two men. When they saw him one turned to run. But the other took three long strides straight for him and aimed a pocket pistol, an over-and-under derringer, at Ethan's head. The storm-tossed lantern at the bow, swaying wildly on its iron hook, cast a shard of light across the face of the man behind the pistol, and Ethan recognized him then. It was Marston. The Englishman identified him in the same instant.

"Well, I say," he murmured. "Look here, Gil. It's your friend, Mr. Payne. Come to see us off, no doubt."

Ethan's bleak gaze swept past Marston and fastened on Gil Stark, who had abruptly terminated his flight now that the Englishman had taken control of the situation.

"Hello, Gil," said Ethan. "Leaving without me?"

"I have no choice, Ethan. Why did it have to be you?"

"You've really done it now," said Ethan bitterly. "I wish I could honestly say I can't believe you'd throw in with someone like this. But I *can* believe it. Did he tell you how easy it would be to steal from those people? How they were rich and could afford to part with a few belongings?"

Marston chuckled. "Really now, you've got it backwards, old chap. It was Gil's idea all along. I helped him pick his marks, occasionally kept them occupied while he purloined the items, and concealed the loot in my stateroom."

Ethan stared at Gil. "It was your idea, for true?"

Gil nodded, forcing one of those crooked smiles. "Sure. Being the cook's mate and saloon steward, I was in and out of the staterooms all the time. Before long I knew what the passengers had with them and, often as not, where they kept their valuables."

"And, as he *is* a steward," added Marston, "if anyone saw him entering or leaving a stateroom they would think nothing of it."

"Where are the things you stole, Gil?" asked Ethan.

Gil tilted his head toward the sounding boat. "In there."

Ethan held out a hand. "Give them to me."

"I think not," said Marston. "We're going ashore in this boat, and I'm taking the loot with me. I'm afraid I'm going to have to shoot you dead, Mr. Payne. Your bad fortune to have been here tonight."

Gil had reached into the sounding boat and grabbed the carpetbag—Ethan identified it as the one Marston had carried aboard at Vicksburg. Now he held the bag over the railing and snapped Marston's name, causing the Englishman to half-turn.

"You shoot my friend," warned Gil, "and all that money you won in Vicksburg goes into the river."

"Put that bag down!" gasped Marston.

Ethan saw his chance, and seized it. He wrapped his left hand around the derringer, pushing it down, and threw a right hook that caught Marston a glancing blow across the cheek, a blow that knocked the Englishman off balance. He fell back against the sounding boat, but held on to the pistol. So did Ethan, knowing that if he let go Marston would surely shoot him. He threw his body into the Englishman. The sounding boat swayed out on the ropes securing it to the stanchions, and the impact of Ethan's body sent Marston toppling backward over the railing. With a strangled yelp of fear he clutched at Ethan as he fell, and Ethan felt himself being pulled over the railing by the sheer weight of Marston's tumbling body. He grabbed frantically for the rail with his right hand, and managed to hold on. The derringer that Marston still grasped slid out of Ethan's left hand, and he looked down in time to see a pale face, stricken by an expression of horror, before Marston disappeared into the river. Ethan reached up with his left hand, took hold of the rail, and hauled himself back aboard. Gil was peering down at the angry black surface of the river.

"Jesus," muttered Gil. "He told me he couldn't swim. That was why we had to steal the boat."

"That's funny. He told me he could swim like a fish.

But who knows what was true about him—if anything." Ethan studied the river. It was running fast and was filled with debris, but they were moored close to the eastern bank. "He might make it."

"Come with me, Ethan. We've got Ash's money now. He took over a thousand dollars in hard money from those Vicksburg yahoos. More than enough to get us to California, and pay for all the supplies we'll need once we get there, too. Hell, if it will make you feel better we'll leave the things I stole here on the *Dru*."

"No. Captain O'Rourke gave us work and passage. He's been more than fair with us. I won't betray his trust."

"Everyone will get their property back. How is that betraying O'Rourke? Okay, wait. Maybe I don't have to run at all. I'll take the money, throw the carpetbag over the side. We'll stay on board and . . . and you can tell O'Rourke that you caught Ash trying to escape in the sounding boat. Yes, that's it! And he fell overboard in the struggle, but you grabbed the bag of loot. You'll be a big hero. And all you have to do is keep quiet about my part in all of this."

Ethan stared at his friend in disbelief. "So all you want me to do is lie to the captain."

"Well," said Gil, with a helpless shrug, "I guess you could turn me in, if that will make you sleep better at night. And then you can go on to California alone while I rot in some stinking prison."

"Damn you!" said Ethan through clenched teeth. He didn't like any of it—but he knew he would do as Gil had suggested. He couldn't just leave Gil to pay the piper for what he'd done, regardless of the fact that he had done wrong and deserved to be punished. Gil's plan would work, and Ethan marveled at his wayward friend's uncanny ability to think on his feet in a time of crisis, to devise a plausible scenario that enabled him to wiggle off the hook. This wasn't the first time Gil Stark had walked through a pile of manure and come out smelling like a rose.

"Come on, Ethan," said Gil cajolingly. "We're friends,

aren't we? You know I would do the same for you."

"No, you wouldn't," said Ethan flatly. "But I'll do it. I shouldn't, but I will."

"Thanks." Gil flashed a grin of relief. "Now I'd better get out of here. Otherwise, you might have to share the glory with me." And he laughed.

Ethan watched him go, carrying Marston's carpetbag. Then, with a sigh of resignation, he picked up the bag of loot and headed for the pilothouse.

# CHAPTER SIX

Three weeks later Ethan was standing on the deck of the steamship *Tampico*, peering across the emerald surface of a shallow bay at a collection of cane huts and a couple of disreputable-looking clapboard buildings. On a high point of land to the north of the bay stood the ruins of an old Spanish castle. Ethan wondered what the Spaniards had found so valuable about this place that it needed protecting. Beyond the town rose steep jungled slopes—in fact, it looked to Ethan as though the jungle was on the verge of reclaiming the strip of shore where the town of Chagres stood. Chagres was hardly what he had expected, but then the journey from Roan's Prairie to the Republic of Nueva Grenada had been filled with unexpected events, so that these days Ethan found himself hardly fazed at all by disappointment, accepting what came his way with a fatalism that reminded him, unpleasantly, of his father.

Still, he *had* hoped for a bit more from Chagres, which, he'd been given to understand by members of the *Tampico* crew, was the major port on the Caribbean side of the republic, and which lately had become the jumping-off point for California-bound gold seekers willing to brave the jungle crossing of the isthmus to Panama City, located about fifty miles away on the Pacific. Ethan had entertained the notion that once they made landfall he might find a decent meal and a bath, neither of which was available aboard the *Tampico*. He was heartily sick of the fare on this ship—

salt pork and rancid whaler's bread. And he had become host to a colony of body lice, to boot. All in all, the voyage from New Orleans had been an ordeal. Apart from a cargo that consisted of casks of rum, bolts of cheap cloth, and crates filled with sundry trade goods—all destined, or so Ethan was given to understand, for the poor primitive natives of Nueva Grenada—the *Tampico* carried over two dozen male passengers, every last one of them bound for the gold fields of California.

Like the rest of the passengers, Ethan found himself with too much time on his hands. One had little to do to while away the hours. Reading, writing, card-playing, and weapon-cleaning were the chief preoccupations of the other gold seekers. Staying below in the dark and dismal quarters provided for the passengers was unbearable, so everyone spent their waking hours on deck, even when a summer squall rushed in to drench them with a heavy rain, as happened almost daily. Ethan could not read very well, nor could he write worth a damn; the only thing more deplorable than his spelling was his penmanship. He had considered getting a letter off to Lilah at New Orleans. He had, after all, promised to write. But he wasn't about to ask Gil to help him in so personal and private an endeavor, and in the end he couldn't think of the right words anyway. He realized the only news Lilah would want to hear was that he had changed his mind about going to California, that he was coming home. But that simply wasn't the case.

Now that New Orleans was behind them, he doubted that any letter he might write would stand a chance of getting to her—at least not until he got to California. The *Tampico* was owned by the United States Mail Steamship Company, and carried several mailbags destined for California, but according to crewmembers, some mishap or other usually befell those bags so that the odds of getting them through was, according to one old salt, no better than four to one against. Ethan had heard that there were plans afoot for an overland stage route connecting California with the eastern states. He hoped that this was true, as he did not want Lilah to worry that he'd died or, worse still, forget about him. This meant he was going to have to find the right words, and get that letter sent sooner rather than later.

He didn't play cards, either. Gil did—constantly—and it seemed to Ethan that his friend lost more often than he won, so much so as the days wore on that Ethan began to worry they might not have any money left for supplies once they reached California. He tried to talk Gil out of sitting down to a game of chance with men obviously more skilled with the dice and the pasteboard than he, but to no avail. Gil insisted that with a little luck he would win back everything he'd lost before, and then some. When he did win, though, he was quick to lose it again. Eventually Ethan stopped belaboring the point. Gil had told him that half the money was his—something over five hundred dollars, which was more money than Ethan had seen in his entire life—but Ethan was ambivalent about the arrangement. The money had been Marston's, which meant it had probably been acquired in an underhanded way, and Ethan reasoned that maybe it would be just as well if Gil lost all of it on the *Tampico*. Then he wouldn't have to wrestle with his conscience when he made his fortune in California on a grubstake of stolen money. As for supplies—Ethan figured he wouldn't try to cross that river until he came to it.

So there was not much else for him to do to occupy his time except clean weapons—the bowie knife and the five-shot Whitney revolver that Captain O'Rourke had presented to him as a gift upon his departure from the *Drusilla*. O'Rourke had wished him good fortune. "But a man can't always leave everything to luck. Just remember, Ethan—riches and friendships are uncertain, and it's wise not to put your faith in uncertain things. Depend on yourself above all else—your instincts, your judgment. I've not known you long, but it's been long enough, I think, for me to believe that both your judgment and your instincts are sound. As for the pistol, well, the law is the most uncertain thing of all out west. From what I've read and been told, the law of the gun prevails still in California. Are you a good shot?"

"I'm fair, sir." He was being modest—everyone in Roan's Prairie had claimed he was one of the best rifle shots around. But he had scant experience with pistols like the Whitney.

"Become better than fair. A steady hand is preferable to a quick one. Shooting a man is a very serious business, so it's best done with all due care and deliberation."

Ethan thanked him for the pistol and the advice. He could tell O'Rourke was genuinely concerned for his welfare, and he was touched. "Don't worry about me, Captain," he said. "I'm not looking for trouble. I'm just going to hunt for gold and mind my own business."

O'Rourke chuckled. "Some people attract trouble, and I'm afraid you might be one of them, son, whether you like it or not."

Ethan shrugged. He couldn't fault the *Drusilla*'s captain for holding that opinion, as in a single downriver journey he'd tangled with a roustabout named Claude and a thief named Marston.

"And I'm fairly certain I don't need to tell you this," added O'Rourke, suddenly very somber, "but as long as you associate with the likes of Gil Stark you'll find staying out of trouble an impossible task."

Ethan had sensed from the first that O'Rourke had never fully accepted his story of how he'd recovered the stolen loot from Marston—particularly that Gil Stark had not been involved in the larceny. The captain had noticed that Gil and the Englishman had been fast acquaintances. In fact, they'd been thick as thieves. But O'Rourke had kept his suspicions to himself, primarily because he didn't want to call Ethan's integrity into question, and reconciled it all by deciding that if Ethan Payne was dissembling he had to have a good reason for doing so. Besides, the stolen items had been returned to the passengers, and, as they had arrived at the end of their journey, Gil Stark was no longer going to be O'Rourke's problem.

During the voyage of the *Tampico* Ethan kept the pistol well oiled and the bowie knife sharpened—and on seeing Chagres and the jungle that lay beyond he was glad that he had. There'd been some talk among the passengers and the crew about the multitude of perils that awaited those who dared the overland crossing. Ruthless bandits, deadly fevers, venomous snakes, treacherous quicksand—all these and more lurked in the jungle. Yes, crossing the isthmus could shave months off a sea voyage to California, but sailing round the continent of South America was, generally speaking, a safer option. For all that, Ethan was looking forward to being back on dry land. Bandits, fevers, snakes, and all else be damned.

The *Tampico*'s captain wasted no time lowering the boats and getting his passengers and their belongings off the ship, for with that done he could commence to unload his other cargo, including the mail bound for California. Then the ship would sail north for the Mexican port that was its namesake, and Tampico had many more amenities attractive to the sailing man than did Chagres. From there the steamship would return to New Orleans, the place that most of the crew called home.

The boats deposited them on the rickety, weathered wharf—Ethan worried whether the structure was dependable enough to hold the weight of all the gold seekers and their luggage. Some, like Ethan, were traveling light. Others, though, were transporting all manner of trunks, crates, and valises. He was very glad he didn't have more than what he could carry in the burlap sack to get across the isthmus to Panama City. Some of the other passengers were trying, with a notable lack of success, to get local men to help them with their belongings. The locals seemed to Ethan a lethargic lot; someone aboard the *Tampico* had subscribed to the notion that the climate was responsible for the laziness of the natives, and he didn't wonder—the day was breathlessly hot, with a suffocating humidity. The slightest exertion and one was drenched with sweat. Which was why the gold seekers sought help. But the people of Chagres were generally indifferent to the arrival of foreigners to their village. Thousands of men from distant lands, all infected by the gold fever, had landed here in past months. So Ethan and the other passengers from the *Tampico* were hardly a novelty, and scarcely worth attention.

For a few moments Ethan watched, amused, as the men he had sailed with from New Orleans went about trying to recruit carriers. The only locals inclined to work appeared to be in a gang under the supervision of a white man who seemed to be in charge of the *Tampico*'s cargo of trade goods. He wore a battered sombrero of straw, a short blue peacoat that could not contain his barrel chest, and filthy white dungarees. He carried a rattan stick, four feet in length, with which he persuaded his workers to labor more diligently by laying it across their backs with a sadistic pleasure, cursing vociferously all the while. And that was why the local men in the gang were inclined to work. The man in the blue peacoat looked like someone to stay away from, as far as Ethan was concerned. But Gil Stark had other ideas. He approached the man as the latter strode past, menacing a native struggling under the weight of a large crate that was balanced precariously on one shoulder.

"Hey, mister," said Gil. "My friend and I—"

"You drop that, you stinking son of a pig, and I'll flay the skin off your worthless bones!" roared the man.

Seeing the pain and exhaustion and fear in the native's face solicited Ethan's sympathy—and a quick dislike for the man wielding the bamboo stick.

"Hey, there," said Gil, louder this time. He reached out and grabbed the sleeve of the man's peacoat. The man whirled, jerking free of Gil's grasp and raising the bamboo rod as though to strike.

"Just who the hell you think you are, putting your hand on me," he growled.

Ethan swung the burlap bag off his shoulder and reached inside, groping for the pistol that Captain O'Rourke had given him. Seeing this movement out of the corner of an eye, the gang foreman lost interest in Gil and peered warily at Ethan.

"What you got in that sack, boy?"

"Just this." Ethan brandished the revolver. "And I'll use it, too, if you're thinking about caning my friend."

The gang foreman squinted even harder, as though he were trying to see right through Ethan and gauge his degree of resolve. Ethan's gaze was as steady as the hand that held the Whitney, and the man lowered the bamboo, apparently convinced that Ethan would indeed shoot if provoked further. His mouth twisted into a leering grin that contained more menace than humor.

"You'd gun me down without blinkin' an eye, wouldn't you, boy. I can see it in your face. You're a born killer. That's what you are."

Ethan had to laugh. "I'm nothing of the sort."

"I ain't wrong about such things."

"We just want to know who to see about getting to Panama City, that's all," said Gil.

"You see Queenie, that's who. Over at the Crescent Hotel." The gang foreman nodded at one of the clapboard buildings that faced a small plaza just off the wharf. "She'll see to it that you get in a boat, for a price."

"A boat?" groaned Ethan. "I've had my fill of boats. I thought this crossing was overland."

"Then you thought wrong. You go by boat to the headwaters of the Chagres River, about twenty-five miles as the crow flies, but really more than twice that far, on account of how the damned river twists and turns back on itself. Then at Gorgona or Cruces you'll start over the mountains to Panama City."

"Who is Queenie?" asked Gil.

"She runs most things around here. Go to the Crescent, she'll be there." The gang foreman whirled and with relish laid the bamboo rod across the back of another cargo-laden local. "Move faster, you lazy heathen, damn you!" he roared. "God in heaven, you're as worthless as the rest of your kind!" He moved on, stalking along the line of native porters moving along the wharf with the cargo from the *Tampico* on their backs, searching for his next victim, Gil and Ethan evidently forgotten. Having been standing downwind of him, Ethan was glad to see him go, and started to put the pistol back in his bag. Then, thinking better of it, he stuck it under his belt instead. Chagres looked like the kind of place where a man was wise to keep his weapons close at hand.

They headed for the plaza, passing a row of thatch-roofed huts. Men and women filled the doorways of these hovels, some of them smoking pipes, all of them dispassionate observers of the new batch of gold seekers passing by. They weren't in the doorways because they were interested in the goings-on outside their homes. It was just that the doorway was a better place to be than inside the wretched huts. Children, naked and dirty, played in the street where pigs and lanky, vicious-looking dogs prowled. The Crescent Hotel was as derelict a structure as any Ethan had seen, with warped and weathered planking for walls, and wooden shutters, paint peeling and dangling precariously from old and rusty hinges. One end of a narrow, second-floor balcony extending across the front had collapsed and, while it was obvious that the damage had been done some time ago—possibly by a storm, thought Ethan—bits of the wreckage still lay about. Ethan hesitated, casting a critical eye over the rest of the hotel, thinking there was a fair-to-middling chance that the whole place might collapse at any moment.

"What are you waiting for?" asked Gil. He paused to let one of their fellow passengers from the steamship hurry by them, heading into the hotel and straining under the weight of a trunk balanced on a shoulder. "We better secure our passage upriver, Ethan. You don't want to be stuck in this

Godforsaken place, now do you?" It was a rhetorical question, so Gil didn't wait for a reply. "Look, just let me do
the talking, okay? I'll handle this Queenie, whoever she is.
Do us both a favor and keep that pistol of yours right where
it is."

"Guess I should have let that man lay your back open
with his cane."

Gil smiled. "Always pulling my fat out of the fire, aren't
you?"

"Starting to look that way," said Ethan dryly.

The gold seeker who had rushed past them reached the
hotel doorway, only to collide with a local man who was
coming out. The latter was old, his Indio features, beneath
the brim of a battered straw hat, deeply etched by time and
travail. The soiled and sweat-stained cotton shirt and trousers he wore hung loosely on a frame that was slightly bent
and reed-thin. The gold seeker was considerably taller and
had twice the heft, yet when the collision came it was as
though he had walked into a wall of stone. He staggered
backward, off balance, and dropped the trunk. It fell right
through the rickety floor of the Crescent Hotel's narrow
front porch, shattering several planks into kindling.

"Goddamn it!" roared the gold seeker. He whirled and
threw a reckless roundhouse punch. But the local man was
as nimble as a cat. He danced effortlessly out of the way.
The gold seeker had put everything he had into the blow—
and when his fist met nothing but air he was thrown off
balance yet again, and careened off the wall of the hotel.
Enraged, he groped under his frock coat and brought out
an Allen pepperbox pistol, threatening the old man with it.
"I ought to blow a hole right through you!" he growled.
"Why don't you watch where you're going, you damned
greaser!"

Ethan was amazed to see that the old man displayed no
fear whatsoever. Sublimely unperturbed, he looked at the
pepperbox pistol being waved in his face, and then at the
man who was waving it.

"I beg your pardon, *señor*. You are right. I was not paying attention as I should have been. Here, let me help you with your trunk."

The gold seeker stared, lowering the pepperbox. "I was beginning to think none of you people understood a word of English, much less spoke it."

"Many of us understand it. Sometimes, though, we would rather act like we didn't."

Ethan had to laugh out loud at that.

"I have a boat," continued the old man. "I will take you and your friends to Gorgona, if you wish."

The gold seeker glanced at Ethan and Gil. "We sailed together on that steamboat, but they're not my friends. I'm not sure I even remember their names."

Ethan wasn't offended. He couldn't recall the man's name, either.

"I will get you safely to the end of the river, *señor*," said the old man. "I promise you that. I know where the bandits lay in wait for travelers."

"You work for Queenie, then?"

The old man stiffened, and Ethan got the impression that he found the gold seeker's assumption offensive.

"I am an honest man, *señor*."

"The fellow down on the wharf said I should rely on Queenie to get me to the headwaters of the Chagres."

"He says this because he works for her. But you would do better to rely on me to see you safely up the river."

"And why should we believe that?" asked Gil.

"Because I do not lie," replied the old man, matter-of-factly. "Ask anyone in the village if Juan Mendez ever speaks anything but the truth."

The gold seeker pulled his trunk out of the hole in the shattered porch. "I'll take my chances with Queenie, just the same," he said, and went inside the Crescent Hotel, dragging the trunk along behind.

"Yeah, and so will we," said Gil.

"Not so fast," said Ethan. He peered curiously at Mendez. "Tell me why we would do better with you."

Mendez looked around to see if anyone was within earshot. "If I say too much my throat will be cut as I sleep."

"By who?"

The old man just looked at him, a blank stare.

"Let me guess. Queenie—or someone who works for her. Am I right?"

Mendez neither confirmed nor denied this deduction. His countenance was completely impassive.

"Come on, Ethan," said Gil, taking a step toward the hotel. "This old coot is just trying to take our money. He probably doesn't even have a boat."

"No, I believe him when he says he's an honest man."

Gil looked at Mendez again, opened his mouth to argue the point, then shrugged. "Well, if I take issue with you on that you'll just tell me I wouldn't recognize an honest man if I saw one." He grinned at Ethan. "You would do that, wouldn't you?"

Ethan nodded. "More than likely."

"Then we should settle on a price. How much to get us to Gorgona, Mr. Mendez?"

It was the old man's turn to shrug. "Ten dollars . . ."

"Apiece?"

Mendez nodded. "You would pay five times as much with Queenie. And you do not have to pay me until we reach Gorgona."

Gil was suspicious. "So why are your services so inexpensive? Especially if they're better? Why don't you ask for a larger fare?"

"I am not a greedy man. It is all that I need."

"Forgive me for saying so, Mr. Mendez, but if Queenie can get fifty dollars a head for hauling folks up the river and you only charge ten, that makes you a pretty poor businessman."

"I am not a businessman," said Mendez flatly. "Now come. I will show you the boat you do not believe I have."

# CHAPTER SEVEN

Juan Mendez did indeed have a boat. His *bungo* was a long, extremely narrow canoe, with the aft section covered by a thatch roof lashed to a pole frame. The old man placed their belongings in the bow and introduced them to two young men, Jose and Joaquin, his sons. Ethan noticed that neither of the young men spoke a word of English in his presence, and when Mendez spoke to them it was entirely in their native tongue. Jose and Joaquin manned the oars, sitting amidships, while Ethan and Gil were assigned to the section shaded by the thatch, and Mendez took his place in the rear of the *bungo* with a long-handled oar he would use as a rudder. While his sons provided the motive power to fight the current of the Chagres during their upstream passage, Mendez would steer. This, as Ethan learned, was no easy task; the river had many twists and turns. In places it was deep and narrow, while in others it ran shallow and quick, widening as it swept over stretches of rocky bottom.

There was room in the *bungo* for several more passengers and their baggage, but Mendez did not offer his service to any other gold seekers. Most of these had already booked passage in boats belonging to Queenie. Ethan got a look at her before they set off upriver. She left the Crescent Hotel and came down to the riverside to see her flotilla of *bungos* off, and her passage through the village was the most bizarre procession Ethan had ever seen.

Queenie was an immensely large woman. Her body was

grotesquely fat, with great rolls of flesh stacked one on top
of another, and all of it encased in a garish crimson and
canary-yellow Chinese robe fashioned from a vast quantity
of expensive silk. Her long black hair was streaked with
silver, and done up in a thick braid that had been piled
tightly on top of her head and held there with pearl-
encrusted pins. As was sometimes the case with obese people, her age was hard to gauge. But Ethan assumed that the
reason she hadn't walked down to the river but rather rode
in a most unusual conveyance, was due not to the infirmi-
ties of old age but to her bulk.

The conveyance was a divan, fitted with iron loops along
the base, two on either side, through which long stout poles
had been fitted. Four burly natives bore her along, two at
each pole, the poles resting on their muscled shoulders.
Behind came a fifth native, this one a stocky woman who
looked only marginally less muscular than the porters. She
held aloft a yellow umbrella adorned with crimson tassles,
which provided Queenie with some protection from the tro-
pic sun. Behind this woman marched another man—a black
giant who stood, Ethan guessed, close to seven feet tall,
with shoulders as wide as a wagon tree. He wore a leather
vest that exposed to view the bulging muscles in his arms
and chest, and yellow dungarees cut off right below the
knees, and he carried on his belt a scabbard of crocodile
hide containing a machete. His head was completely
shaved, and a gold ring in one ear glimmered in the sunlight. Though Ethan had never seen a pirate before, he decided that this man had to be just that. An honest-to-God
buccaneer. He couldn't be anything else.

Queenie had five *bungos* in operation, with four of them
carrying three gold seekers, and the fifth carrying four.
Each *bungo* also carried four oarsmen, and one also carried
a man named Bega, who was the *segundo*, or captain, of
the expedition. After wishing the passengers Godspeed,
Queenie spoke briefly to Bega in low tones, and they
looked to Ethan like conspirators hatching some nefarious

scheme. He glanced at Juan Mendez, who was also watching Queenie and Bega, his eyes hooded beneath the brim of his battered straw hat.

"Shouldn't we get going?" Gil asked him. "If we hurry we can get ahead of this bunch." He nodded at Queenie's boats.

"We do not want to get ahead of them," said Mendez.

"Why not? We want to get to Panama City quickly, mister. We didn't come all this way for a pleasure jaunt, just to see the sights."

"It may be," said Mendez, "that you will get to Panama City long before the others do."

"That doesn't make any sense," protested Gil. "If they leave before us, they'll get there sooner. We *are* taking the same river, right?"

Mendez merely shrugged, and said no more.

Soon Queenie's boats were off, and only then did Mendez nod to his sons, who dipped their oars deeply into the brown waters of the Chagres River and put their backs into rowing. Up ahead, Bega exhorted his rowers to greater exertion, and before long the other *bungos* pulled ahead. That seemed to suit Mendez. An hour later, Queenie's flotilla went out of sight around a bend in the river and Ethan never caught sight of them again.

The Chagres wound its way through towering walls of jungle foliage, an impenetrable mass that stretched as far as the eye could see in every direction, covering the highlands as well as it did the low places. Sycamores and palms mingled with the mango and cciba trees. Plaintains and cane and giant lilies lined the banks. Blossoming vines lent the verdant jungle dashes of yellow, crimson, and purple color, outdone only by the vivid coloration of the parakeets and butterflies that they saw by the hundreds. The pungent aroma of rotting vegetation filled Ethan's nostrils. There wasn't a breath of wind, and the stifling heat left him drenched with sweat.

He offered to take a stint with an oar later that day, but

Mendez would not hear of it. Even after hours of constant rowing his sons were still going strong. As much as it made him uncomfortable to sit idly by while others were hard at work, there was nothing else Ethan could do. For his part, Gil suffered from no such scruples; he lay back with hands behind his head and watched the jungle go by for a while, then drifted off to sleep. He was abruptly awakened by a thunderstorm, a torrent of rain that burst upon them without warning. The thatch cover kept Ethan and Gil fairly dry, while the deluge didn't seem to faze Mendez or his sons in the least.

When the downpour stopped—the storm passed as suddenly as it had come—Mendez told his sons to cease rowing, and Joaquin moved to the bow, took up a length of rope and tossed it over a sycamore limb that dangled low over the river. He tied both ends of the rope to an iron grommit at the bow of the *bungo*, and in this way the craft was anchored against the current. Mendez provided a simple meal of biscuits, fruit, and fresh water. Ethan accepted the food gratefully. Simple though the repast was, it was far better than anything he'd eaten aboard the *Tampico*. Gil wolfed his portion down and then complained that there wasn't meat to be had.

"We will find meat for supper in a village called Gatun, which lies some miles yet up the river," said Mendez. "But it is not good for the body to have meat during the heat of the day."

Gil rolled his eyes and lay back down to resume his slumbers.

"How did you come by such good English, Mr. Mendez?" asked Ethan.

"When I was young I went to work on the plantation of a man named Rollin Bayard. He was a good man, concerned for the well-being of those who worked for him. All who wished it could go to a school at the plantation one day a week. In time I became his *segundo*. I admired him, and he trusted me. In all matters but one."

"What was that?" asked Ethan, noticing the deep regret in the old man's voice.

"I tried to warn him that his wife harbored ill will towards him. She could not be depended on, but his love blinded him to the truth. She was pretty in those days, and a woman's beauty makes fools of men. He was some years older than she, but he was a strong man who often worked in the canefields alongside us, and I think she was greatly vexed when he did not die long before his time, as so many Anglos do in this country. One night her patience ran out. She killed him with poison. Then she bribed those she had to, with money in some cases, with her favors in others, and escaped justice. Earthly justice, at least. One day she will pay for her sins, which have been compounded many times since *Señor* Bayard was murdered."

"This woman . . . she wouldn't be Queenie, by any chance?"

Mendez nodded. "She is an evil person."

As the day waned they arrived at the village of which Mendez had spoken, a collection of bamboo huts with thatch roofs. They were made welcome by the inhabitants, and given a supper of pork and coffee. From the villagers Mendez learned that Queenie's *bungos* had stopped here briefly, only to press on upriver less than two hours earlier.

"They'll keep going all night?" asked Gil.

"Yes. But it is not safe to travel on the river at night."

"Yeah, well, if we don't they'll get to Panama City long before we do."

"So what?" asked Ethan. "What are you worried about? Think there won't be any gold left by the time we get to California? You said there was more than enough to go around when we were talking about going. And you also said we wouldn't have any trouble finding a ship at Panama City to take us the rest of the way."

Gil grimaced. "I know what I said. I guess I just don't like the idea of anybody getting there before me, is all. Not that it will make any difference in the long run. That's not what I'm saying."

They slept in hammocks in a hut down by the river. Mendez woke them before dawn and told them it was time to go. After a quick breakfast of coffee and fresh fruit they climbed into the *bungo* and proceeded upriver. They had not gone far before Gil spotted what he thought was some clothing caught on some plaintain roots near the bank. Mendez spoke to his sons and the *bungo* veered in that direction. As they drew closer, Ethan realized that there was a body wrapped in that clothing. Mendez's sons grabbed the corpse, untangled it from the roots, and rolled it over.

"That's one of the passengers on the *Tampico*," exclaimed Gil. "His name was Bailey and I think he was from New York."

"He has not been in the river long," observed Mendez, scanning the Chagres with narrowed eyes.

"Looks like he was shot in the head and the chest," said Ethan. "You think bandits are responsible for this, Mr. Mendez?"

Mendez nodded. "It was an ambush, probably last night, not far upriver, where it is narrow and twists one way and then bends the other."

"Maybe the others made it through," said Gil.

"No," said Mendez gravely. "None of them got through. Those that were not killed by the bandits along the banks were taken care of by Bega and his men."

"What?" Gil stared at the old man. "My God. Do you realize what you're saying?"

"Of course, or I would not have said it. But they were careless. Usually, no trace is ever found of their victims. I think they lash the bodies to heavy stones and drop them into the deepest part of the river."

"My God, so this has happened before?" asked Gil.

"So Queenie is in league with the bandits," said Ethan.

Mendez nodded. "They leave her other enterprises alone. This is how she pays them off. That is the bargain they have struck. Every now and then she will sacrifice an expedition. Not often, but enough times to keep the bandits happy. There can never be any survivors. No one lives to tell of these things."

"If you know all this, how come she lets you live?" asked Gil, nervously peering at the jungle that loomed on all sides.

"You cannot exercise power over a dead man."

"But if she leaves you alone," said Gil, "that means we'll be left alone, too, since we're with you. Right?" He was looking for much-needed reassurance.

Mendez shrugged. "Maybe. Maybe not. She does not command the allegiance of the bandits. She only has an arrangement with them. Who can say what they will do? We must take no chances. The bandits, I think, will still be close by, celebrating the success of their ambush, dividing up the things they took, boasting of how many men they killed, and how easy it was to kill the Anglos. And they will drink up any liquor they may have found. We will go overland, that way." He pointed west. "Soon we will come to the river again, and it will be safe then to put the boat back in the water."

Dubious, Ethan looked at the jungle. He could only imagine how difficult carrying the *bungo* through that seemingly impenetrable mass of vegetation would be.

"Wait a minute," said Gil. "How is Queenie going to explain why Bega and his men came through the ambush without a scratch, when all the passengers lost their lives?"

Mendez shook his head. "You do not understand. She does not have to explain anything to anyone. No one will seek justice for the men who died today."

"Doesn't seem right," muttered Ethan. "Most of those men probably had families. Loved ones. Wives and children—they will never know what became of their husband, or father."

"It is because you are young," decided Mendez, "that you still believe there is such a thing as justice in this life.

There is none. You must wait until the next if it is justice you want."

"Well," said Gil, "there's nothing much we can do about it."

Ethan was inclined to disagree. But he kept his mouth shut. It irked him that Queenie and her bandit henchmen could commit murder and get away scot-free. He understood why Mendez would do nothing. The old man had his sons to consider. Yet, even while he understood, and even though he liked Mendez, he didn't approve of the man's cold-blooded pragmatism. Surely *something* could be done. There had to be someone, perhaps in Panama City, who would want to bring the bandits to heel, who would desire the curbing of lawlessness that ran rampant throughout the Republic de Nueva Grenada. And it looked to Ethan like it was up to him to take action. Someone had to, if this murderous enterprise was going to be shut down.

They left the river, the old man leading the way, his sons following and carrying the *bungo* on their shoulders, and Ethan and Gil trailing along behind, packing as much gear as they could to lighten the load for Jose and Joaquin. Mendez wielded a cane knife to blaze a trail. Mosquitoes as big as horse flies swarmed around them, but Mendez had uncorked a bottle and made them rub its viscous, foul-smelling contents over their exposed skin before they'd departed from the village of Chagres, and Ethan didn't get a single bite.

In two hours' time they came to the river again, about five miles, said Mendez, above the spot where they'd left it. The overland jaunt had been rough going; every vine seemed intent on tearing at their clothing, and every root conspired to trip them up. By the end of the passage Ethan was exhausted, and more than ready to get back in the boat. Even Jose and Joaquin looked tired for once, though they did not complain. They had not once done so since the journey had begun. Without any show of reluctance or a moment's hesitation they always obeyed Mendez, perform-

ing without question any task the old man set for them.
Ethan was pretty sure that had Mendez told them to carry
the *bungo* the rest of the way to the Pacific Ocean they
would have done so without a word.

There was no sign of the bandits, and Mendez was confident that they were out of danger. Continuing upriver until
mid-afternoon, they reached the village of Gorgona. Nes-
tled between rocky heights and the river, Gorgona was
about the size of Chagres; in fact, there was little to distinguish one village from the other but for the absence of any
clapboard buildings at Gorgona. Instead there were several
squat adobe structures. One had a red tile roof, the others
were thatch. What drew Ethan's attention to the former was
the presence of a soldier. He stood guard at the door, leaning against the wall in a thin strip of shade, wearing dirty
white dungarees and a green tunic, sweat-soaked and half-
buttoned. There were sandals on his feet and a shako on
his head, and a rusty percussion rifle with bayonet attached
was cradled carelessly in his arms.

When he mentioned the soldier to Mendez the old man
nodded. "A squad of soldiers is stationed here. It used to
be a posting reserved for men who were being punished by
the army for some misdeed."

"I can see why," said Gil. "Can't imagine anyone *wanting* to be stuck in such a Godforsaken place."

"You said 'used to be'," said Ethan. "Not anymore?"

"No," said Mendez solemnly. "Not anymore."

By now Ethan felt he knew the old man pretty well, and
he could tell Mendez was being intentionally cryptic.

Jose and Joaquin had secured the *bungo*, bow and stern,
to one of several docks jutting out into the river. Ethan
gathered up his bag of belongings and, without a word to
anyone of his intentions, walked down the dock and headed
resolutely up a dusty street populated by naked children and
grunting pigs toward the adobe hut guarded by the soldier.

Halfway there he heard footsteps behind him—someone
who was in a great hurry—and he turned, curiously, to see

Mendez. The old man was carrying the cane knife and had a grim, purposeful countenance that alarmed Ethan.

"What's—" It was all Ethan had time to say. Mendez grabbed him by the shirt front and propelled him out of the street, pressing him against the wall of a hut. Ethan experienced firsthand the old man's wiry strength. For one who appeared so frail he was surprisingly strong. Ethan liked being manhandled as little as the next guy, and he stiffened, grabbed Mendez by the arm, and was on the verge of fighting back when the old man spoke.

"You must not tell the soldiers what happened on the river."

"And why not?" asked Ethan angrily. "Isn't that why they're here? To deal with bandits and such?"

"You do not need to tell them what they already know."

"Already know? How could that be? Who would have told them about the massacre? The only people left alive were involved in the crime."

Mendez nodded. "Yes, that is true. Listen."

Ethan listened—and heard voices, the voices of two men in the street, both of them speaking Spanish, and then laughing heartily together. Mendez peered cautiously around the corner of the hut and, after a quick look, pulled back and gestured for Ethan to have a peek. Ethan did, and was shocked to see the black goliath, the one he had last seen with Queenie back in Chagres village, standing now with another man in the street in front of the adobe hut that had been Ethan's destination a moment before. Obviously the two men had been inside and had only this moment emerged. The black's companion wore an officer's uniform, and wore it badly; his slovenly appearance was a telling clue to his lack of regard for what the uniform stood for.

"How did he get here?" whispered Ethan.

Mendez knew he was referring to the black giant, and in the Latin way approached the answer obliquely. "His name is Alonzo. They say he has killed over a hundred men. He comes from Santa Domingo, and he was once a prize fighter. But too often he killed the men they put in the ring against him. When he began to kill men in quarrels outside the ring, they decided they would have to do away with him. But he escaped them and came here, and was a bandit for some years, until Queenie hired him as her body-guard."

"Yes, but how—"

"He came up the river, as everyone must. He was behind us, until we stopped for the night at the village of Gatun. And then he slipped ahead of us under cover of the night. She sent him to make sure the ambush went according to plan, and that none of the intended victims survived. Also, to pay off the lieutenant, so that he will keep quiet about what has happened. As he can be relied on to do, if he is rewarded."

"My God," said Ethan. "The soldiers are in on it, too? Are there any honest men in this land? Besides you and your sons, I mean."

"Sometimes honesty is a luxury you cannot afford. Or survive. The lieutenant gets only a small amount of money. But he will do Queenie's bidding because he is afraid of Alonzo."

"Who wouldn't be," muttered Ethan. "So that's why she sends him. As a reminder to the lieutenant that it's healthier to keep his mouth shut."

Mendez nodded: "If you had walked in there to tell the lieutenant what you had seen, they would have killed you. Even if Alonzo had not been there the lieutenant would have killed you. His job is to make sure no one gets past Gorgona that would tell of what happens on the river."

Ethan just sighed, and shook his head. He understood even more so, now, why Mendez did nothing about Queenie. There was nothing he *could* do. Her wicked influence was too far-reaching. Her principal weapons were greed and fear, and those were very potent weapons indeed. Ethan felt as though this experience, while an unpleasant one, had taught him a very valuable lesson. Survival was the only law that mattered in some places, and so self-interest trumped justice every time. If he said anything he would be placing Mendez—and probably the old man's entire family—in jeopardy. That meant Queenie and her cutthroats *would* indeed get away with murder.

"Neither Bega nor the bandits would dare tell Alonzo that they lost the body of one of the victims," said Mendez. "That is all that has saved us. Otherwise, Alonzo would make sure none of us lived to see another day, just on the chance that we had seen the body. That we might not have would not matter. He is not one to take chances, and killing means absolutely nothing to him. Come, my friend. There are several hours of daylight left. The sooner you are on your way over the mountains to Panama City, the better. You can be started in an hour, as I know of someone who lives here that you can trust to guide you."

"Fine," said Ethan, disgusted. "Let's go see him." He didn't tell Mendez, but he was ready to put the old man's country behind him. They said California was a rough and lawless place. But he didn't see how it could be any worse than this bloodstained land.

# CHAPTER EIGHT

The United States Mail Steamship Company, which owned the *Tampico*, had as its counterpart the Pacific Mail Steamship Company, which, apart from its government contract to carry the mail from Panama City to San Franciso, also employed a fleet of steamers to transport gold seekers who had survived the land crossing to the promised land. Each PMSC vessel—the *California*, the *Oregon*, the *Panama*, the *Tennessee*, and the *Unicorn*—could carry two hundred passengers, and each made about ten or twelve round trips a year. In addition, a number of individually owned ships carried passengers to California. Ethan heard the story of Darius Ogden Mills, who tired of waiting in Panama City for a ship and purchased a schooner in Peru, sailed it back to the Republic of Nueva Grenada, and there sold one hundred berths on her before sailing on to San Francisco, making a handsome profit in the deal. Convinced that he possessed a soul as enterprising as Mills's, Gil Stark tried to persuade Ethan that they should also buy their own ship, using the money in Marston's carpetbag, and do as Mills had done. But Ethan would have none of it. He reminded Gil that they had come all this way for the express purpose of prospecting for gold in California, and that was exactly what he intended to do. Besides, Gil was underestimating the funds required to buy a reliable vessel. But that was Gil's way—never acknowledging that the devil was in the details. Whenever an attractive scheme occurred to him he seldom stopped long enough to consider the consequences, to think it through. More often than not it was this failing that landed him into so much trouble.

Ethan found Panama City to be a place where life was cheap—and everything else was entirely too expensive. By all accounts it had been a sleepy village only a year or so ago; now it was filled with entrepreneurs and confidence tricksters. Regardless of the category into which a man fell, he was there for the sole purpose of making a profit at the expense of the men returning from California—a good many of whom had gold in their pockets. While technically Panama City was part of the Republic of Nueva Grenada, it looked to Ethan as though an American invasion had taken it over. Every hotel, store, saloon, and brothel was owned by an American. Both the local newspapers were, as well. This had engendered no small amount of resentment among the native population. Ochoa, the man who was a friend of Juan Mendez and who had guided Ethan and Gil across the mountains from Gorgona, warned his charges that the streets of Panama City were not a safe place to be after the sun went down. Robbers would cut their throats for the money in their pockets—and some locals would do the same just because they were gringos.

The twenty-six miles of winding trails, steep climbs, and perilous descents between Gorgona and Panama City had been uneventful, if arduous. As Mendez had said, Ochoa owned "reliable" burros, and that made all the difference, as Ethan learned when he found himself on a narrow trail with a sudden chasm falling away beside him. Nothing could perturb the burros, and Ethan was reminded of the dependable old plow mare he had left behind on the Payne farm. He'd been gone for more than two months now, and wondered what fate had befallen the mare, and the farm—and his father.

Fortunately, one of the PMSC steamers, the *Unicorn*, lay in the harbor at Panama City when they arrived, and Ethan wasted no time in determining that he and Gil could still buy passage to California aboard her. There was room in steerage, he was told, and as this was the cheapest fare available, Ethan did not hesitate to buy the tickets. To Ethan's surprise, Gil was disappointed. The *Unicorn* would sail that very afternoon, giving them less than five hours to spend ashore.

"That's a shame," lamented Gil. "Look at all the gambling dens! Have you seen all the bordellos they've got here? If I had a single day here I could probably double our money at the gaming tables. And if I had a single night I could get real acquainted with one of these pretty *señoritas*."

Ethan shook his head. "I thought you were in a rush to get to California before they picked up all the gold off the ground. Besides, you'd probably lose what's left of the money. And you know what Ochoa said about the women of ill repute. I don't know about you, but I don't fancy a case of syphilis."

"I've been a long time without a woman. You're a virgin, so you don't know what you're talking about, anyway. I wasn't expecting you to take up with a soiled dove."

Ethan laughed. "You've never been with a woman, either, Gil. Becky Shriver doesn't count. She's just a girl." He ignored the "virgin" comment, as he did not care for the subject of Lilah Webster to come up, as it inevitably would.

"Well," said Gil, resigning himself to the fact that he did not have the time to sample all of Panama City's enticements, "I guess I'll just have time for a little female companionship, then. Maybe I'll find a good game of cards or two aboard the ship."

They agreed to meet at the dock where the *Unicorn*'s launches were picking up passengers and cargo. That suited Ethan. He had decided it was time—past time, in fact—to get a letter off to Lilah. There was a mail office in Panama City, through which passed all the mail going to and coming from California. He'd been pondering what to write for quite some time now, and figured that, given a few hours, he could get the job done. It would be an ordeal, but he'd given his word. After two months Lilah was probably worried sick for not hearing from him. An equally unpleasant thought was that she might be mad as hell that he hadn't written sooner. Or, God forbid, that she'd found someone else to interest her and had forgotten about him.

Ethan made his way to the mail office. He carried no writing materials with him, so he went inside and purchased two sheets of paper for a penny. A long table stood to one side, with four chairs and as many pens and inkwells. A young man in his twenties sat in one of the chairs, bent over a sheet of paper, laboriously scratching words onto it. Ethan quietly sat at the other end of the table, trying not to disturb the man, but he looked up, smiled tentatively, and removed his spectacles.

"Writing a letter to my wife back in Boston," he said. "Just received one from her. She's with child. Our first. She tells me that all is well. Still, I can't help but worry. Her mother died giving birth to her, and she's always been terribly afraid. . . ." The man closed his eyes and pinched the bridge of his nose. "I should never have left her. We'd been married less than six months. But the job I had, clerking in a law office . . ." He shook his head ruefully. "My wages were hardly enough to make ends meet. So I joined an association. The Boston and California Mining Company. Fifty subscribers, and each of us put up five hundred dollars. I had to borrow the money from my uncle. I told him I would strike it rich in California and pay him back within a year's time, with interest. The interest wasn't his idea, it was mine. I also insisted on a contract being drawn up. Twenty-five of us set sail ten weeks ago, and the rest are going overland. Ten weeks—but it seems like ten years since I last saw her. I should never have left." He attempted another half-hearted smile. "I'm sorry. I don't mean to ramble like this. I shouldn't burden you with my troubles."

"It's not a burden," said Ethan. He wasn't certain what

else to say. "I'm sure your wife will be fine. And your baby, as well."

"Of course. Thank you." The man returned to his letter, and Ethan bent to his own task. *Dear Lilah*, he wrote—and then the man said, "I should be there when the baby is born, though. But I won't be." Ethan looked up, but the man didn't; even so, Ethan could see his eyes gleaming with tears. Made uncomfortable by the stranger's show of emotion, he looked quickly away.

He finished his letter in less than an hour. As it turned out, he did not have that much to tell her, except that he was healthy, and but a week or two from California, and to reiterate his pledge to return to her a wealthy man who could provide for her every need. He left out a good deal of information—the trouble he'd had with Claude over the bowie knife, the bad business with Ash Marston, the band of gold seekers murdered by Queenie's cutthroats. To mention those events would serve no useful purpose. If she knew of them it would only cause her to worry more about his welfare. He folded the letter twice, then encased it in the second sheet he had purchased and wrote *Lilah Webster, Roan's Prairie, Illinois* on the outer face. The clerk at the counter sealed the letter and took Ethan's payment.

"How long will it take for that letter to reach Illinois, sir?"

The clerk shrugged. "There ain't no telling. Sorry, kid."

As he left the mail office, Ethan noticed that the young man from Boston was still bent over the table, still agonizing over the letter to his pregnant wife. Ethan wondered how many lives had been ruined by the gold fever. Lilah aside, his situation back at Roan's Prairie had been pretty grim, so he felt confident that whatever fate lay in store for him, it could not be any worse than what he'd left behind. But he'd met over a hundred gold seekers during his journey, and many of them had given up a lot—wives, families, comfortable homes, lucrative employment. Some would go home wealthy men. Others would be broken men. And still others, mused Ethan, grimly thinking of the corpse they had discovered in the Chagres River, would not go home at all. He hoped the man at the table got safely back to Boston and his family.

Leaving the mail office, Ethan paused just beyond the threshold and scanned the bustling street, uncertain how to pass the time until the *Unicorn* sailed. He had hard money in his pocket—pay for his stint as one of the *Drusilla*'s roustabouts. Perhaps a hot bath and a decent meal were in order. But before he could take a step his attention was drawn to a sudden commotion in an alley that ran alongside the mail office. Curious, he turned that way—and then a woman cried out, and he rushed forward. A pair of men, locals by the looks of them, were accosting a woman. She was wrestling with one of them for possession of two valises, fighting like a wildcat. This man was shouting at his compadre, no doubt urging the latter to become more actively involved in the fray. The second man was brandishing a knife that had a narrow, wickedly curved blade, and he seemed to be waiting for a chance to slip in behind the woman and, assumed Ethan, slit her throat.

Considering what Ochoa had said about Panama City, Ethan had taken the precaution of transferring the Whitney revolver and the bowie knife from his bag to his person, securing both weapons under his belt at the small of his back. Now, instinctively, he reached for them. "Leave her alone!" he shouted, and the two men took one look at him—more specifically, took one look at the pistol and knife he had in his hands—and ran away. In his haste, the one with the knife collided with the woman and knocked her down. Ethan ran forward to give her assistance. Putting up his weapons, he took her by the arm to help her to her feet. She came up swinging one of the valises and cursing like a sailor. The valise struck Ethan squarely in the chest. It was surprisingly heavy, and the impact knocked him right off his feet. He landed flat on his back and lay there a moment trying to get his wind back.

The woman loomed over him. Ethan thought she had to be a few years older than he. Her hair was black, her eyes a beautiful sea green, her nose aquiline, and her lips full and red. Her naturally milky-white complexion was burned in places by exposure to the tropical sun. She was of medium height, and slender. He thought at first that she must be of Latin descent, perhaps with a direct lineage back to the Spanish *conquistadores* who had tried to tame this land a few centuries ago, as clearly there was no Indio blood in her veins. But when she spoke, standing there and staring suspiciously at him, Ethan realized his mistake, for her accent was unmistakably English.

"And just who the bloody hell might you be?" she asked.

Ethan told her his name. "From Illinois," he added. Drawing a ragged breath, he realized with relief that his lungs actually were going to function properly again. "I'm bound for California."

"Are you, now." Some of the suspicion faded from her countenance. "Then perhaps I owe you an apology. I thought you might be just another cutthroat. There seem to be more than a few in this place."

Ethan sat up. "Do I look like a cutthroat?" he asked, exasperated.

She tilted her head to one side and smiled— a smile that cooled Ethan's anger and resentment.

"Well, now," she said—and he suddenly realized that her husky voice was rather seductive—"you look like you *could* be dangerous, in one way or another."

"No cause to worry. I don't want anything from you."

"Nothing?" She dropped the valise with which she had assaulted him a moment earlier, and gave him a hand up. He noticed her hand was small, with long, slender fingers, but her grip was stronger than he had expected. There was more to this girl than met the eye. "Not even a kiss, out of gratitude for coming to my rescue?"

"A kiss?" Ethan was taken aback. It was a bold offer— bold even if made in jest—and he began to wonder if she might be one of those women of easy virtue they said populated Panama City in great numbers. She didn't *look* like one, or what he imagined one would look like, as she was very pretty, and dressed conservatively in a blue serge traveling outfit.

"Yes, a kiss," she said, a twinkle of pure mischief in her eye. "Haven't you ever had a kiss from a girl before? Oh, surely you must have, a handsome devil like you. I'll wager all the girls in Illinois simply swooned when you walked by."

Ethan blushed furiously. "Not hardly." A handsome devil? He was thoroughly flattered.

"Well, Mr. Ethan Payne, my name is Ellen. Ellen Addison. And I, too, am California-bound. Aboard the *Unicorn* this very afternoon." She raised a questioning brow. "How are you making the passage?"

"I'm going on the *Unicorn*, too."

She gave a delighted laugh. "I'm so very glad to hear that!"

"You are? How come?"

"Just in case I have need again for a knight in shining armor, of course."

Ethan couldn't figure out if Ellen Addison was making fun of him or not.

She seemed to be able to read his thoughts. "I really ought not to say this. It isn't proper for a young lady to come right out and tell a young man she's happy to be sailing on the same ship as he because she's taken an instant liking to him. But then, I'm not a proper young lady, as a whole host of governesses have pointed out down through the years, and as my own father would admit were he not prone to dote on me."

She smiled at him again, and Ethan was completely beguiled. So much so, in fact, that he could think of nothing to say. She spoke in such a breathless rush, the words tumbling effortlessly and headlong from those full red lips, imparting so much information so quickly that he just didn't have time to think of anything.

"I was on my way to the dock when those heathens accosted me," she continued. "I don't think they wanted to kill me, but rather were after my belongings, yet I wasn't about to give those up without a fight. I suppose the very upbringing that makes me something less than proper stands me in good stead on occasions such as these. I know how to fight, though I fare better with sword and pistol than in fisticuffs with a man. That's understandable when you consider my disadvantage in terms of weight and strength."

"You know how to use a sword and a pistol?"

"Oh, absolutely. I am a crack shot, and I learned the sword from Cavella, the foremost master in Italy. Though my father was against the idea initially, I confess. Still, the poor fellow simply cannot say no to me."

"I bet he's not the only one with that problem," murmured Ethan.

"What a nice compliment. Now I really must kiss you. Would you mind terribly if I did?"

"Well, um, I, uh . . ."

She laughed softly and leaned forward, laying her hands lightly on his shoulders and brushing her lips very softly against his cheek, about an inch to the left of his mouth. Ethan felt his cheeks burning furiously.

"Now," said Ellen, her voice growing even more seductive, "if you'll accompany me to the dock, and make certain that I'm not attacked again by those awful men, I may give you another of those—someday."

"Yes. Yes, of course," he said. "Here, let me take one of those. They're very, um, heavy."

Ellen smiled. "You can certainly attest to that, can't you, you poor dear."

He grinned back at her. With valise in one hand and his bag in the other, he followed her out of the narrow alley and, once on the street, fell into step alongside her.

"My father is Sir Edward Addison," she told him. "He's a mining engineer. He has been employed as a consultant by the Eldorado Mining Company out of San Francisco. Have you heard of the company?"

Ethan had to confess his ignorance.

"I'm told its board of directors contain some of the richest men in the country. They want to open several mines in California. That's where my father comes in." She gave him a speculative look. "I take it you are bound for California to get your share of the gold, too. I'd be happy to put in a word for you with my father about getting a job."

The idea of working in a gold mine, deep beneath the surface of the Earth, held no appeal for Ethan. Yet, for some reason he was not inclined to turn Ellen down flat.

"I don't know," he said, being as noncommittal as possible. "I'll, um, I'll sure think about it."

They arrived at the dock and Ellen pointed out a white-haired man in a nicely tailored tweed jacket and doeskin trousers tucked into high black riding boots. The broad-brimmed straw sombrero on his head looked incongruous considering the rest of his attire. Sir Edward managed to look both dignified and eccentric at the same time. Approaching from one side, Ethan was particularly struck by the Englishman's profile. His forehead, adorned with very thick white eyebrows, jutted sharply out over deep-set eyes, while a hawkish nose protruded above a thin-lipped, disapproving mouth. His long white sideburns flared like the outstretched wings of a bird about to take flight. His body was oddly constructed, with a thick, barrel-chested upper torso atop long, thin, horse-warped legs. Ethan could only assume that Ellen had gotten all her physical attributes from her mother.

"Ah, there you are, my child," said Sir Edward, upon seeing Ellen. 'What kept you? They were about to take me out to the ship, as you can see, and I don't think I could have delayed them for very much longer."

"I'd just left the hotel, Father, when I was set upon by a pair of ruffians. Thanks to Ethan here, I stand before you none the worse for that dreadful experience."

"Indeed?" Sir Edward took a moment to scrutinize Ethan. "Why, he's just a boy, isn't he?"

"Pay my father no attention," Ellen advised Ethan. "At times he's simply much too droll."

In spite of her advice, Ethan bristled at that remark, and found it difficult to refrain from commenting on the kind of father who would leave his daughter to wander alone in the streets of a place as perilous as Panama City.

"Yes, quite right," agreed Sir Edward. "My apologies, young fellow. And my heartfelt thanks to you for assisting my daughter. I'm afraid I sometimes forget that Ellen is a young woman in need of protection. You see, I've hauled the poor girl to the far corners of the world. She has survived Thuggies in India, Zulu warriors in Africa, and head-hunting aborigines in Borneo. She is courageous, resilient, and clever, and as dangerous as the king cobra if you get her dander up."

Ethan smiled. Clearly Sir Edward was no indifferent father; you could tell he did indeed dote on his daughter. His words merely reflected the fondness with which he gazed at Ellen as he sang her praises.

"Well, come to think of it," said Ethan, "she was pretty much holding her own against those two men when I came along."

"Nonsense," she scoffed. "He saved my honor, Father—and, if not that, my baggage at the very least."

Sir Edward chuckled, and took another look at Ethan. "If I had to guess I'd say she was a bit smitten with you, sir."

"Hush, Father!" exclaimed Ellen. "You'll scare him away."

Sir Edward chuckled some more. "Well, young man, are

you to be a passenger aboard the *Unicorn*, then? Good, good—then please share this launch with us, and you can tell me all about yourself. The look in my impetuous daughter's eye alerts me to the probability that I will be seeing a great deal of you during our voyage to golden California, so it behooves me to know what you're about. Ah, I see they've got my trunks lashed down. So come along, we'll be off."

He clambered into the launch and then helped Ellen aboard. Ethan hesitated only an instant before joining them. He wasn't even close to being ready to part company with Ellen Addison, as he'd never met anyone quite like her, and doubted he ever would again.

# CHAPTER NINE

San Francisco was a sprawling collection of frame buildings and tent cabins and adobe structures, perched on the
slopes of barren hills overlooking a splendid natural harbor
filled with sea-going vessels, some appearing completely
deserted. Standing at the *Unicorn*'s starboard rail and gazing at the scene spread out before him, Ethan felt both
immense relief and growing anticipation. It wasn't anything
like the fever-pitch excitement that he'd experienced back
in Illinois—back when he and Gil had talked for long hours
about setting out for the gold fields, and dreamed of what
their lives would be like after discovering the mother lode.
The long journey from Roan's Prairie to San Francisco had
stripped Ethan of the naïveté required to feel that kind of
euphoria. During that journey he had heard a thousand stories about California, and while he realized that many of
them were no more than wild speculation without any
grounding in fact, others he believed, and those were
enough to convince him now, as he arrived at his destination, that just because California finally lay within reach
didn't mean all the hardship and peril were behind him.

One of the stories he had heard—and believed—was
that whole ship's crews, infected with gold fever, had deserted their captains upon arrival here. Hence the empty
ships rocking forlornly at anchor in the harbor. The *Unicorn*'s captain, Ethan knew, was resigned to the likelihood
that he would lose a good portion of his crew within forty-

eight hours of their arrival; it happened every time the
steamship dropped anchor in the bay. The captain wasn't
overly concerned, as he also knew from experience that he
could easily replace the deserters with men selected from
the swollen ranks of the disillusioned, the homesick and the
broke who loitered along the waterfront looking for some
means of getting home. Many of these men would jump at
the chance to sign on with the *Unicorn*, even if they had
no sailing experience; they would seek some way across
the isthmus at Panama City, and at Chagres they would
hope to find passage to New Orleans or Charleston or even
New York.

Ethan took a look about him. Nearly all of the *Unicorn*'s
passengers were on deck with him, all eager for that first
glimpse of San Francisco as the ship passed through the
Golden Gate. Yet he saw no sign of Sir Edward Addison
or his daughter. The former, like as not, was in the dining
room drinking port—a habit, Sir Edward had said, that he'd
picked up while spending four years in India on a project
to control the Indus River, which frequently flooded, rav-
aging the countryside, killing thousands, and contributing
to the spread of contagions. An English physician who had
spent most of his adult life in India had assured him that
one or two glasses of port daily would make a white man
virtually immune to the multitude of exotic diseases that
had claimed the lives of so many *sahibs*. Whether there
was any truth to this claim Ethan couldn't say with any
certitude, and he was fairly sure Sir Edward was using the
port prescription as a justification for his drinking habit. It
was quite a habit, too, so conspicuous that Ellen often felt
compelled to make excuses, telling Ethan that her father
had increasingly turned to strong spirits after the death of
her mother in a riding accident. Astonished, Ethan had told
her about his own father, who had suffered the same fate.
It was a story, embarrassing in every respect, that he ordinarily would not have shared with anyone. But, oddly,

where Ellen was concerned, he felt comfortable divulging his secrets.

Now, standing at the rail, the voyage from Panama City concluded, he found himself dreading the moment when he would have to part company with Ellen Addison. He wondered where she was at this moment, and missed her with a terrible ache in his chest, especially as the few remaining moments available to them to spend together were so precious. Perhaps, he mused, growing more despondent, she was too busy packing to spend time with him. Maybe these last moments weren't as precious to her as they were to him. A terrible thought, and one at odds with the fact that she'd seemed inclined to spend all of her time with him during the sea passage.

"Why the long face, bucko?"

Ethan snapped out of his reverie, saw Gil slipping through the press of other passengers like an eel through rocks to join him at the rail. Gil was grinning from ear to ear as he made a sweeping gesture toward the shore.

"There she is! California! The land that's going to make us rich beyond our wildest dreams."

"Yeah," said Ethan, looking over Gil's shoulder, still searching for Ellen, still hoping against hope. The notable lack of enthusiasm in his voice prompted Gil to peer curiously at him. Then that crooked smile crept across his lips. At such times Ethan found that smile nothing if not infuriating. He hated that Gil could read him like a book.

"Where is Ellen?" asked Gil, looking around with feigned innocence. "Kind of surprising to see you without her. The two of you haven't been more than a foot apart since we left Panama City, seems like. And, um, usually a lot closer than that."

Ethan scowled at him. "What are you trying to say?"

"Who, me? Nothing. Not saying anything but what I said. Hey, I don't blame you, *amigo*. She's very pretty. I admit I was jealous at first. She hardly paid me any attention at all. Only had eyes for you. And that's puzzling, to

tell you the truth. I mean, what does she see in you? What
have you got that I don't have?"

"Shut up, Gil."

Gil punched him playfully in the arm. "I'm just joking,
Ethan. Cheer up! Now, I just hope and pray you're not
going to start moping about Ellen, like you've done over
Lilah ever since we left Roan's Prairie. You pining over
one girl was bad enough. Just keep in mind that when you
strike it rich you'll have your pick. Ellen or Lilah or any
other girl you want. Come to think of it, I'd hate to be the
one to make the choice between Ellen and Lilah. Who
knows, maybe I'll settle for the one you don't want—"

Ethan lost his temper then, grabbing Gil by the front of
his shirt and slamming him against the rail. The passengers
who stood nearby quickly backed away, giving them more
space, expecting a fight. Ethan knew there wouldn't be one.
Gil's first instinct was to resist being manhandled. But then
he thought better of resistance—just as Ethan had expected.

"I've warned you before," said Ethan coldly. "You have
a big mouth. You talk too much. And it gets you into trouble."

Gil looked at him through hooded eyes that gave nothing
away. "Take your hands off me, Ethan."

"Not until you stop talking about Ellen. And Lilah. Not
until you promise to mind your own damned business."

"Fine. I'll mind my own business. And you mind yours."

Ethan let go, but couldn't resist giving Gil another shove
before stepping back. Gil's cheeks were mottled by the anger rising in him—anger he was trying hard to keep bottled
up.

"Maybe we should just part company," muttered Gil.
"Go our separate ways. We don't seem to get along very
well anymore."

"That suits me," said Ethan, though he wasn't sure if it
really did. The suggestion caught him by surprise. Gil often
infuriated him, but he'd never given any thought to striking
out on his own.

"I'll even give you half the money."

Hurt, Ethan stubbornly shook his head. "Keep the money. I want no part of it."

"Oh, yeah, that's right," said Gil, his tone dripping with sarcasm. "You don't like the way Marston came by it, and you're too good to have anything to do with it as a consequence."

"That may be because he has integrity."

It was Ellen—and they turned to see her standing there, in the circle of space made for them by the other passengers, most of whom had resumed their inspection of the city on the hills above the sheltered bay.

"No," said Gil, her implication that he lacked integrity feeding his resentment and loosening his tongue. "It's because he's a fool."

Ellen slid her arm under Ethan's and leaned her body against his, and Ethan thought it likely that she was doing this just to further antagonize Gil, doing it because she knew in the mysterious way that her gender knew such things that Gil was attracted to her and envious of Ethan, doing it because she knew this intimate posture would get under Gil's skin.

"I happen to disagree with you," she said. "As far as I can tell, the only foolish thing Ethan has done is to remain your friend for so long."

Ethan thought that was going a little too far. Her words wounded Gil like daggers, and it pained him to see this. Gil was stunned. Usually, he was able to summon that crooked buccaneer's smile to mask his feelings, but this time he couldn't, and that alone was ample proof that Ellen had cut him to the quick. Ethan felt as though he should come to Gil's defense, as he had often done in the past, on all those occasions when Gil would do something wild or reckless or underhanded, and people would shake their heads in dismay and say that he was no good, a troublemaker, a scoundrel. But this time Ethan said nothing. For one thing, he couldn't bring himself to contradict Ellen, especially when she was defending him, and when she was leaning up against him like she was at this moment, as though she belonged to him, or he to her. And, for another, he was still fuming over what Gil had just said about Ellen, and Lilah.

Seeing that Ethan was not going to speak out, Gil nodded, his countenance as grim as Ethan had ever seen it.

"So that's how it's going to be," said Gil. "Well, I never figured we'd end up like this. Guess I thought our friendship was the one thing I could always depend on. Pretty ironic, I'd say, that after everything we've been through to get to California, that this would happen right when we finally reach the promised land." Gil shook his head. "I hope you find what you're looking for, Ethan." He glanced at Ellen and added, "If you haven't already." He started to turn away.

"Gil?"

"Yeah."

Ethan felt Ellen tighten her grip on his arm. And he said, "Good luck to you."

Gil nodded and walked away.

"I know you think you've lost a friend," said Ellen earnestly. "But believe me, you're better off going your own way."

Ethan freed his arm, pulled away from her, and leaned heavily against the rail, the picture of dejection. "You're not the first to say that. But Gil's not all bad, the way some people think. The ones who don't know him like I do." He looked bleakly across the bay at the shore of California and shook his head. "He's right about one thing. We stick together through hell and high water to get here, and when we finally do, this happens."

"What are your plans now?"

Ethan shrugged. "I came to look for gold. I guess that's what I'll do. But I don't have a grubstake. Most of the money I made on the Mississippi is gone. So maybe I can find a job in that town yonder. Earn enough to buy the supplies I need."

"You could come with us," said Ellen.

Sir Edward, as an employee of the Eldorado Mining Company, was bound for the field office located at the headwaters of the Stanislaus River, in the foothills of the Sierra Nevada, about a hundred miles due east of San Francisco. The Eldorado was planning on digging a mine there, and after that, a couple more, and that was where Sir Edward's expertise would come into play.

"I don't think I'd like working down deep in some tunnel," admitted Ethan.

"Then we'll just have to find something else for you to do, won't we?"

He had to smile. It was one of Ellen's cardinal virtues that she refused to let obstacles deter her from getting what she wanted.

"Your father might have something to say about this."

"My father likes you. He's simply not one to wear his emotions on his sleeve. You can't tell, but I can. And besides, he wants me to be happy. And you, Ethan Payne, contribute to my happiness."

"I do?"

"Of course you do. Don't be silly."

Ethan's heart began to soar—and then an errant thought, a thought of Lilah, sent it plummeting.

She read his expression. "You're thinking about her, aren't you?" She said it without acrimony.

"Her?"

"The girl back home. The one you didn't tell me about. The part of your life that you left out when you were telling me all about your life." She smiled. "It's quite all right, Ethan. I understand, really I do."

"How did you—?"

"Gil told me."

"He did?"

"Yes."

"Why would he go and do a thing like that?"

"Can't you guess why? But his little scheme didn't work, did it? I'm still here. Knowing that she exists changes nothing as far as I'm concerned, except perhaps to make me more determined than ever."

"Determined? To do what?"

"To keep you."

Ethan stared at her, not knowing what to say, and she laughed softly at his expression.

"To keep you here, with me, for as long as I'm able to do so," she elaborated.

"Well, um, I'm not planning on going anywhere," he said lamely.

She laughed. "My, how romantic you are, Mr. Payne! No matter. Come on, let's go find my father and tell him the good news."

Ethan wasn't convinced that Sir Edward Addison would consider it "good news" that he was being saddled with a flat-broke Illinois farm boy. In fact, it seemed that Sir Edward had only been tolerating his more or less constant presence in Ellen's vicinity, assuming perhaps that the romance apparently blooming between the pair of young people would be of short duration, specifically until the *Unicorn* dropped anchor in San Francisco Bay. It hadn't escaped Ethan's notice that Sir Edward regularly spoke of this fine young gentleman or that—either in England or some other civilized part of the world—who belonged to this important family or that one. And he would scowl (but not too sternly, as he was never too stern where Ellen was concerned) when his daughter made some disparaging remark about each of the young men about whom he waxed so eloquent. She dismissed out of hand her father's contention that any of them would make do as a suitable husband, one who could provide for her, and provide well. So Ethan was pretty sure Sir Edward would not be overjoyed. Ellen knew it, too. But she simply did not care. And why should she? After all, Sir Edward would comply with her wishes.

As would one Ethan Payne. Even though he was nagged with pangs of guilt where Lilah Webster was concerned. He didn't know if he should be going to the headwaters of the Stanislaus River with Ellen Addison and her father, or not. The only thing he *was* sure of was that he *would* go, because Ellen wanted him to.

# PART II

PART II

# CHAPTER TEN

Even though he had seen the place for the first time over a year ago—and nearly every day since then, except during the trips he made to San Francisco with the supply train—Ethan Payne still found the Eldorado Number One mine an awe-inspiring sight. Clinging to a steep rocky slope long since stripped of the last viable piece of timber (just like much of the land for about a mile in any direction) was the stamp mill, a huge structure consisting of four levels. A rail emerged from the upper section, crossed a short and sturdy trestle bridge, and then entered the main entrance of the mine itself, about two-thirds of the way up the slope. Ore was transported out of the mine tunnels by hoist, then placed in ore cars, which were pushed by burly trammers along the rail and into the top of the mill.

The ore was then pulverized by steam-powered crushers on the upper level before being dropped into the ten stamps on the level below, which reduced the ore even further. Leaving the stamps, the ore passed through screens and onto vanners, belts which carried it into pans on the third level where workers separated the gold from the ore by cooking it in a mixture of water, salt, mercury, and bluestone. On the bottom level were the massive wood-burning boilers that produced the steam that in turn powered all the machinery. These boilers had consumed the forest that once covered the adjacent hills, which were part of the western shoulder of the Sierra Nevada, whose snow-draped peaks had proven a considerable obstacle to the gold seekers who had chosen to come by way of the overland route.

Five years ago, those mountains had conspired with a harsh winter to destroy a group of emigrants known as the Donner Party, and they had killed a good many more since. Still, the people came, some still bent on finding gold, though the fever had died down some in the year and a half that had passed since Ethan's departure from Roan's Prairie. More and more these days the survivors of the westward trek turned out to be farmers, lured by the talk of California's fertile valleys and mild winters. This was a golden land in more ways than one.

As he rode in the lead wagon of the supply train, Ethan could hear the pulsating stamps of the mill as far down the canyon road as the mining town of Angel Camp, more than a mile from the Eldorado. It was a pounding tattoo that went on and on for sixteen hours a day, except on Sundays. In the beginning, the mill had operated 'round the clock. But Eldorado Number One's rich veins were beginning to play out. In another year, according to the scuttlebutt among the jackers and trammers employed by the company, this mine would be closed down. The machinery would be sold, or dismantled and shipped elsewhere. The tunnels would be left to collapse, as timber gave way to the inexorable pressure of the mountain combined with the immutable laws of gravity and decay. The stamp mill would become an empty husk, slowly disintegrated by the patient elements. The creek that ran down the canyon, now polluted with effluvium from the mine, would eventually return to the pristine condition that it had enjoyed when Ethan first laid eyes on it. The forests, though, would never be as before. Such was the price of progress.

None of it would have happened without Sir Edward Addison. As a mining engineer he had few equals, and not even his propensity for strong spirits had any effect on his abilities. Ethan admired his expertise. Eldorado was lucky to have him, and the board of directors knew it. Sir Edward could have had great success and lived out his life in comfort, had he chosen to stay in England. But it seemed he could not bear to do so.

"My poor father," Ellen had said. "When we are away he misses England terribly. Yet when we come within sight of her shores, even though we've been in a foreign land for years, he becomes physically ill. Nearly ten years have passed but he simply cannot stop grieving for my mother, God rest her soul."

"He must have loved her very much."

"I have never seen nor heard of a love like theirs." Ellen sighed—and gave Ethan a sidelong look. "I've always hoped to find a love like that. It is quite rare, you know. Most people will go through life without experiencing anything like that."

And then she stood there, watching him, obviously expecting something more from him. Ethan had no idea what that might be, or what he was supposed to say. Ellen Addison often spoke of love in his presence, and it never failed to make him distinctly uncomfortable. Because over time he'd become convinced that she was in love with him, or at least *thought* she was. Somewhere along the way he'd ceased to wonder if he was just a diversion for her, a plaything with which she could while away the time. There had been plenty of other diversions available to her since— plenty of unmarried young men in the employ of the Eldorado Mining Company, or on their own in the goldfields, and she could have had her pick. Wonder of wonders, though, he discovered that her interest in him was enduring, to the exclusion of all others. Though he still couldn't figure out why a girl like Ellen— a girl so pretty, so well educated, so refined, so vivacious, and so sought after—would want to spend so much time with him.

He figured any other young man would have counted his blessings and accepted his great good fortune. And yet, as happy as he was to be the apple of Ellen's eye, it also made him miserable. This was because of Lilah Webster.

The memories were not so compelling when he was at the mine, with Ellen almost always present. But when he went to San Francisco with the supply wagon, the thoughts of Lilah became stronger and more frequent, and he would usually end up writing her a letter. Nine times in the past year he had gone to San Francisco—thrice the monthly caravan had been called off due to weather that made travel with heavy wagons impossible. Eight out of nine times he had written, telling Lilah about everything that had transpired, even the disintegration of his partnership with Gil Stark—about everything, that is, except Ellen. And only once—on this trip—had he found an answering letter waiting for him in San Francisco. He carried it now under his shirt and, having read it a dozen times, knew it by heart:

*Dear Ethan:*

*I was so happy and relieved to read your letter. It is the first one I have received and I was worried sick that you had come to harm. I know now by your letter that you have written to me before this. You were worried, too, as you had not heard from me either. But I never got any of your previous letters. Even so, I would have written to you before this, except that I did not know where to send it. I am glad you are well and still thinking of me, and know that you are always in my thoughts. I was surprised, though, to read that you are working at a mine. I thought you and Gil were going to prospect for gold. You wrote that you do not know what has become of Gil. I suppose the facts behind that statement were in one of the letters that I never got. If something has happened to your friendship, then I am truly sorry. I will not pretend that I ever liked or trusted Gil, but I know he meant a lot to you. All is well here. Your father is still on the farm. Do you remember Mr. Griggs, the man who left his family to go to California, only to return without a coin in his pocket, to have his family move away, and his farm taken over by the bank? They found him drowned in the Rock River three months ago. Some say it was an accident, but others believe he threw himself into the river in a fit of dark despair. Gabriel Stark was very angry with Gil over the horse, but as time has passed he has become less so, and now he seems just very sad. I can tell he misses his son terribly and wishes him home. I miss you terribly, Ethan, and I wish you were home, too. Just know that I will wait as long as I have to for the day you return to me. That day will be the happiest of my life.*

*Lilah*
*P.S. I have found the stone.*

Ethan was at a loss what to do. Lilah loved him—loved him so much that she was willing to wait indefinitely for his return. And she had continued searching for the heart-shaped stone. Her finding it—was it an omen of some kind? Reading between the lines of her letter, he could tell she wanted to know why he wasn't looking for that bonanza that would make him wealthy. After all, that was why he and Gil had set out for California in the first place. Instead, he was working for a mining company, and while Lilah could not know that he made twenty dollars a month, she had to be aware of the fact that he would never become a rich man on company wages. The unasked question, therefore, was *why did he stay in California if he wasn't going to pursue his dream?*

It was a question he had often asked himself. He *could* have worked for Eldorado just long enough to earn a grub-stake and then struck out on his own for the goldfields. But he hadn't, partly because the gold rush seemed to be dying down. Gold camps were being abandoned. Angel Camp, once filled with prospectors, now consisted primarily of gamblers and prostitutes and purveyors of cheap rotgut, all of whom eked out a living by pandering to the appetites of Eldorado men. Most people were moving on to other things. But mainly he stayed because Ellen wanted him to. Or was it more because he wanted to?

Ethan rode shotgun in the lead wagon. He had acquired the role of supply train guard thanks to his accuracy with the rifle, demonstrated on the occasion of his first ride with the supply train, when he'd borrowed someone's rifle and brought down a deer at four hundred yards, on a dare, in front of the entire company. Next thing he knew he had a shotgun in his hands instead of harness leather. The supply trains were attractive targets for the Indians and bandits that infested the stretch between the coastal settlements and the gold camps and mines in the mountains. For this reason Eldorado put a shotgunner with every wagon.

As the wagons drew nearer the stamp mill, Ethan saw right away that something wasn't right. The stamps were still pounding away at the ore that the trammers were hauling out of the mine, but it looked like everyone who did not have some essential duty to perform at that moment was gathered in front of the superintendent's cabin. Normally, the arrival of the supply train was cause for a great deal of excitement among the Eldorado employees, as it meant the sutler's would be fully stocked with tobacco and sugar and other luxuries—and that some of them might be getting mail from home. But this time Ethan noticed with surprise that their arrival elicited only moderate interest. The men were far more intrigued by a discussion going on between John Maller, who ran the mine, and several of his lieutenants, on the porch of the superintendent's cabin. One man did wander curiously over to the wagons, and the driver sitting next to Ethan asked him what was going on.

"Outlaws stole the gold shipment," was the reply. "That makes twice in a row now, you know. They killed a man this time, Johnson. Wounded a couple more."

"Damn shame," muttered the driver. "I knew Johnson. Good man."

Ethan spotted Sir Edward, standing behind Maller on the porch. The mining engineer seemed content to listen rather than contribute to the heated debate presided over by the superintendent. Setting the sawed-off shotgun down, Ethan jumped off the wagon and made his way through the press of onlookers so that he could hear what was being discussed.

"Makes no sense to me how the robbers could know with such certainty which shipment contained the gold," said Maller grimly. He was a short, slender man, a tireless human dynamo who drove his employees hard, and drove himself even harder. "We send out three details, spread out a day apart, and all taking separate routes. Two of them carry a strongbox filled with rocks. I marked the first robbery down to dumb luck on the robbers' part. But not this time, boys. The odds are long that they could be that lucky twice in a row. One of the sons of bitches rides an Appaloosa—a horse that sticks out like a sore thumb in these parts—and our men have reported seeing it during both robberies."

"Maybe we should have listened to Addison," said Benedict, one of Maller's subordinates. Like most of the other men at the mine, he could not bring himself to address the mining engineer as Sir Edward, and Sir Edward, being well acquainted with the idiosyncrasies of Americans where titles were concerned, had not bothered to insist on this particular prerogative. "He said we should send the gold with the supply train instead of on the back of a mule to the railhead at Copper Creek."

"It was merely a suggestion," said Sir Edward mildly. "Such weighty matters I prefer to leave entirely in the hands of you gentlemen."

"If we did that there'd be gold on every supply train," said Maller. "Lots of it. We can't send out decoy caravans, as we lack the wagons, the livestock, and the manpower. Before long, every highwayman in California would know that an Eldorado supply train carried gold. Then guess what would happen? No. We have to have the supply trains because the railroad charges too much for us to ship all the provisions and tools and everything else we need. Besides, the railhead is just two days' ride away. The gold is in a bank vault in San Francisco within four days of it leaving the mine. It takes a week to ten days for the wagons to get to the coast. The board of directors liked that idea and so did I. We expected a holdup now and again. These damned hills are chock full of bandits these days. Lot of 'em are Americans who came to dig for gold and didn't find any and got fed up with trying to get it the hard and honest way. But the decoy shipments gave us an edge, or so we thought. And I still believe it would. Except that I'm smelling a rat."

Benedict glanced at the other lieutenants. There was Richter, who was in charge of security for the mine—and, by extension, was responsible for the protection of the gold shipments. He was a burly ex-soldier who had seen plenty of fighting in the recent war with Mexico. And there was Collery, the young, college-educated Philadelphian who handled the mine's books.

"What are you saying?" asked Richter, suspiciously.

"I'm saying," replied Maller, enunciating each word carefully so that no one could possibly misunderstand him, "that these robbers are either the luckiest bastards on the continent or they know which detail carries the gold."

"An inside man?" asked Collery.

"Why not?" asked Benedict.

"Got any ideas who?" asked Richter, staring at Maller as though he was daring the superintendent to accuse him of treachery.

"Sorry to say that I don't," replied Maller, giving Richter a look that made it plain he was not intimidated by the man's size, and that if he'd had any evidence against Richter he'd have made the accusation. "All four of us know what day the gold leaves, and by what route it goes to the railhead. So do a few others in the camp. Fact is, too damned many people know. It's been a slipshod operation, Richter, I'll say that much. You've gotten careless."

Richter fumed, tight-lipped. To Ethan he looked about twice Maller's size, looming over the superintendent. Yet Maller didn't notice. Nothing rattled him. That was why the Eldorado Mining Company's board of directors had put him in charge of everything. And Richter wasn't about to challenge him. It wasn't size that mattered, but grit, determination, and attitude. That was a lesson Ethan had learned long ago, back when he'd had to fight so many fights with the other boys around Roan's Prairie—the ones who made fun of him and put him down because he was Abner Payne's son. A lesson that it was obvious Maller, who stood there staring Richter down, daring the big man to take offense to the criticism just leveled against him, had learned as well.

"So what do we do about it?" asked Collery.

Maller's smile was about as amiable as a wolf's. "I'm paid a salary to get the gold out of these damned mountains and into a San Francisco bank vault. That's what I intend to do. It's my responsibility. Always has been. I just made the mistake of delegating it to others. Now I'm taking it back."

"Wait just a damned minute," said Richter. "You saying I can't do my job?"

"The facts speak for themselves," said Maller dryly.

"Then you're firing me, is that it?"

"No," said Maller, exasperated. "You're still on the payroll. Still in charge of security here at the mine. But I'm going to see to the next gold shipment personally." He took a look around, spotted Ethan, then looked beyond the crowd at the supply train wagons, and Ethan got the impression that he hadn't noticed them at all until this very moment. He turned his attention back to Ethan.

"Any trouble?"

"Some renegades got a little too interested in our mules one night, but we took care of things."

Maller nodded. "Mr. Collery, check in those supplies.

Mr. Benedict, disperse this crowd. By God if they don't have anything better to do than just stand around all day, find something for them to do. Get half of them to dig a trench and the other half to fill it up again." He turned to enter the superintendent's cabin, then stopped and looked back at Ethan. "What's your name again?"

"Ethan Payne, sir."

"He, um, came with me, John," volunteered Sir Edward.

"Oh, yeah. Payne, step into my office for a minute. I want to talk to you. You too, Mr. Addison."

Ethan followed Maller and Sir Edward inside, uncomfortable because he had been singled out. The room was cluttered with a desk, several tables, and some chairs, all covered with charts and papers. Maller went straight to the desk, plucked a Mexican cheroot out of a humidor, stuck it between his teeth, and fired up a sulfur match to light the tip. All Ethan could do was wait and wonder what Maller wanted with him. Sir Edward took the liberty of cleaning some reports off a chair and sitting down.

"I remember now," said Maller. "You're supposed to be a crack shot. That's why we turned you into a shotgunner. What else can you tell me about this young man, Mr. Addison?"

"My daughter knows him better than I," replied Sir Edward, with more than a trace of irony in his tone. "But I can say that he strikes me as an honest young chap, with plenty of backbone. He rescued Ellen from a gang of cutthroats in Panama City."

"Did he, now," said Maller.

"Hardly a gang, sir," corrected Ethan. "There were only the two of them."

Maller nodded. He puffed vigorously on the cheroot and peered speculatively at Ethan through the blue smoke that quickly pervaded the cabin. "How old are you, Payne?"

"Eighteen," replied Ethan. "Well, nearly."

"I've already got about thirty thousand dollars' worth of gold dust that needs to be in a bank vault in San Francisco.

Can I rely on you to get it to the railhead at Copper Creek?"

"Yes, sir. How many others will be coming with me?"

"You'll be going alone, son."

"I say, John," exclaimed Sir Edward—but that was all he *did* say.

Ethan couldn't believe his ears. A band of robbers had just made off with a second Eldorado gold shipment, killing one man in the process. It was likely they would be lurking near at hand, hoping for a shot at a third shipment. And here was Maller sending him off with thirty thousand in gold *all by himself*? Had the man gotten into some loco-weed?

"That's right," said Maller, reading Ethan's expression. "Tomorrow I'm sending a strongbox out with a guard of six men armed to the teeth. Far as anyone else wil know, there'll be gold in that box. But there won't be any gold. Hopefully, six men—double the number Richter was sending out—will deter those bandits from trying another holdup. But it will surely get their attention. Should be a good enough diversion that you can get the gold through to the railhead without a problem. What do you think?"

Ethan nodded. "I can get the job done, sir."

"Yes, I believe that you can," said Maller. "I don't need to tell you to keep your mouth shut about all this. Speak about it to no one. I mean no one, you understand?"

Ethan said that he understood.

"You really think that someone in our ranks is in collusion with the highwaymen?" asked Sir Edward idly as he scanned the room looking for a bottle of whiskey.

"I'll tell you what I don't think," replied Maller crisply. "I don't think there's any such thing as a coincidence."

"I'm flattered that you trust me," said Sir Edward. "But also rather curious as to why."

"I don't believe a bunch of long riders and an English gentleman would have much in common," said Maller. "Correct me if I'm wrong."

"You're quite right, actually. Quite right."

Maller nodded and turned his attention back to Ethan. "The decoy shipment leaves at dawn. You'll go before first light. Leave the mine without being seen. I'll have the gold waiting for you a ways down the road, along with a saddle horse."

"Yes, sir."

"One more thing, Payne. If you lose that gold, I don't want to see you come back here any other way but dead."

# CHAPTER ELEVEN

Ethan went to the mess hall to get his supper. It was the usual fare, meat and potatoes and biscuits, but it was still better than what he had gotten on the trail, except on the occasions when he or some other hand with a rifle brought down some wild game for the cook fires. He had never been finicky in his eating habits, but this time he couldn't muster up much of an appetite. All he could think about was the task that Maller had put before him. It sounded like a real handy way to get himself killed. If for some reason Maller's decoy scheme didn't work, he would find himself standing alone against a pack of desperados who had already demonstrated their readiness to kill anyone who tried to get between them and the Eldorado gold they were after. Such thinking tended to rob a man of his taste for food.

After picking over his meal for a while, Ethan gave up and went to the bunkhouse where he was quartered, along with twenty-three other employees of the company. There were several such barracks, long narrow wooden buildings with external stone fireplaces on either end. Inside they were all identical—twelve narrow wooden beds with thin mattresses lined up along either long side, and two split-log tables in the middle accompanied by split-log benches.

There were a half-dozen men in the bunkhouse; some of them acknowledged Ethan as he entered, while others did not bother to look up from whatever they were doing. Ethan had made no enemies among the other company

men, but neither had he made any friends to speak of. Sir
Edward had labeled him a loner and Ethan supposed that
this was true. He had always been so. But for Gil Stark
he'd not had any real friends in his life. He was beginning
to think it just made life easier. So he tended to keep to
himself, minding his own business and declining to partic-
ipate in any of the extracurricular activities indulged in by
so many of his colleagues during their off time. He didn't
play cards or gamble in any other way, nor did he enjoy
drinking, nor did he have much desire to find his way to
the nearby camp where the calico queens were always willing to spread their legs for two dollars in hard money.

His bunk was at one end of the room, and he went
straight to it and was just sitting down to pull off his
boots—which, but for one or two occasions, had been on
his feet for the better part of three weeks—when one of the
other inhabitants of the bunkhouse came through the door,
looked for him, and bellowed his name.

"Hey there, Payne. Someone out here wants to see you."
He hooked a thumb over his shoulder.

"Who is it?" asked Ethan wearily, loathe to get up now
that he had planted his trail-weary bones.

"I ain't no doorman," said the other, "so I'm not inclined
to make introductions." Then he grinned. "But now if
you're too busy to keep her company tonight, I'll just go
on back out there and see if maybe she'll settle for me in
your place."

It was Ellen! Ethan was mortified, realizing that he had
forgotten all about her, so preoccupied was he with the
business of the gold shipment that Maller had dropped so
unexpectedly into his lap. He had one boot off—now he
strained to get it back on over his swollen, sweaty foot, an
arduous task that he continued halfway to the door, hopping
on his booted foot along the way. As he passed one of the
tables, a man who sat there reading a month-old newspaper
tried to suppress a grin. "You smell pretty ripe for a feller
about to go a-courting," he drawled.

Horrified, Ethan had to acknowledge that the man was right. Ordinarily he would have gone up the creek far enough to find fairly clean water, washed himself, changed into his spare shirt and trousers, and gone to see Ellen, who resided with her father in a small cabin upslope from the superintendent's place. And since he hadn't done that, Ellen had come looking for him.

He stepped out onto the porch and shut the door behind him to make eavesdropping that much harder for the men inside the bunkhouse to accomplish. Ellen stood there in the twilight gloom, lovely as always in a blue dress with a ribbon of lace at the high collar and around the sleeves, and her black hair had been brushed to the point that it fairly gleamed in the waning light, tied back from her pretty face with silken ribbons.

"Well, there you are," she said, pouting, hands on her curvaceous hips. "Were you not going to come see me, then? Did you not miss me after all the time we have been apart?"

"Yeah, sure I missed you, Ellen. I just, well, I—I had a lot of things on my mind." Immediately he said it, Ethan knew he shouldn't have.

"Oh, did you, now. And here I was, unable to think of anything but the happy moment I would see you again, feeling so lost and lonely every minute you've been away. I suppose I should be glad you didn't suffer as I did, that you had more important things to think about, things that would not make you as miserable as I was without your arms around me."

"That's not what I meant," protested Ethan, with a certain element of fatalism creeping into his voice. He knew this was a debate he was destined to lose.

"And do tell, why are you being so standoffish? What are you doing way over there? Don't I at least deserve a kiss? I declare, Ethan Payne, you do know how to test a woman's patience."

Ethan blushed—and was grateful for the gathering night

shadow, hoping that it was already too dark for Ellen to see the reddening of his cheeks.

"Well," he said, reluctant to speak of it, yet knowing he really had no choice in the matter. "Well, if you must know, I haven't had a chance to bathe just yet. I've been on the trail for more than a fortnight and, I, um, well, I smell like it."

Ellen took her hands off her hips—and suddenly she was smiling. Just like that. And Ethan wondered if her ire had been entirely manufactured. Had she been toying with him again? Thing was, with a woman you could never be certain.

She stepped up onto the bunkhouse porch, reached out, and captured his hand. "I don't mind," she said. "Really, I don't. Walk with me, Ethan. We need to talk."

Ethan stifled a groan. When it came to conversation, especially on important subjects—and her tone of voice indicated that the subject she had in mind for discussion was very important indeed—he was at a terrible disadvantage. Particularly with Ellen, who talked so well, and at such great length and rapid pace that she inevitably left him far behind, bobbing helplessly in her verbal wake. But there was no escaping this walk. He had to agree—and did.

They walked along the creek, going upstream, passing below the stamp mill, a hulk looming above them, its immense size forbidding in the deepening darkness. The first stars were just now appearing in the soft indigo blanket of the night sky. Soon the moon would rise above the sierra. It wasn't safe to venture too far from the buildings, day or night, without being well armed; but Ethan didn't say anything, knowing it would be fruitless to make any objection no matter how valid the reasoning, and trying to assure himself that Ellen didn't intend to go much farther up the creek anyway.

He was wrong, as he so often was where she was concerned. She took him by the hand when he hesitated and looked back to gauge just how far from safety they had come, pulling him along as she pressed resolutely forward. About a quarter of a mile from the mill they came to a place where the creek tumbled down a steep rock slope; above the slope was a deep pool, rimmed by large boulders. Ethan had never been here; he'd never had any reason to come this far up the creek, but he sensed that Ellen was familiar with the spot. He worried about bandits, figuring they wouldn't have strayed too far from the mine, and thinking that this was a watering hole that varmints of both the two- and four-legged varieties might want to make use of.

"I think we should go back," he told her as she led him up to the top of one of the big rocks.

"Oh, come now. Don't tell me you're afraid."

"Afraid for you, yes."

"And I'm afraid for you, Ethan," she said, peering at him with sudden earnestness.

"Me? How come?"

She sighed. "My father told me what you've agreed to do."

"He what?" Ethan was astonished. "Damn it, Ellen. He wasn't supposed to tell anyone."

"Don't fret so. He told only me, and will mention not a word of it to anyone else, you can be sure. And he wouldn't have told me, except that—except that he knows how fond I am of you."

"Fond of me," echoed Ethan wryly. "Is that all? Just *fond* of me?"

Ellen smirked. "Well, perhaps that is an understatement, and then again maybe it isn't. But there is one thing about you that I am not at all fond of."

"Oh? And what is that?"

"The way you smell," she said. She put her hands on his chest, and for an instant Ethan thought she was going to slide them up around his neck. Instead, she gave him a hard shove. He toppled backward off the boulder into the pool, and his shout of surprise was abruptly cut short as he hit the water with a great splash. The water was cold, colder than he would have expected, due to the depth of the pool. He flailed to the surface, spitting water, searching for the bottom with his feet and, failing to find it, sank beneath the surface yet again. As he came up a second time he began to swim. He reached the edge of the pool and found his footing. Looking up at Ellen on top of the boulder, he was just in time to see her step out of her dress. Stunned, all he could do was stand there, waist-deep in the pool, and stare at her, marveling at the alabaster whiteness of her skin, the proud, full, dark-tipped breasts, the narrow waist, the inviting curve of her hips. The dress lying in a heap at her feet, she glanced at him and giggled shyly—and that was the one and only time he would ever see Ellen Addison display any sort of self-conscious behavior. She dove headlong into the pool, her pale body slicing into the water. Ethan expected her to surface immediately, and when she failed to do so he was seized by a moment of alarm. Then she came up, right next to him, laughing delightedly at the startled expression on his face.

"Now, Ethan," she said, "you can't very well wash yourself while wearing all those clothes, can you?"

He mumbled an unintelligible assent, unable to take his eyes off her breasts as she unbuttoned his shirt, and he remembered skinny-dipping with Lilah Webster in the Rock River, recalling that Lilah had managed somehow to deny him such an intimate look at her body, and even as he thought of Lilah her letter, which he had put under his shirt for safekeeping and had forgotten all about, fell into the water as Ellen tugged the last button loose. Ethan reached for it, but Ellen snatched it deftly off the dark surface of the pool.

"What is this?" she asked, looking him straight in the eye.

"A letter. From Lilah."

She nodded and, with a very serious look on her face, carried the letter and Ethan's shirt out of the pool, placing them on top of a rock with the letter partially beneath the shirt. That done, she turned and waded back into the water, quite unselfconscious about her nakedness now, and when she got to him she reached out and took him by the wrist and placed his left hand over her right breast. The nipple was hard against his palm and seemed to send a bolt of lightning shooting straight through his body. She took his right hand and put it on her left breast, then set to work on his belt buckle, and when she had it undone she slid her hand under his trousers, making a soft, husky sound of desire, her eyes widening with delight and wonder as she felt his manhood. He swept her up in his arms and carried her out of the water, laying her pale, dripping body down between two boulders and shedding his soggy trousers, and as he lay down on top of her she opened her arms and legs like a flower opening to the sun. The heat of her passion was far greater than any the sun could produce. And as they became one she clasped her arms and legs tightly around him and held him deep inside her. Their bodies moved in an instinctual harmony that needed no choreographing, a graceful ballet that escalated into feverish thrashing, accompanied by her quiet moans of ecstasy, and then into a moment of rapturous convulsions. Their passion spent, they lay entwined, heaving for breath, bodies atremble. She kept him cocooned in her grasp and he didn't mind, didn't want to move, didn't want to separate his body, or his soul, from hers.

Eventually, though, they rose and dressed with the haste of the guilty, and Ethan worried because Ellen was strangely subdued, worried that she was regretting what had happened between them. He felt as though it was incumbent upon him to say something, but he was—as seemed to be the case with him all too often—at a loss for words. At such a moment a man had to careful not to say the wrong thing. He knew this intuitively. When he was dressed, Ethan took Lilah's letter, still damp from its submersion in the pool, and slipped it back inside his shirt. It was odd, he mused, how so often in his life reality veered so sharply from a person's expectations. He had never expected that he and Gil Stark would end their friendship. Nor had he expected to be working as a gun guard for a mining company once he reached California. And he had certainly never expected to make love to anyone but Lilah Webster. He'd always assumed that if and when that ever occurred it would be with her. These past months he had speculated on what it would be like to make love to Ellen, but he'd never really *expected* it to happen.

As they walked back to the mine hand in hand, no words passing between them, Ethan felt the letter clinging wetly to his skin—and felt stabbing pangs of guilt. Lilah hadn't asked him for a promise that he wouldn't be intimate with another woman during his absence. She had felt it unnecessary to do so. That he would not was implicit in his commitment to her. Certainly he had expected her to resist any temptation while he was away. So he had betrayed her trust in him. There was no way around that. How was it, he wondered, amazed by the irony of it all, that something so wonderful as what had just transpired could be so terrible in its implications at the same time?

They were nearing the mill when Ellen stopped suddenly and turned to face him. Her face was especially radiant in the pale silver light of the moon that had only recently climbed above the jagged peaks of the sierra, and in spite of all the disturbing thoughts rattling around in his head, Ethan found himself desiring her again. She looked as solemn as he had ever seen her. It was rare indeed to see someone as vivacious and cheerful as Ellen so pensive, so grave.

"You had better not get yourself killed, Ethan Payne," she told him sternly. "I so wish you hadn't agreed to take that gold to the railhead."

"But Mr. Maller asked me to do it. What was I supposed to say? No?"

"Yes. Oh, why do you have to be so brave?" she asked petulantly.

He had to smile at the pout on her lips, and he had to summon all the willpower at his command to refrain from kissing it away. He didn't only because he wasn't sure how Ellen would respond.

"I'm not brave," he said. "I guess I just didn't want Mr. Maller to think I was afraid to do it, to be honest."

"You must promise that you will come back to me."

"I promise, Ellen," he said earnestly.

She tilted her head to one side. "You made the same promise to Lilah long ago, didn't you?"

"Well, yes. Yes, I did."

"I'm ashamed, for I've put you in an awful position by asking you to make that same promise to me. How can you keep your promise to me and your promise to her? Because you know, don't you, that I don't mean that I simply want you to come back. I want you to come back and be with me. Every night from now on I want you to love me the way you loved me tonight. Is that asking too much? Am I being selfish—again?"

"Why no, I—"

"Father says I always expect too much from others."

"I don't think so," he said lamely.

"No, I think he might be right. I do ask a lot. But I'm worth it, don't you think?"

"Yes, you are."

"But then, if you do come back to be with me always, you must break your promise to her. You realize that, don't you?"

Ethan didn't say anything, thinking bleakly that he had already broken one unspoken promise to Lilah—and wondering why God had given women such an uncanny knack for reasoning men into a corner. Especially *this* woman.

"I must go," she said. "My father will be very worried by now. I'm surprised he hasn't had Mr. Maller send out a search party." She stood on her tiptoes, draping her arms langorously over his shoulders, and kissed him softly. The touch of her lips made him delirious with desire. "I love you," she whispered, with her lips still very close to his—and then she was gone, not waiting for him to tell her that he loved her, too.

In a sort of witless daze, Ethan wandered back to the bunkhouse. It was late—where had the time gone?—and the lamps were turned down low. Most of the bunks were filled with men fast asleep and snoring, and Ethan was glad of that, particularly glad that the man who had told him Ellen had come calling wasn't awake. He was in no mood for any ribbing, good-natured or otherwise, about being out so long with Sir Edward's winsome daughter. Cat-footing his way to his bunk, he pulled off his boots and stretched out, hands clasped behind his head, knowing that he could benefit from getting some shuteye in the few hours that remained before day broke, and knowing too that there wasn't much chance of it happening. Jumbled thoughts caromed through his overwrought brain—thoughts of how Ellen had looked, standing on the boulder with her dress down around her ankles, how Lilah had looked sitting on the limb of that old lightning-riven oak at the Rock River meeting place, how Ellen had felt squirming and gasping beneath him as their passion exploded, and how Lilah's copper-colored hair, smelling of sunlight and flowers, had fallen across his face as she kissed him goodbye—for the last time. He experienced a sudden strong urge to get on a horse and ride like hell for Illinois, to ride without stopping until he got home, even though this was impossible, just to see Lilah again. Her voice, her eyes, her smile had always made him feel that all was right with the world even when the reverse was true, and he realized for the first time that nothing had really felt right since he'd left her behind. Yet he wasn't sure he could bring himself to leave Ellen. Ellen loved him, desired him, needed him—and he wanted her, too. Did he love her? That was a good question. He wasn't sure. He wasn't really sure about much of anything.

Ethan groaned, rolled over on his side, and closed his eyes, tried to stop thinking. He figured there was a fair chance he would get himself killed in the next day or two anyway, so why torture himself so over a decision he probably wouldn't live long enough to make?

# CHAPTER TWELVE

He was at the appointed place at the appointed time, having slipped out of the bunkhouse an hour before dawn while the rest of the Eldorado men still slept, then stealing away from the mill on foot without—he was fairly certain—being seen by anyone. He proceeded down the canyon by way of the road that led to Angel Camp, and reached the place where Maller was waiting for him.

"Right on time," said the superintendent, checking the sky instead of the timepiece in his vest pocket. "I've got everything you need," he added, gesturing at a tall roan saddle horse and a pack mule, the latter secured to the saddle of the former with a lead rope. Maller moved alongside the mule and patted the tarp-wrapped bundles strapped to the stout wooden frame on the animal's back. "The gold is here, in ten sacks. I decided not to put it in strongboxes. There's no mistaking the shape of one of those for anything but what it is. With any luck you'll make it to Copper Creek without seeing another living soul, but just in case you don't, they'll like as not take one look at you and move on."

"Yes, sir," said Ethan, trying not to sound as dubious as he felt, and wishing he could be as confident as Maller.

"Okay, then. What kind of weapons do you carry?"

"I've got this," said Ethan, taking the five-shot Whitney revolver from his belt. "And this." He patted the bowie knife sheathed on his left hip.

Maller nodded. "Handsome knife." But he looked skeptical as he glanced at the pistol, and nodded at the saddle horse. "You'll notice there's a sawed-off ten-gauge on the rig there, and in a boot on the other side is a .50 caliber percussion rifle, manufactured by Sharps, for long-range work. You ever had to kill a man, Payne?"

Ethan thought of his struggle with Ash Marston aboard the *Drusilla*, the one that had ended with the Englishman plunging into the river. He preferred to believe that Marston had survived—had somehow made it to shore. But even if that wasn't the case, he still hadn't been *trying* to kill Marston. Rather than attempt an explanation of the circumstances surrounding that event—and all of his rationalizing over it—to Maller, Ethan simply shook his head.

"No, sir, I don't think so."

"You don't *think* so?"

"I mean, I've shot at some Indians who were trying to make off with company livestock on the last trip to San Francisco, but I'm not sure I hit anything. It was a dark night. We couldn't see much of anything."

"Think you could kill a man if you had to?"

Ethan recalled the man back at Chagres, the one who had taken one look at him and declared him to be a natural-born killer. Ethan had thought him mad, but the man had spoken with an unshakable conviction.

"Yes, sir, if I have to I'll pull the trigger."

Maller nodded again, apparently satisfied. "I think you can, too. Well, you'd better get going. It will be light before long. Get this gold to Frisco, Payne, and there'll be a bonus in it for you. How much do you get paid?"

"Twenty dollars a month."

"That'll change. If you make it back alive."

"I will, sir."

Maller smiled. "Then it's a deal. Good luck to you."

And that was all. The superintendent went to his own horse, mounted up, and started back up the trail for the mine without a single backward glance.

Ethan stood there for a moment, feeling suddenly very alone, very exposed, and very burdened with a responsibility he did not relish. There was thirty thousand dollars' worth of gold dust riding on that mule, and it was in his keeping. Thirty thousand dollars! He had to wonder how Maller could be so sure he would take the gold to San Francisco and not steal it himself. He could take that thirty thousand and go back to Illinois. A man could live quite comfortably for a good long time on that kind of money. It would be so easy. He would just ride east instead of west. Would they come after him? There was a possibility they might just assume the robbers had waylaid him. Assume that he'd been killed and the gold stolen. They might look for sign, or a body, but even if they never found either they might still decide to blame the loss of the gold on the desperados who had already made off with two shipments.

There was just one small problem. His conscience. It would get in the way. It wouldn't allow him to live that life of ease without an accompanying guilt, a guilt so durable and pervasive that it would probably take all the joy out of living, even if no one ever suspected. And why would they? He could tell them he'd struck it rich in a gold field—he would still despise himself. This Ethan knew with a certainty that he did not have to put to the test.

So, instead, he would try to get the company's gold to a bank vault in San Francisco—and quite possibly get killed for his trouble.

With a sigh he climbed into the roan's saddle. Too bad, he mused, that he wasn't more like Gil Stark. Gil would have had no compunctions about absconding with the Eldorado Mining Company's gold.

Of course, Maller was too good a judge of character to put someone like Gil in charge of thirty thousand dollars' worth of gold dust. Ethan tried to tell himself that the trust a man like John Maller put in him was worth much more than all that gold. It was some consolation, at least.

He proceeded down the trail until he neared Angel

Camp, then veered off into the brush. If he pushed hard he could reach Copper Creek and the railhead by tomorrow night. Once he had the gold on the train he would feel a lot better about things. Until then he had to stay alert, keep his eyes open, be prepared for anything—and try to adjust to the crawling sensation along his spine, the feeling a man gets when he knows he's been made a target. It was a feeling Ethan suspected would not dissipate until he reached Copper Creek.

The entire day passed without incident, and he saw no one. Even while he understood that this didn't necessarily mean no one had seen him, or that he wasn't being followed, Ethan felt a little more confident of his chances when he made camp for the night in a bosque of scrubby oak trees thirty yards uphill from a creek in a rocky ravine. The night was cool, but he decided that a fire would be too risky. Maller had provided him with provisions—some biscuits, some jerked beef, a can of beans that he opened with the bowie knife. This and creek water constituted his supper. Maller had also included a sack of coffee, and Ethan thought he might get away with a fire in the morning just to brew up some java. The prospect consoled him as he lay in his blankets, the reins to the roan's bridle and the pack mule's lead rope tied to his left arm. If either animal moved suddenly it would awaken him.

He drifted off to sleep—and the roan's soft whicker startled him awake. He wasn't sure how long he had slept. Minutes? Hours? The canopy of interlocking branches overhead blocked his view of the stars, so he was unable to calculate the time that had passed by the movement of the heavens. Lying very still, he strained eyes and ears. A carelessly placed foot snapped a twig. Yes, there was definitely something moving through the bosque. Moving, more or less, in his direction. Ethan sat up slowly and transferred the roan's reins and the mule's lead rope to the trunk of a sapling that stood near at hand. Then he reached for the shotgun that was on the ground beside him. If he had to fire the greener he didn't want the animals attached to his arm; they could spook, and he didn't cotton to being dragged through the brush.

Whatever was coming through the bosque apparently wasn't striving for a quiet passage, and Ethan took some solace in that fact. If it was the bandit gang he figured they would be trying to Indian-up on him, jump him before he could get off a shot, or perhaps even cut his throat while he was sleeping. Still, he didn't relax. Sitting cross-legged on the ground—a standing man made an easier, more recognizable target in the dark—he rested the shotgun across his lap and thumbed back both hammers as quietly as possible. The sounds suddenly ceased. Ethan had to remember to breathe. Utter silence reigned for a moment that seemed to drag on for hours. And then the intruder called out.

"Hello the camp!"

Ethan instantly recognized the voice—and, shocked, wondered if he wasn't dreaming.

"Don't shoot, Ethan. It's me, your old friend Gil."

The sounds resumed, and a few seconds later Gil Stark came into view, emerging from the brush with a saddle horse, an Appaloosa, in tow. Ethan couldn't make out much, couldn't see his friend's face. Gil was wearing a sombrero and a long, dark coat. And Ethan figured he was also wearing that old buccaneer's smile of his.

"Howdy, Ethan," said Gil, stopping about a dozen paces away. "How are things with you these days?"

"What the hell are you doing here, Gil?"

Gil chuckled softly. "That's a fair question, under the circumstances. I didn't come to chew the breeze, I can tell you that. Not interested in talking about the good old days, I must admit. Not that I'd mind. But my partners, well, they're not what you'd call patient men. So I guess I'd better get right down to business, if it's all the same to you."

"Partners?" Ethan scanned the surrounding darkness. He saw and heard nothing. But he remembered what he'd

heard just yesterday, in front of the Eldorado superintendent's cabin, about the bandits. *One of the sons of bitches
rides an Appaloosa—a horse that sticks out like a sore
thumb in these parts.* And an Appaloosa had been seen
during both of the previous robberies.

"Yeah, they're out there," said Gil. "You just didn't hear
them. You'd be amazed how quiet a wanted man gets to
be."

The back of Ethan's neck started to tingle. Gil's partners
were wanted men. So that settled it.

"Reason I'm here," continued Gil, "is to take that gold
you're carrying. So do me, and yourself, a big favor. Put
aside your weapons. You might just get out of this alive,
if you do."

White-hot anger surged through Ethan. "I should have
known," he said bitterly. "Any low-down thievery going
on, you'd be a part of it."

"I've struck it rich, Ethan, just like I said I would. With
my share of this shipment, plus my cut of the first two, I'll
be headed east. A big city, though not sure which one. But
my days as an outlaw are soon over. I'll live like a king.
The way I see it, that'll be my fair share of California's
gold. Now I ask you, why should a handful of rich men
just get richer because they sit on the Eldorado's board of
directors? God knows they've got no use for all that gold.
They've probably got more in their coffers now than they
could spend in a whole lifetime."

"It's because they put up the money to dig the mine,"
said Ethan. "Don't bother trying to justify what you're doing, Gil."

"Spoken like a loyal employee." Gil shook his head con-
temptuously. "How much do they pay you, my friend? Ten,
twenty dollars a month? You'll never get rich at that rate,
hoss. You'll never get back to Roan's Prairie and Lilah
Webster at that rate, I can tell you. Assuming you still want
to get back, that is. I hear you and that English girl are
getting along pretty good."

Ethan remembered then what Maller had said. *Either these robbers are the luckiest bastards on the continent, or they know which detail carries the gold.*

"I just want to know one thing, Gil," he said flatly. "How did you know I had the gold?"

Again Gil shook his head. "Sorry, amigo. If I told you that then you'd get killed tonight for sure. As it is you're up to your neck in hot water. My partners wanted to blow your head off outright. But soon as I saw it was you I knew I had to talk them out of it. Sure, we've got a little bad blood between us right now, you and me. But I still think of you as a friend—a good friend. Maybe the best I'll ever have. And so I told them to let me come in and talk to you first. Try to make you see reason. My aim here is to keep you alive, Ethan, but I'm going to need your help if I'm to get that job done. Put that scattergun aside. And the bowie knife that I'm sure you still carry. Don't reckon you'd ever part with that, seeing as how you went to so much trouble to keep it back on the Mississippi."

Ethan quickly scanned the night shadows again. Was Gil bluffing? Could he be alone, and just *saying* he had partners out there to discourage resistance? And even if he *was* telling the truth, and there *were* cutthroats out there just itching to kill him and make away with the gold shipment, how could he be sure that Gil wasn't lying about wanting to keep him alive? One thing had always been certain where Gil Stark was concerned—he had never been wed to the truth.

"What's it going to be?" asked Gil, impatience edging into his voice.

Ethan swung the scattergun around and pulled one trigger, blasting a load of buckshot into the ground at Gil's feet. He was close enough to blow a hole clean through Gil, even in the dark, but in spite of everything he simply couldn't bring himself to kill someone who had been his only friend for so many years.

Gil let out a yelp of surprise and jumped backward,

twisting his body away instinctively, and raising an arm to shield his face. The muzzle flash was blinding, the discharge of the scattergun a deafening one—and a quick flurry of gunfire from the woods just added to the din. Ethan was getting to his feet when the shooting started— now he knew that Gil was telling the truth about having partners—and then he threw himself onto the ground as the bullets flew around him. Looking up, he saw the roan and the mule straining against their tethers; the sapling was within reach and Ethan drew the bowie knife from its belt sheath and slashed both the reins and the lead rope. The mule took off into the trees, braying and kicking as one of Gil's cohorts came out of hiding and lunged for it. The mule evaded the man's grasp, and the outlaw tripped and fell as he started to pursue. As the man got to his feet, Ethan triggered the other barrel of the shotgun. The distance was too long, but some of the buckshot hit the mark, enough to launch the desperado into a fit of howling and cursing as he limped hastily back under cover.

Several other men were still shooting at him from the brush, and Ethan figured the only reason he was still alive was because it was night and they could not make him out clearly as he lay on the ground. He might have been quite content to stay on his belly and crawl for cover, except he had a more immediate problem than the one posed by the outlaws. The roan was completely spooked and, instead of running, was rearing up on its hind legs. Of course, as in all other things, what went up had to come down, and those flailing iron-shod hooves were coming down entirely too close to Ethan for comfort. Ethan tossed the empty shotgun at the roan, but that had no visible effect on the animal. Then Ethan rolled away, groping for the revolver in his belt, reconciled to the possibility that he might have to shoot the horse to keep from being trampled. A single blow from one of the hooves could break a bone, or crush a skull.

But he didn't have to shoot the horse—one of the outlaws did it for him. Hit in the head by a stray bullet, the roan died instantly—and suddenly Ethan was confronted by a thousand pounds of dead horse coming down on top of him. He scrambled out of the way and the carcass caught his heel and made him stumble. Sprawling, he tried to get up again, and only then realized he'd been shot. His arm was numb. He groped for the wound, felt the warm sticky blood between his fingers. Then the pain came, surging through him, and he felt dizzy, nauseated. No longer interested in putting up a fight—what was the point? The gold was gone—his instinct was to get away as quickly as possible. If he could get deeper into the woods they might lose track of him in the darkness. And they might not wait around until daylight just to find him and finish him off. It was much more likely that if they spent any time looking for something, it would be the mule that carried the gold.

He fired the revolver as he got to his feet—fired it until all the cartridges were spent, throwing lead in the general direction of the outlaws, based on the location of the muzzle flash from their guns. In a glance he could see that the Sharps percussion rifle in its saddle boot was inaccessible—the horse had fallen on the side where the boot was located. He hoped to keep their heads down long enough for him to reach cover. It seemed to work. The outlaws' gunfire slacked off a bit, and he reached a bunch of scrub trees growing close together, paused there for a heartbeat, and then moved again. A loose stone underfoot betrayed him—he stumbled, and then, abruptly, the ground fell away beneath him and he was falling, tumbling head over heels into the steep-sided ravine with the creek at the bottom of it. He hit the slope first with his shoulder, flipped over, and gasped in pain as a sharp rock jabbed him mercilessly in the lower back, mere inches from his spine. The pain paralyzed him momentarily, so that he could not catch himself, and he pitched forward helplessly, scrub tearing at his clothes and flesh. He tried to curl up in a ball but landed awkwardly on his shoulder among the rocks strewn along the creek bottom.

He lay there in the shallows, battered and bleeding and working at sucking air into his lungs, marveling at the fact that he was still alive, even while he wondered if he had broken anything important, like his spine. Before he could concern himself further about such possibilities, he looked up to see Gil Stark looming over him, silhouetted against the sky. Gil had a pistol in his hand; Ethan couldn't see his face beneath the sombrero's brim, but he could clearly see the barrel of the revolver, and he watched, almost mesmerized, his mind refusing to acknowledge what he saw, as the barrel came up—and spit flame.

"Did you get the bastard, Gil?"

This came from a man standing somewhere up above, on the rim of the ravine.

"Yeah, I got him," said Gil flatly. He lowered the pistol and looked down at Ethan and muttered, "Lay still. Don't move. Don't make a sound." He started to turn away, but thought of something. "And don't come after me. If you do I might have to shoot you for real next time."

Ethan didn't say anything. He couldn't if he'd wanted to. He didn't have the breath for it. So he just lay there, amazed that he was still among the living.

Gil Stark walked away.

# CHAPTER THIRTEEN

Ethan lay there in the creek bottom for a while, giving the outlaws plenty of time to clear out, and hoping they wouldn't want to linger long anyway. With the gold strapped to the back of a runaway mule there wasn't much to keep them here. Eventually he moved, gingerly testing his arms, then his legs, trying to find out if anything was broken. Nothing seemed to be. That amazed him. The gunshot wound in his arm was intensely painful, but closer inspection revealed that it was only a deep graze; he wasn't carrying any lead. It was with a great deal of difficulty that he sat up. Once he'd managed that he sat for a spell in the shallows, doubting that he had the strength left to get to his feet. The worst part of it all was that he couldn't think of a good reason to do so. Maller had told him not to come back to the mine if he lost the gold shipment and, sure enough, he'd lost it. He had no place to go now and, since the roan was dead, no good way to get there. Sure, he could walk back to Eldorado Number One and tell Maller that the gold had been stolen; he could probably reach the mine by late tomorrow, if he pushed hard. It wasn't as though the superintendent would actually pull a gun and shoot him down in cold blood just because he had failed. John Maller was a hard man, but not that hard.

But Ethan didn't cotton to the idea of trudging back to the mine and admitting failure. He didn't want to face Maller, or the other men—and he especially didn't want to face Ellen. Mark it down to foolish pride, but he just couldn't bear the thought of doing that. He could find his way to Illinois, and Lilah. But, there again, he would have to admit failure of an entirely different sort. Ethan shook his head. Through a process of elimination he was left with only one viable alternative.

"Damn it," he muttered angrily, and forced himself to get up, telling himself to stop sitting there in the creek, soaking wet, feeling sorry for himself. His whole body, a solid mass of pain, protested the exertion, but he ignored the protest and tried to ignore the pain. There was something much more important to focus his attention on.

He was going to have to get the gold back. Even if Gil Stark and his owlhoot friends had found it, which they may well have done by now. And if that turned out to be the case, he would just have to take it away from them.

Just the thought of Gil Stark made him seethe with anger. Thanks to Gil he was still alive. But he wasn't sure that was something he should be grateful for. In his present state of mind, he had to wonder. He blamed Gil for this. For everything. And this time he was not going to let Gil get away with it. Always in the past he had turned a blind eye. But not anymore. He wasn't going to allow Gil Stark to take advantage of his forgiving nature. No, he was going to get the gold back, and if Gil got in his way, well, then that would be his bad luck.

Ethan looked up the steep slope of the ravine. He had lost his revolver in the fall, and he realized that he would have to wait until daylight if he wanted to find it among all the rocks and brush. But up above, somewhere, was his scattergun. There were extra loads of buckshot in his saddle panniers. And he was relieved to find that the bowie knife was still sheathed at his hip.

First he had to tend to his arm. Ripping off the blood-soaked sleeve of his shirt, he managed to wrap it tightly around the wound, knotting this makeshift dressing with one hand and using his teeth to pull the knot tight. Then, using his anger for fuel, he stoked up his willpower and began to climb.

It took everything he had, but Ethan made it to the top. He found the empty scattergun, not far from where the roan's carcass lay. He was relieved to see that the panniers were still strapped to the saddle, and he could get to one of them. But his relief was short-lived. The bandits had probably been in a hurry to begin searching for the mule that carried the gold—but not in so big a hurry that they had forgotten to ransack the pannier. They had made off with all the shotgun loads. Except one. Elated, Ethan fed it into the shotgun. Only belatedly did the absurdity of what he was about to do register with him. With a half-loaded double-barreled shotgun and a bowie knife, he was going in pursuit of a gang of desperate outlaws, and he didn't even know how many of them there were. To top that off, he was on foot. Ethan shook his head. But he was unwilling to mull over all his options again. That was too depressing. So he headed deeper into the bosque to a place where the brush grew thick, and found a good place to hole up until dawn. He couldn't do any tracking until daylight, and he didn't want to blunder into the outlaws in the dark. And though he didn't think he'd get any sleep under the circumstances, he did drift off, waking with a start to find that a new day had come.

Finding the tracks he was looking for was an easy task— he could easily distinguish between the sign of the smaller mule and that of the horses belonging to the outlaws. After a long and careful scrutiny of the ground in the bosque, he decided that there were at least three outlaws besides Gil, and that they had spent most of the night fruitlessly searching for the mule. Three times their tracks crossed those of the mule, and it wasn't until the third time that they turned their horses in pursuit. This, Ethan assumed, must have occurred at first light. The mule, he thought, was headed for home—the mine. Ethan was pretty certain that the bandits would catch up to it long before it reached its destination.

The tracks proved him right. Around midday he arrived at the spot where Gil and his outlaw friends apprehended the mule. Mule and horse sign both abruptly turned east. So did Ethan. He was tired, hungry, thirsty, and footsore, but he didn't stop moving until the sun had sunk below the horizon in a blaze of orange glory. And the reason he stopped was a pinprick of light in the distance that, upon closer inspection, turned out to be lamplight escaping through the window of an adobe hut. The hut was backed up against a barren, rocky hill. There was a small clump of dusty trees at the base of the hill, and Ethan speculated that they marked the location of a spring. He hadn't seen any other water for many miles—and so what else would prompt someone to build out here except the presence of a spring? Since the tracks he had been following all day headed straight for the adobe, he further speculated that this remote shelter was the outlaw gang's hideout.

He waited patiently for the last threads of daylight to depart before moving. Instead of heading right for the adobe, he circled around to the backside of the hill and climbed to the rim. From there he could clearly see a corral behind the hut, which he had not been able to see before. Now he was sure that the men he was after were in the adobe, for there in the corral was the mule, relieved of his gold dust burden, Gil's Appaloosa, and several other horses.

That the outlaws hadn't bothered to post a guard outside bothered him, and for a long while he remained flat on his belly, on the rim of the hill, searching the shadows around the hut and under the trees, thinking that maybe a sentry had been posted and he just hadn't spotted him. Eventually he came to the conclusion that Gil and all his cohorts were inside. Probably splitting up their ill-gotten gains and celebrating with some rotgut whiskey. Ethan hoped they were drinking, anyway. The more snakehead they imbibed, the better his odds became. As for the absence of a guard, all the men down there, with the exception of Gil Stark, thought he was dead. They probably thought it would be a couple more days at least before the Eldorado Mining Company discovered that yet another gold shipment had been stolen. In Gil's case, he most likely just assumed that Ethan was too smart to come after them. Ethan smiled thinly. He could hardly wait to see the look on Gil's face—even if it was the last thing he saw before he died.

He started down the hill in a crouch, trying to make as little sound as possible, and angling for the clump of trees. When he got closer, the horses in the corral began to stir, and just as he reached the trees one of them let out a whinny—a signal, an alarm to the others that something was slipping through the trees, possibly something dangerous. It served as an alarm for the men inside the adobe, as well. That suited Ethan. He had sketched out the bare bones of a plan—admittedly, a plan that did not bear careful scrutiny—and if by some miracle everything fell into place he had a slim chance of coming out of this alive.

Crouching in the night gloom beneath the trees, Ethan kept his eyes glued to the adobe, hoping now that the men inside, if they *were* drinking, hadn't imbibed so much that they would ignore the racket made by the horses, which were nervously circling the corral. He would stand a better chance, he thought, if they came out to him, instead of his having to go in after them. Ethan realized he was downwind of the corral; the horses couldn't smell him but they heard him, and he thought it possible that they were acting up like this because they couldn't tell *what* he was—maybe a bear or mountain lion come down to drink from the spring.

He was beginning to think he would have to get in closer and stir the ponies up some more, just to get a reaction from the bandits in the adobe, when suddenly the door flew open, spilling a rectangle of yellow lamplight across the hardpack in front of the hut. A man stepped out. Thirty yards away and with the man's back to the light, Ethan couldn't make out his features. But he was a burly man, much larger in stature than Gil Stark. That was a good thing, in Ethan's opinion—since he was going to have to kill this man. The bandit peered at the horses in the corral and then engaged in a long, wary scrutiny of the rest of his surroundings.

"See anything out there, Rudd?" came a voice from inside.

"Hell no," growled the man Ethan could scc. "It's slap dark. I can't tell what's got them so spooked. I reckon I'll go check it out."

With that he headed for the corral, a rifle cradled in his left arm, a holstered pistol flopping against his right thigh. He reached the corral and paused there to take another long look around. One of the horses—no doubt Rudd's own—calmed and went to its master, draping its head over the corral's top pole. The other horses took their cue from this one and began to mellow. The mule had remained impervious to the alarm from the first. It stood apart from, the horses, head lowered as though sleeping through the commotion, and belatedly Ethan realized it was tethered.

*Don't think about it,* Ethan told himself. *You need his guns. All you've got is one load of buckshot. It's kill or be killed.*

And that meant he had to lure Rudd closer. Had to get him to this side of the corral. He couldn't fire until it was close range, because he couldn't afford to miss, or just wound the bandit. He had to kill him outright. Everything else depended on that. Ethan felt around on the ground. His hand closed around a stone, which he tossed over his shoulder. The stone struck a tree with a dull *thunk!*, then hit the ground and clattered against some rocks. Rudd tensed, bringing the rifle around to bear and moving around the corral. Ethan slowly, slowly eased the shotgun's hammer back. He had to give credit where credit was due. Rudd might be a desperado, with few redeeming qualities, but he was certainly no coward. He had no idea what was lurking in the trees, but whatever it was, it was spooking the horses, and he was going to put a stop to that.

Ethan waited until Rudd was nearly to the trees, less than ten feet away, before standing up. Rudd saw him, saw the scattergun, and just had time to register shock and dismay on his face before Ethan triggered the shotgun. The blast shattered the night; the impact of the load of buckshot in the chest lifted Rudd off his feet and hurled him backward. Sprawled on his back on the ground, Rudd convulsed once, twice, and then lay still.

Tossing the empty shotgun aside, Ethan steeled himself to walk over to the body and pry the rifle out of a dead grip. He relieved Rudd of the pistol, too. He forced himself to look into the face of the dead man. That look of surprise he'd glimpsed on Rudd's face, in the light from the shotgun's muzzle flash, was frozen there. The outlaw's eyes were staring blankly up at the sky. Ethan marveled at how easy it was to snuff out a life, leaving the body just an empty, useless husk. Even a man like Rudd, who was big and brawny and in the prime of his life, could be gone in an instant, thanks to tiny pellets of lead. Fighting the nausea that threatened to overcome him, Ethan got up and headed for the corral.

He had removed one pole from the gate and was lifting the second when two more bandits emerged from adobe. Ethan fired the revolver three times in their direction, not taking the time to aim. Even so, the lead he slung came close enough to send the outlaws scurrying back inside. That gave him the time he needed to drop the second pole. Inside the corral, the horses were worked up and milling again. Ethan circled to the back of the corral, a maneuver he hoped would flush them out. It worked. The horses bolted. Tethered to a pole, the mule could not go with them. And that was the way Ethan wanted it; he needed the mule to carry the gold to the railhead at Copper Creek. That was the job Maller had given him and by God he was going to get it done—assuming he survived the night.

A bullet smacked into one of the corral poles. An outlaw had ventured out of the adobe, running for the cover of the nearest brush and firing his pistol as he ran. Ethan knew it was damned near impossible to hit your mark when you were running. He stood his ground in the middle of the corral, with the bullets flying around him, and methodically drew a bead on the running man. He squeezed the trigger. His bullet struck the desperado in the thigh, knocking the leg out from under him, and he fell, sprawling. Moving to the corral gate, Ethan fired his last two rounds. The outlaw returned fire, to no avail. Ethan retrieved the rifle he'd put down to handle the gate poles. The outlaw was out of ammunition now, and was trying to crawl for cover. Without hesitation Ethan raised the rifle, took aim, and killed him with a single shot.

At that moment a third man bolted out of the adobe. This one didn't waste any time shooting at Ethan. He just ran for all he was worth, and disappeared around the corner of the hut before Ethan could get off a shot. Ethan figured he was headed for the rocks on the hillside, whirled, and ran back through the clump of trees, scrambling up the slope by the route he was familiar with. He thought he spotted the outlaw once—a shadow moving among the shapes of the boulders—but it wasn't a target worth shooting at. So he waited, biding his time, stopping halfway up the hill and focusing his attention on the rim, about where he thought the desperado would pass over the crest. He suspected that if he got a shot at the man it would have to be a very quick one; he doubted the outlaw would linger at the top of the hill. He was right. His target was silhouetted against the night sky for only a second or two. But Ethan was ready. He snapped off a shot and, squinting through the drift of powder smoke, saw the outlaw throw up his arms and topple forward, out of sight.

Ethan's first thought was that he needed to climb to the top of the hill and make sure the man was dead. But there was one more robber in the cabin. Gil Stark. And Gil was with the gold. Ethan decided he couldn't risk giving Gil the time to make his escape. So he hurried back down the hill. Running past the corral, he was relieved to see that the mule was still tethered there. Reaching a corner of the adobe, he pressed his back up against the wall and took a quick look around the corner. The door was still open. The interior of the hut was dark now—Gil had extinguished the light. Ethan heard no sound from inside. Had Gil slipped away? There was only one way to find out.

"Gil!"

There was no response.

"Gil, it's Ethan."

Still nothing from within the cabin.

"Your friends are dead. I killed them all. Don't make me kill you, Gil. Light that lamp. Throw out your guns, and come out with your hands over your head."

He waited—ten seconds, twenty, thirty—scanning the darkness, wondering if he'd made a mistake by chasing the third man up the hill, wondering if Gil was out there somewhere, maybe drawing a bead on him at this very moment. Or maybe on the run, with all the gold he could carry. . . .

Light from the lamp inside the adobe spilled out over the hardpack again. Ethan watched it—saw the shadow of a man blot much of it out as Gil Stark stood framed in the doorway for a moment.

"Well," said Gil. "I guess that man was right."

Rifle to shoulder, aiming it at Gil's chest, Ethan came around the corner of the adobe.

"What man?" he asked.

"The one down in Chagres. Remember? The one who said you were a born killer. Those three I rode with, they were rough hombres. But you made short work of them."

"I had no choice," said Ethan flatly.

"Not taking any prisoners, eh?"

"Taking the gold back, that's one thing. Taking the gold back while trying to keep an eye on four prisoners?" He shook his head. "It was too risky."

"You're probably right. Besides, you never would have taken Rudd alive. He never ran from anything in his life, I don't think. I can see how you had to kill him. But not the other two. Wiley and Cochran, they were just trying to get away."

"I couldn't let them. And I didn't have the advantage of knowing them like you did," said Ethan dryly. "All I know is they were sure trying to fill me full of lead last night."

Gil nodded. "They were desperate men, true enough. I regret that they killed that other Eldorado rider, back when we took the second gold shipment."

"Speaking of the gold, where is it?"

Gil tilted his head in the direction of the adobe. "We were splitting it up. Tomorrow we would have taken our shares and ridden off in different directions and stashed them somewhere. If you're looking to retrieve the other gold shipments, you're out of luck. I have no idea where the others hid their shares. And since you killed them all, I guess no one will ever know."

"I'm not worried about the other shipments. Just the one I was put in charge of."

Gil gave Ethan a long look, as he would a stranger he was trying to understand. "You sure have changed since I last saw you. That Illinois farm boy I came to California with is gone. Someone else is standing in his place."

"I wish I could say you've changed, Gil. But I can't. You're still up to your old tricks. Still trying to get something for nothing."

"So what are your plans for me? Going to kill me like you did my partners?"

"That's up to you."

"Up to me? How do you figure?"

"I want to know who you're working with."

Gil Stark flashed that crooked grin of his, and made a sweeping gesture. "I'd introduce 'em to you, Ethan, but it's a little too late for that. You've sent them all to meet their Maker."

"No, I mean the man who's with Eldorado. The one who told you boys about the gold shipments."

"Oh, him." Gil chuckled. "You mean to tell me you haven't figured that out yet, Ethan? I mean, way I understand it, not too many people knew of your little trip to Copper Creek. Shouldn't be hard to figure out."

"You saved my life last night," said Ethan grimly. "So I'm going to let you go. But only if you swear you'll leave California and never come back. I don't ever want to run into you again."

"Fair enough."

"And one other thing. I want the name."

Gil nodded. "But you're not going to like what you hear."

"Just tell me."

And Gil Stark did just that.

# CHAPTER FOURTEEN

When Ethan got back to the Eldorado Number One, he could tell right away that things were different. His arrival was cause for a great deal of excitement among his fellow exployees. They greeted him like a conquering hero. He didn't know what to make of it all, until Maller told him what had happened.

The superintendent's cabin was not where he intended to go first—he'd long ago made up his mind that he needed to talk to Ellen the minute he got back. But Richter was among those who came out to meet him, and it was Richter who informed him that Maller wanted to see him right away. When Maller wanted to see you, you didn't keep him waiting. Ethan figured the superintendent was going to rake him over the coals for nearly losing the gold shipment. Instead, Maller shook his hand enthusiastically, bade him sit down, and offered him a drink. Ethan took the chair but declined the whiskey. But Maller insisted, and Ethan had the drink. The whiskey burned his throat, but it seemed to even out his nerves, relax him, make him feel better about things, even though realistically there was no reason to feel better.

"You did a damned fine job, Payne. Robards sent me all the details."

"I see," said Ethan, noncommittal. Robards was the company representative in San Francisco that Ethan had dealt with, the man to whom he'd handed over the gold and related all that had transpired during his journey. Well, not all. He'd left out any mention of Gil Stark. As far as anyone knew, there had only been three desperados involved in the attempted robbery, and all three of them were dead. Ethan had told Robards about everything else, keeping his narrative sparse, free of any embellishments. The robbers had hit his camp in the middle of the night. They had killed his horse and wounded him. The mule carrying the gold had bolted. He had escaped. The following day, he'd tracked the outlaws. They had found the mule and then ridden east to the adobe hut where, that night, Ethan had found them. In the gun battle that followed, all three of the outlaws lost their lives. Ethan had recovered the gold, taken it to the railhead, then accompanied it on the train to San Francisco, where he'd handed it over to Robards. And that was the long and short of it.

He had assumed that Robards would just send a terse telegram to the Eldorado mine—a telegram that would go to the end-of-line station at Copper Creek and from there would travel by mounted messenger to the mine—informing Maller that the gold had been safely delivered. He hadn't expected the Eldorado representative to relay all the details of his clash with the bandits. But that was precisely what Robards had done. Maller told him so.

"Robards was very impressed by what you did," said Maller. "I'm sure the members of the board are, too."

"I was just doing my job."

"What you did went beyond just doing a job, son."

Ethan shook his head adamantly. "I don't see it that way, sir."

Maller shrugged. He wasn't going to argue the point. "I sent some men out to find that adobe after I got Robards's telegram. Didn't turn out to be that hard to find. The buzzards led them right to it."

"Buzzards? I buried the dead."

That wasn't exactly true—he'd had Gil bury the three dead men. He figured that was the least Gil could do for his partners in crime. And besides, it was very satisfying to watch Gil do some hard physical labor. It wasn't something Gil cottoned to at all.

"Yes, they told me they saw the graves. Coyotes and such must have dug them up. There wasn't much left of the bodies—certainly not enough to identify them. You didn't get the name of even one of them?"

"No, sir." Ethan was afraid that if he started handing out the names of Rudd, Wiley, and Cochran, and the Eldorado started doing a little investigating in an attempt to discover the whereabouts of the gold from the first two shipments, at some point along the line Gil Stark's name might crop up. And Ethan didn't want that.

"And no sign of the other gold shipments," said Maller.

"Nope. My guess is they split the gold up, then each man rode off a ways and buried his share. They wouldn't trust each other with that information. It's not likely you'll ever find that gold, sir."

"No, not likely, I agree. One of the men I sent out is half Modoc Indian. He told me there looked to be four outlaws at that adobe, at one time or another. But you saw only three."

Ethan's face was like a mask carved of stone. "There were only three men there."

"How many horses?"

"Four horses. But only three men."

"Hmm." Maller looked away. "One of the guards on the detail with the second gold shipment that was stolen said he was sure he saw four robbers."

"Maybe one of them got away without my seeing him. It was dark."

"That could be. Or maybe, if there was a fourth man, he rode away before you got there. Though why he would do that without his share of the gold, I don't know. Anyway, you did a damned fine job, Ethan. I knew you had grit. But to track those desperados down like you did, and then beard them in their den. . . ." Maller shook his head in wonder. "Not many would have the *cajones* for that kind of work."

"Thank you." It was all Ethan could think to say. He didn't want to be having this conversation, and certainly had no desire to prolong it.

"Well," said Maller, sensing Ethan's eagerness to be away, "there's only one regret I have, and it's that we may never know now if there *was* a man on the inside helping those bandits."

"Sorry."

"Don't be." Maller clapped him on the back. "You've done well by the Eldorado, Ethan. I promised you a raise in pay. Thirty dollars a month, as I recall. It's effective immediately."

"Thanks."

Once Maller had shown him out, Ethan was confronted by at least a dozen Eldorado employees who were loitering in front of the superintendent's cabin waiting to get a glimpse of him. Ethan was unmoved by their enthusiasm, and stubbornly shook his head in response to their persistent requests for details of his adventures. Tight-lipped, he plowed through them, took up the reins to his horse, and walked away.

He had some unpleasant business to attend to, and that was all he could think about.

Reaching the Addison cabin, he tethered his horse—it was a company horse that had been awaiting his arrival by train at Copper Creek—went to the door, raised a fist to knock, and hesitated. Second thoughts assailed him. Did he really have to do this? Was it necessary now? And if he did it, what would the deed cost him? This last consideration was the one that worried him the most.

He was about to turn away, but then the door flew open and Ellen rushed across the threshold, arms outstretched and pure delight on her lovely face, and he was instantly trapped in her tight embrace.

"Ethan!" she gasped. "Thank God you're home safe!"

She covered his face with kisses, and then laughed softly as he took her by the arms and gently pushed her away, looking around; she knew he was embarrassed by this public show of affection. She took his hand and pulled him inside. "Father!" she called. "Here's my hero!"

Sir Edward was sitting in a chair by the cabin's window. He had been peering out at the stamp mill, an elbow resting on the arm of the chair and his chin propped on a hand. He seemed to be lost in thought. The entrance of Ethan and Ellen shook him from his reverie, and when he looked at Ethan it was in the way of a man desperate to fathom a vital truth—a truth that his life depended on knowing. He rose slowly, as with a great weariness, and extended a hand to Ethan.

"Welcome back, son," he said gravely. "You have acquitted yourself well, I hear."

Ethan thought Sir Edward was genuinely glad to see him back safe and sound, even though the fact that he was spelled the engineer's doom. He took the proffered hand and shook it—but didn't let go. He forced himself to look Sir Edward squarely in the eye, reminding himself that this was the man who had signed his death warrant by telling Gil Stark that he was carrying the gold to Copper Creek.

"I wish I could say the same for you, sir."

Sir Edward blinked and looked away. The looking away simply confirmed for Ethan what he already knew—that Gil Stark had told him the truth.

"I suppose it was your friend who informed you about me," sighed Sir Edward.

Ethan nodded. "I didn't want to believe it, either. Gil's been known to stretch the truth a bit. Shoot, he's as good at lying as anyone I've ever met. Ever since he told me I've been trying to talk myself into believing it was a lie. But down deep I knew it wasn't."

"What's going on?" asked Ellen. She was alarmed by the expression on her father's face. "What are the two of you talking about?"

Ethan purposefully ignored her. "I just want to know one thing, sir. Why? You couldn't need the gold."

Sir Edward pried his hand loose from Ethan's grip. "It's a common enough misconception, you know. Everyone thinks that because I'm *Sir* Edward that I must be a wealthy man. Nothing could be further from the truth, actually. I'll have you know I was not born into the nobility. I was knighted for my service to the realm as an engineer. Men with my education and skills are highly regarded by society, but poorly paid, as a whole."

"Father, what are you saying?" asked Ellen.

Ethan glanced at her then, and saw what he didn't want to see—the growing horror in her expression.

Sir Edward didn't want to see it either, and turned away, moving to the window. "For some time now I've wanted to find a home for you, my dear. A place to settle down. I've felt a certain degree of remorse for having dragged you hither and yon, from one dusty outpost of civilization to the next, ever since you were a child. That's no life for a young lady like you."

"I never complained."

"No, you didn't." Sir Edward smiled faintly. "My dear girl, you've been entirely too devoted to your father, I'm afraid."

"But the company pays you well," cried Ellen, still not willing to believe that what she was hearing was true. She was too intelligent to need it spelled out, realized Ethan; she knew exactly what was being said here. "All the people you've worked for have paid you well, haven't they?"

Sir Edward nodded. "But not well enough. And then we came here. And there was so much gold. I suppose I justified what I did by telling myself that the loss of one or two gold shipments would do hardly any damage to the company."

"That sounds like something Gil would say," remarked Ethan.

"With the gold we could have settled down," said Sir

Edward, his back still turned. "For once, dear Ellen, you would lived in a house you could call your own. We would have lived comfortably. You would have had a house servant, a carriage, nice dresses. . . ."

With a shock, Ethan realized that this was uncannily similar to the dream he had shared with Lilah Webster. These were all the things he'd wanted to provide for Lilah, the reasons he had come to California in the first place.

"Oh, Father," said Ellen, distraught. "What makes you think I would ever want those things if they were bought at the cost of your honor? Or Ethan's life? I've never asked you for them. Never wanted them anyway."

Sir Edward finally turned to face his daughter. He was very pale. A sad smile touched the corners of his mouth.

"It's true, you've never once asked for anything of the sort. I suppose it was for my sake that I wanted to give you all those things. Perhaps to compensate you for the loss of your home and friends—and your country—when I left England because I thought I could escape my grief for your mother."

Ellen just stared at him for a moment. Then she looked at Ethan. "You mentioned your friend. Why?"

"Gil was a member of the holdup gang. He was the one your father contacted about the gold shipments."

Ellen sank into a chair at the table that was the centerpiece of the room. "Father," she whispered. "Father, how *could* you?"

She was close to tears, and seeing this pained Ethan. He regretted coming here, exposing Sir Edward. He cursed himself for not keeping his mouth shut. And then Ellen reminded him why he'd felt obliged to do this. She cast an angry, accusatory glance in her father's direction, and said, "Men have lost their lives because of what you've done!"

Sir Edward shook his head morosely. "I never wanted that to happen. You must believe me, Ellen. I shall never forgive myself."

"I hope I will be able to, someday," she murmured, bitterly. "What did you expect would happen? The law of the gun rules in this land, Father, and life is cheap. And—and worst of all, Ethan might have been one of those who died. You say you were concerned for my happiness? Then how could you have put Ethan in harm's way? He is the source of my happiness."

"Gil Stark assured me . . ." But Sir Edward didn't finish, knowing there was no defense he could muster that would exculpate him in Ellen's mind.

Ethan decided it was best not to mention that he *had* nearly been killed; the gunshot wound in his arm was well on its way to healing, and caused him only slight and occasional discomfort now. In San Francisco, Robards had insisted that a doctor take a look at it. But the wound was even then starting to heal, and there had been no infection to deal with.

"What I want to know is when you and Gil first spoke about this," Ethan said. "He knew on the *Unicorn* that you were going to work for the Eldorado Mining Company. When did he show up here? Was this his idea to begin with? And if so, what made him think you would go along with it?"

Sir Edward appeared surprised. "He didn't tell you? I assume you spoke to him."

Ethan nodded grimly. "Yeah, I talked to him. He *did* save my life, so I let him go. After he gave me the name of the inside man. I guess . . ." He glanced at Ellen. "I guess I was too busy trying to think through certain things after that to ask him for details. I had him bury his friends and then I let him walk away."

"I see." Sir Edward sat down in the chair by the window. "Well, Ethan, if it will make you feel any better, this wasn't Gil's idea at all. It was mine entirely. And I broached the subject with him while we were aboard the *Unicorn*."

Ethan was astonished.

"You conceived of this . . . this thievery even before we got here?" asked Ellen.

"I confess it occurred to me the moment I learned that the Eldorado Mining Company was going to dig gold out of these hills."

"You took an awful big chance," said Ethan. "What if Gil had told me about your plan?"

Sir Edward smiled. "I was fairly confident that he wouldn't. And after we spoke about it, he agreed not to. You see, my boy, I assumed even then that you would be coming to work for Eldorado. I expected Ellen to come to me with the proposal that you do so, that I put in a good word for you. I assumed also that Gil Stark would also be employed here. After all, the two of you were best of friends. You had come all the way from Illinois together, seen each other through the hardships and adventures of the journey. I thought that he and I would have plenty of time to work out the details. Imagine my surprise when the two of you had your falling out aboard the ship! He told me not to worry. That he was still interested, and would keep in touch with me. I didn't hear from him for several months. And then one evening, a couple of months ago, I was taking a walk along the creek, and he suddenly appeared before me." Sir Edward laughed softly. "At first I didn't recognize him. I thought he was a robber. When I said as much he just smiled and said that I was right."

Ethan noticed that Ellen was staring at him. She hardly seemed aware of what her father was saying. There was a question in her gaze—and he knew exactly what it was before she put it into words.

"I didn't tell Mr. Maller," he said.

"Are you going to?" she asked.

He shook his head.

"Why not?"

"Don't you know?"

She looked down at her hands, which were clasped tightly together in her lap, so tightly that her knuckles were white.

"I'd better go," said Ethan. "I feel like I could sleep for

a week. And I . . . I reckon the two of you have some talking to do."

"Wait," said Sir Edward. "You hold all the cards now, son. What do you expect me to do?"

Ethan's gaze was cold. "I've done what I felt I ought to. Now it's your turn."

He walked out of the cabin. Ellen caught up with him before he'd taken two steps away from the door.

"Ethan?"

"Yes?"

She just stood there, staring at him again. It was the only time he could recall her being at a loss for words. It was understandable, given the circumstances.

"I do love you," she said, finally. "Whatever happens, that will never change."

He nodded—and with a strong premonition of disaster leaving a bitter taste in his mouth, he trudged wearily toward the bunkhouse.


When one of the miners shook him awake, Ethan was groggy, coming out of a very deep sleep, and the miner had to repeat himself several times before Ethan gave an indication that he understood. John Maller wanted to see him right away. Groaning, he swung out of his bunk and looked at the window. It was very early in the morning; the sun had not yet climbed above the mountain peaks to the east, and the light that existed was a pearly gray. He rose, stumbled to the table at the end of the bunkhouse where a wash basin was located, and splashed some water on his face. Then he got dressed, slightly perturbed. He'd just gotten back from delivering thirty thousand dollars' worth of gold to San Francisco, killing several men in the process and being wounded himself—and they wouldn't even let him catch up on his sleep. He could only hope that Maller didn't have another shipment that he wanted delivered. Not this soon.

Trying to tame his unruly black hair by running his fingers through it, Ethan left the bunkhouse and walked across the hardpack to the superintendent's cabin. He glanced at the Addison cabin as he walked—it was visible further up the hill, behind Maller's place. There was no activity there. He wondered if Ellen had gotten any sleep last night.

Reaching the superintendent's cabin, he knocked on the door, and Maller's stentorian voice ordered him in. The superintendent was behind his desk, grimly scratching out a letter—or maybe it was a report, Ethan couldn't tell. He stood in front of the desk, waiting, but Maller kept writing furiously for a moment before glancing up. Ethan could tell that the man was not pleased.

"You should have told me yourself," said Maller.

Ethan's mind raced. There was only thing that he could think of that he should have told the superintendent, and that was about Sir Edward's connection with the robbers.

"I reckon so," he said.

Maller put his pen down and sat back in his chair with a weary sigh. He looked like a man who had been up all night. "Not going to make any excuses?"

"No."

"Then just tell me why you didn't mention the fact that Addison was involved when you were in here yesterday. How's that? No excuses. Just the facts."

"I wanted to talk to him about it first. Hear it from him. All I had to go on was an outlaw's word. After I talked to him—when I left his place last night—I was under the impression that he was going to tell you himself."

"As a matter of fact, he did. He must have come down here shortly after he talked with you. Gave me all the details. Said he met a young fellow of dubious morals on the boat up from Panama City, and hatched the scheme right then and there. You came up on that same boat, didn't you?"

"That's right."

"But I guess you were spending all your time with Addison's daughter, and you didn't notice who he was associating with."

Ethan sighed. He'd been a fool to think that he could keep Gil Stark out of this. Even if Sir Edward hadn't told Maller that he and Gil had been traveling together, the Eldorado supervisor knew, down deep, that there was more to the business than met the eye.

"I know now who he was talking to," said Ethan. "It was Gil Stark. He came from Illinois with me to hunt for gold. But we had an argument in San Francisco, and he went his way while I went mine. I didn't know about him and Sir Edward—not until one night a few weeks ago, when I killed his compadres and recovered your gold. And set him free."

Maller just sat there for a moment, tight-lipped, staring at Ethan, and Ethan couldn't even begin to guess what the man was thinking—or what he was about to do next.

"I admire honesty," he said, nodding. "Even if it's a little late in coming. Sir Edward came clean last night. I let him go. But I told him that I was going to write a full report to the board of directors. What action they might take against him, I don't have any idea. That's why I'm not sending that report for a couple of weeks. Gives Sir Edward and his daughter time to get clear of California."

"His daughter?"

Maller nodded. "They left a couple of hours ago. I loaned them a company wagon."

Ethan was speechless. He couldn't believe his ears. "Ellen—I mean, Miss Addison—left, too?"

"That she did." Maller rescued an envelope from the clutter on his desk and handed it to Ethan. "She asked me to give you this."

Ethan looked at the envelope. She had written his full name on the front. Her handwriting, he noticed, was graceful and bold at the same time. It suited her, he thought, feeling somewhat overwhelmed by a sudden, powerful melancholy.

Watching him, Maller read the expression on his face. It made the superintendent feel uncomfortable. He got up and walked to a table over against the wall where a bottle of whiskey stood among some charts of the Sierra Nevada and blueprints of the stamp mill and the mine. He poured two glasses and handed one to Ethan.

"Here," he said, his tone sympathetic. "You look like you could use some ninety-proof painkiller."

Ethan downed the drink in several gulps. It didn't help the pain. He hadn't really held out much hope that it would.

Maller heaved a sigh. "I don't much care for what you did. Letting your friend go. But I'm not going to fire you over it. I think . . . I think you've lost enough already."

Ethan shook his head. "I'm not staying. I quit."

"I wish you'd reconsider, Payne. You've got a future with the Eldorado. I said it before, and I stand by it. We all should be allowed a mistake or two."

"Thanks, Mr. Maller. And good-bye."

He pocketed the letter and left the superintendent's office.

Walking aimlessly, he looked up to find himself heading uphill, toward the cabin once occupied by Ellen and her father. It looked empty, forlorn—a place he wanted no part of. Quickly reversing direction, he walked down to the creek. He didn't want to go upstream. That route would bring him, eventually, to the place where he and Ellen had made love. It seemed like ages ago. So he turned and walked downstream, instead. He walked for a very long time. He wasn't sure how long. Time didn't have much meaning for him anymore. From now on, he figured, one day would be about as dismal as the next. The sun climbed higher in the sky, and eventually its searing heat made him consider the time of day. It was late morning, and a quick look around informed him that he was just a few yards from the road that led to Angel Camp. Road and creek both were squeezed into a canyon, and never were far apart. By his calculations he was several miles away from the mine.

There was no point in going back there, ever. He had the clothes on his back, the bowie knife in its sheath on his belt, a little money in his pocket. He checked to see how much—and felt the letter. He had no desire to open it. There was no need to. He knew what it said. It said that she loved him, but Sir Edward was her father, and her father needed her now more than ever before, and she simply couldn't let him go off alone. So Ethan left the letter in his pocket and counted his money. There was enough for a few bottles of whiskey and a ticket on the railroad to San Francisco. Maybe there he could find work on a ship sailing around the Horn to the east coast. And from there he could make it back to Illinois. That was as good a plan as any.

Somehow, though, he knew he would never make it as far as Illinois.

# PART III

Five years later

# CHAPTER FIFTEEN

Half-asleep, Julie Cathcott squirmed under the warm covers and reached across to touch Ethan Payne's hard, lean body. In the mornings she liked to nestle in that mat of hair on Ethan's chest, and throw a leg across him, and sometimes he would make love to her again as the amber morning light stole through the calico curtains on the room's solitary window. Even half-asleep she knew that on this particular morning the westbound stage would be rolling in, somewhere in the vicinity of eight o'clock, and that meant she had a great many things to do to prepare for its arrival. But still, there was enough time for Ethan to make love to her. . . .

Only he wasn't there.

Julie's dreamy smile vanished, and her blue eyes snapped open and darkened with annoyance as she threw the covers aside to swing long legs out of bed. She shivered as the brisk cold of the desert morning gave her a rough caress.

"Damn him," she muttered crossly to the empty room. "If he's snuck away again I'll . . . I'll . . ."

She had to smile, then—an ironic smile. What *would* she do? Absolutely nothing. If Ethan had slipped away while she slept, well, it wouldn't be the first time. And, in the end, she would not take him to task for it, if for no other reason than that she did not want to drive him off for good. Ethan was her only antidote to the poison of loneliness—that dire, debilitating, sometimes overwhelming frontier brand of loneliness that drove some people to drink, others to the brink of insanity, and a few to suicide.

Julie listened hard, hoping to hear some sound that would indicate that, early-risen, Ethan yet lingered in the station. But all she heard was the mournful whisper of the wind, and the wind seemed to be mocking her, planting a seed of melancholy in her heart on purpose, and not for the first time, or even the thousandth. She wondered what she was doing out here in the middle of nowhere. And that wasn't for the first time, either.

Because you have nowhere else to go, she reminded herself sternly. So stop feeling sorry for yourself. That was the way life was, a never-ending heartache interspersed with a few, all-too-rare moments of joy, and who was she to expect any special dispensation in that regard? She was a sinner like any other.

Rising, she hurried to put on her frayed cotton wrapper and, barefoot on the cold puncheon floor, stepped out into the dogtrot. The wind tossed her golden hair across her face and whipped the wrapper away from her legs. Her intention was to hurry into the swing station's common room and stoke the fire in the big stove, but the unmistakable scent of rain gave her pause, and she looked west, across the badlands, to the line of jagged peaks, blue in the distance. Black-bellied thunderclouds, painted crimson and gold by the morning sun just now peeking over the eastern rim, were already gathering above the sierra. A storm was brewing, there could be no question about that. Julie didn't mind, though. This time of year, though the nights were sometimes downright cold, the days were blister hot, and a rainstorm would be a welcome respite from the heat.

Then she saw him, standing over at the corral. His back was to her, and he had one booted foot up on the lower pole while his arms were folded over the topmost one, and his rebellious black hair, long almost to the shoulders, as well as the long black duster that he wore, were being swept by the blustery zephyr that in no time at all would blow those thunderclouds across the desert. The horses in the corral were restive. They knew a storm was coming, too. But Julie didn't think Ethan was watching the Overland's livestock. No, she surmised, he was looking far away, farther away than the sierra, farther than the storm clouds, too, farther than she or anyone else could ever see.

Julie sighed. She had a hunch Ethan was in one of his moods. They came of a sudden, when he got to feeling as though things were getting too comfortable, too domestic, between them. These moods usually presaged a long absence on his part. Julie's spirits plummeted. She was in for a good long dose of loneliness.

No longer aware of the chill wind, she squared her shoulders and put on a brave face and went out to join him. He heard her coming—she seriously doubted that a ghost could sneak up on Ethan Payne—and turned to face her. The look in his black eyes confirmed her worse fears, but she made an effort to disguise her dismay with a coy pout.

"You'll be sorry you weren't in bed," she said, scolding him, but not too harshly, "when I tell you about the dream I was having before I woke up."

A half-smile curled a mouth that was hard, almost cruel, in repose. "Julie, you'll catch your death of cold. . . ."

She let go of the wrapper and let the wind sweep it away from her body, and watched him look her over, slowly. The appreciation in his eyes was gratifying to her. She had a good body, and she had hopes of keeping it that way, at least for a few more years. Small consolation for the inability to bear children. But then, every cloud had its silver lining. Her infertility had cost her a husband, but at least other men still found her attractive. Not that she wanted other men. She was quite happy with the lean, dark hombre standing here before her.

"I know what you're thinking," she said. "You think I'm a wanton woman, don't you?"

He reached out, and her pulse quickened instantly into

a gallop, but he gathered in the wrapper and held it closed around her.

"You shouldn't go around outside like that. What about Manolo?" he asked.

"Oh, Ethan, he's just a boy."

"Every day that passes makes him less a boy."

"He would never do anything to me."

"You're too trusting for your own good, Julie."

"And you don't trust anybody."

"No," he said bleakly. "I don't. Not anymore."

"Not even me?" She folded her arms in front of her, relieving him of the task of holding the wrapper closed to cover her nakedness.

He swung wide around that question and looked to the east, beyond the stone and adobe station from where the westbound stage from Jacobsville would come, but of course it was too early to expect the stage. It was rarely on time, and never early. Ben Holloday's schedules were nothing if not optimistic. The reins men said there weren't enough horses west of the Mississippi to keep the stages running as fast as Holloday wanted them to run.

No, Ethan wasn't expecting to see the stage. He was just wishing. Wishing it would hurry up and get here so he could ride away. Julie was stung by regret. She was doing a little wishing of her own—wishing that she hadn't been so desperately foolish as to try to entice this man with her body. Whatever the reason, he'd had enough of her, at least for a spell. She didn't think his indifference was permanent, at least she had to believe it wasn't. That was the arrangement they had made, and though sometimes she hated it, she had to keep up her end of the bargain or she would not have him at all. They had agreed on the specific terms of their relationship long ago. No strings attached. This was at his insistence. He didn't like to be tied down, he said. But she sensed there was much more to it than that. Truth was, he didn't want to be hurt. Didn't want to give away his heart because he'd given it away before and someone

had trampled on it. He'd never told her about his past romantic involvements, and she wasn't one to pry into that
sort of thing, but a woman had instincts—a woman could
tell this kind of thing about a man. So if she tried to change
the rules on him now, Ethan Payne would ride away and
this time he would never come back. And of all the fears
that resided in her heart, that was her greatest fear of all.

So, of course, she had asked a stupid question. He didn't
trust her because she was lonely and in love with him, and
he knew that if he gave her any rope at all, even a glimmer
of hope that he might be inclined to make an honest woman
out of her, she would use it to bind him so tightly that he
would never be able to free himself. Julie loved him, but
she could not have him, not so completely as that, or as
she would have liked, because there was someone else who
owned at least a part of his heart. A woman of whom he
had never spoken, and yet Julie could feel her presence.
Only a woman could make a man hanker so deeply. In
Ethan's case the woman was far away, in both miles and
years, but where true love was concerned, miles and years
were of no consequence. Julie knew this because of the
faraway look in Ethan's eyes. That mystery woman lay
heavy on Ethan's mind this morning. Perhaps, mused Julie
fruitlessly, it was something she had done or said, possibly
during the night before, that had conjured up the memories.

"Well, I'll go brew some coffee," she said in a small
voice, and her words were swept away by the wind roaring
across the great empty desert.

"Julie."

She had started to turn away and did not turn back to
face him. Shaking her head, shoulders hunched against the
cold that suddenly cut right through her, clean through to
the heart of her, she walked quickly toward the station as
though it were some sort of refuge, which was odd considering that most of the time she thought of it more as a
prison. She was in a hurry, suddenly, to get away from him,
because she knew that whatever he said would hurt her,

and she didn't want him to lie, and didn't want him to see her tears, either.

Ethan Payne watched her go with a pang of regret, but was only of brief duration. A regret or two lost in the shadows of his crushing desire to escape. "You're a damned fool," he muttered to himself, and meant it with all his heart and soul. Julie Cathcott was a good woman, and good women were rare as bonanza strikes out here. Her no-account husband had left her two years ago. Just rode away without a by-your-leave, and Ethan had been both surprised and secretly pleased when Julie had stayed on to run the swing station thirty miles west of Jacobsville, in the heart of the Utah desert. He'd wanted her from the get-go. What red-blooded male wouldn't? But he'd minded his manners while Joe Cathcott lingered, even though a blind man could see that Joe and Julie didn't get along and that Julie was starved for kindess, if not romance. Joe Cathcott was a brutish man who did not treat any animal or person well as far as Ethan could tell—and least of all his wife. Ethan couldn't quite figure out why Julie had taken up with the man in the first place, but he'd never probed into the past with her; it hardly seemed fair to do that to her when if she tried it with him he would refuse to provide her with any information. He didn't think she'd ever been in love with Joe Cathcott, so he could only assume there had been a situation where Julie had thought it was her only option. It was the only explanation for finding someone as gentle and compassionate and loving as Julie with a man as cold and cruel as Cathcott could be.

Even after Joe left, Julie hadn't stayed at the swing station on Ethan's account, at least not at first. He knew this for a fact. In was more a case of her having no place else to go. No family back east—this information she had volunteered without his asking. And no other friends to speak of. The reins men who drove through here liked her, but reins men came and went on a regular basis, and it was hard to strike up a long-term friendship with a man in that line of work. All she'd had for a long while was Joe—and Ethan conceded that this might have been why she tolerated the treatment that son-of-bitch had given her for so long.

Quite objectively, Ethan thought that Julie did a fine job running the Wolftrap Station. The company—Ben Holladay's Overland Mail & Express Company—had sent Manolo down to help out as hostler. Manolo was a slender young mestizo with a fondness for knives. He didn't talk a whole lot; he spent words like they were rarities to be cherished. But he knew horses backward and forward. There wasn't anything about horses that he didn't know, as far as Ethan could tell. Ethan trusted him with the stock, but not with Julie, even though he tried to tell himself that he had no right to be jealous. It was just that with Manolo you never knew what he was thinking. He seemed to be everywhere, watching everything, thinking all the time—and yet never sharing his thoughts with anyone, even when asked. Such people you automatically suspected of . . . well, of something.

Ethan's job as Holladay's hand-picked troubleshooter gave him the right to come and go along the route as he pleased, and for two years now he had shared Julie Cathcott's bed whenever he passed this way—which he made sure was on a pretty regular basis when possible. Still, they tried to be discreet. And yet it seemed like everyone on the line, from Denver to the Salt Lake, knew about their arrangement by now. While some didn't approve, no one, not even John Tattersall, the division agent, proposed to make an issue of it. No one wanted to take issue with Ethan Payne on any subject. Although in theory Ethan was supposed to work hand-in-hand with the division agent, in reality he answered only to Ben Holladay. For five years that had always been the way. Tattersall didn't like that arrangement, but what could he do about it?

Holladay wasn't called the Stagecoach King for nothing. He ruled the Overland with an iron hand. His word was law on the three thousand miles of stage and freight lines he owned in Kansas, Nebraska, Colorado, and Utah—the most successful enterprise of its kind in the country. But he wasn't satisfied with all he had accomplished; no, he had plans to expand his operations into Idaho, Montana, and Oregon. In addition to the Overland, he owned a fleet of Pacific steamers, some mills, plants, stores, distilleries, and gold and silver mines, too. He lived in high style in his residence located in Washington, D.C., and he had another fancy place to hang his hat in New York City. Ethan heard that he'd recently acquired a million-dollar, 200-room palace on a thousand acres near White Plains, New York. Born the son of a dirt-poor Kentucky farmer, Ben Holladay had done quite well for himself.

A man of action and rare imagination who craved power, wealth, and influence, Holladay had started with a scheme to deliver manufactured goods to the Mormons of Salt Lake City. The endeavor was a huge success, and very profitable. In lieu of hard money, Holladay accepted cattle from the Mormons in payment for the goods and services he delivered, and, in turn, drove the cattle across the Sierra into California, selling them to the gold hunters at an immense profit.

Not too long ago, Holladay had loaned money to the firm of Russell, Majors & Waddell, whose two ventures, the Pony Express and the Central Overland, had quickly sunk into a quagmire of debt. Holladay was given a deed of trust to the Overland's properties as collateral. Before long he owned the stage line—lock, stock, and barrel. And in the next couple of years he had ruthlessly expanded the Overland, often at the expense of a number of smaller, struggling lines.

Inevitably, Holladay had found that some of the "scrapped up" lines he had acquired were plagued by crooked employees, horse thieves, and rampaging bandits and Indian renegades. To clean up one such stretch of the line, the one between Carson City and Jacobsville, he had hired Ethan Payne.

Ethan thought back to that fateful day when Holladay had found him in a San Francisco alley, face down in the muck and as drunk as any man had a right to be. Holladay had just finished proving he could make a run from Atchison to San Francisco in eleven days, most of it on his own line. It had been more than a publicity stunt; Holladay had just bought the Overland from Russell, Majors & Waddell, was trying to turn the struggling concern around, and the way to do that, he felt, was to offer the best and fastest service available. He wanted to prove to the men under his employ that they could achieve the five-mile-an-hour average that he insisted upon. As for Ethan, he'd had been feeling sorry for himself—Holladay had told him so back then and it had angered Ethan, but Ethan knew now that the Stagecoach King was right. In spite of Ethan's sorry condition, Holladay had put him on the payroll, largely on the strength of a recommendation from his friend John Maller that detailed the short work he'd made of the bandit gang that had been taking the Eldorado gold shipments.

*Do what you have to,* Holladay had told him, *and as long as it is in my best interests I'll back you to the hilt.*

Holladay had proven to be a man of his word, too. Ethan had done his job well—so well that for the past couple of years there had been no real trouble to speak of on his four-hundred-mile section. Until recently, anyway. Now there seemed to be a gang of holdup men operating in the vicinity. They had hit the stages out of Jacobsville on three occasions, usually in the vicinity of the Big Smoke, but never in the exact same place twice. They were an elusive, wild bunch, and Ethan had so far failed to locate their hideout in that rough and mountainous terrain. Though not for luck of trying. Of late he had taken to accompanying the stages running west out of Wolftrap Station, hoping to get lucky. Ethan wanted the blacklegs. Wanted them bad. No passengers or drivers had been killed—yet. But he figured it was just a matter of time before someone's toes got curled permanently. Besides, the success of the long riders was at his expense. His reputation suffered as a consequence of their actions. And out here, especially in the line of work he was in, reputation meant a lot. It kept much of the trouble at bay. It was just safer, in the long run, to have a reputation, because fewer hombres were willing to try you on for size. And then there was pride. Ethan was proud of the fact that his section of the Overland was the one with the least amount of trouble, and he wanted to keep it that way.

As Julie Cathcott disappeared into the station's common room, Manolo, the hostler, came around from behind the station, and when he spotted Ethan he stopped and tilted himself against the corner of the structure and began to pare down a thumbnail with the Arkansas toothpick he never went anywhere without. Ethan's eyes narrowed suspiciously. Manolo was a reed-thin youngster with dark brooding eyes in a face that reminded Ethan of a ferret. Or maybe a fox. Ethan knew nothing of the young mestizo's history. So long as an employee did his job, no questions were asked on the Overland. Keeping enough hired help was a never-ending chore; the average hostler or station agent was generally just a drifter who lasted only a few months before moving on. Like a tumbleweed snagged on a fence line— eventually it was going to shake loose and roll away. That was why a station agent like Julie was such a prize, even though a female running a station was a rare thing indeed.

A few long strides carried Ethan to the station. He paused at the dogtrot steps and fastened a dead-flat gaze on the mestizo lingering at the corner.

"I'll be riding out with the westbound," he said. "Make sure my saddle's on the top rack when we pull out."

Manolo just nodded.

There was something about the boy, an insolence that was carefully masked but detectable nonetheless, and it rubbed Ethan wrong. "By the way," added the trouble-shooter, "that star-faced sorrel in the corral has a hock splint. Hobble her and wrap it tight. If you can't take care of the stock I'll find someone who can."

He waited, looking for a flash of anger from Manolo, a glimmer of insubordination, an excuse to ride the boy harder, but the mestizo youth merely nodded and put away his knife and headed for the corral. Ethan realized that he wasn't being fair. Manolo knew his business, and no doubt the sorrel had come up lame during the night—the horses had been restless for hours, sensing the imminent storm, and an injury was not uncommon among animals packed into such a confined space as the corral. But Ethan didn't care if he was being fair or not. He was in a bad mood and it was just Manolo's bad luck that he had come around the station house when he did, in range of Ethan's foul humor. Besides, as Holladay had pointed out to him on more than one occasion, a troubleshooter wasn't supposed to be well-liked by the other Overland employees. In fact, according to Holladay's theory, any troubleshooter that was popular with the rest of the hands wasn't doing his job.

The door to the common room was open just a crack, and Ethan could see Julie inside, trying to coax a fire out of kindling and last night's embers in the belly of the black iron stove. On the verge of crossing the threshold, he hesitated. He knew exactly why there was such a burr under his saddle this morning. It had nothing to do with Manolo, and everything to do with Julie Cathcott. When he was with her he was happy. The problem lay in the fact that there was something inside of him that just wouldn't allow him to be happy for long. Hell, he didn't deserve to be happy. He sure as hell didn't deserve the love of a woman like Julie. So, when this arrangement became a little too cozy, when it started falling into the routine of her doing all those little things for him, the ones that women liked to do for the men they wanted to keep, he got into one of his moods and, ultimately, bolted like a mustang that sensed a trap. It wasn't fair to Julie, and he knew this all too well. But he just couldn't help himself. It was something deeply engrained inside him and he could no more change it, he thought, than he could change the color of his eyes or the timbre of his voice.

He wanted to go in and put his arms around her and promise her he would return, soon, because he supposed that she was afraid he wouldn't be coming back this time. But he couldn't make any promises. Many years ago, when the urge to yonder had lured him west, with big dreams of striking it rich and becoming something more than a dirt-poor Illinois farm boy, he had promised Lilah Webster that he would return, and that they would be married, and live happily ever after. He wasn't sure if Lilah was living happily ever after—he hadn't heard from her in over a year and a half—but he knew damn well that *he* wasn't living that way.

A promise unkept meant a heart broken. And Ethan Payne was not the kind to make the same mistake twice.

He softly shut the door and settled down on the steps, unmindful of the cold, knifing wind that seemed to cut right through the duster he wore, his other clothing, and his skin, just to hunker down in the marrow of his bones and chill him to the bone. He gazed bleakly at the line of oncoming storm clouds and calculated that before too much longer all hell was going to break loose.

# CHAPTER SIXTEEN

Within the span of an hour the storm had advanced across the badlands, and from his place on the steps, Ethan watched the gray curtain of rain in its relentless march closer, ever closer. When the first heavy drops splattered ominously in the dust around him, he reluctantly stirred, and went inside.

Julie had gotten dressed—a white blouse and a gingham skirt with an apron tied around a waist so narrow that Ethan could very nearly span it with his big, rough hands. Her golden hair was done up now in a severe bun, with a few errant tendrils escaping to lie fetchingly against her slender neck. She'd had time to recover her composure, and she even smiled at him as she brought him a cup of strong, steaming hot Arbuckle coffee. In that smile there was just a hint of sadness—but it was enough to twist like a knife in Ethan's grit and stir up his conscience, something he often wished would lay dormant a little more often than it did.

He sat at the common room's rough-hewn table and sipped the coffee and, later, rolled a cigarette and smoked it, listening to the rain lash at the station while the thunder rattled the glass panes in the window, wondering how much the storm would slow the westbound stage due anytime now. Julie busied herself making breakfast—sourdough biscuits and thick rashers of bacon, enough to feed a coach-load of people and then some. Her cooking was highly thought of by the reins men lucky enough to work this stretch of the division. Ethan was fond of her cooking too, but he found he had no appetite this morning. He kept thinking about what a good woman Julie was—sweet and dependable and loving, and who cared if she wasn't book-read, or very well educated, and she didn't talk very well, certainly not in the league with Ellen Addison, who could have talked the ears off a statue. No, Julie was a quiet girl. A little on the frail side, too. That fooled some people into thinking she had no business being out here on the wild and woolly frontier, but looks could be deceiving. Julie could be tough when she had to be. She could use a rifle as well as most men, and she had the courage of a lioness, especially when it came to defending the station and the Overland stock that was located here. The Wolftrap was an isolated outpost that had a history of being regularly hit by renegades, but that had been in the old days; Ethan would not have felt so confident about leaving her here with just Manolo to back her up if he thought there was much danger anymore from Indians and bandit gangs. Still, in the desert you never could let your guard down completely. You never knew what kind of trouble might ride up. And you had to be prepared, always, to handle it. Julie could handle most trouble, and Ethan admired her grit.

Manolo came in and ate. The mestizo youth was soaked to the skin in spite of the slicker he had donned. Rain, snow, sleet, or shine, his job was to have a fresh team harnessed and ready when the stage pulled in. Ethan checked the clock on the wall. Holladay made sure that every station had one, and it was his standing order that the clocks be kept in perfect working condition, as though a clock that kept perfect time would somehow make the stages run according to schedule, Indians, flash floods, and busted wheels be damned. Restless, Ethan went to Julie's room, fetched his saddle and warbag, and dumped them on the dogtrot. The front of the storm had swept on eastward, and through the lessening rain, far off to the north and west, he could see slants of sunlight through the clouds, like golden ramps to heaven.

He was about to return to the common room when the sound of a horse on the run reached him through the storm noise, and he turned to see a soaked and bedraggled rider, bareback on a harness horse, enter the station yard. As the man dismounted, Ethan recognized him—and knew he had been outfoxed.

"Ethan Payne!" gasped the half-drowned man. "What in tarnation you doing here?"

"Not much good, looks like, Ben."

Ben Riles shook his head. "They hit us about eight miles back, at daybreak."

"Damn." The gang had never before held up a stage east of Wolftrap.

"The big augur in that bunch must be one smart son of a bitch," said Riles. "You come here to ride with us the rest of the way? Just in case they hit where they usually do?"

Ethan nodded, smiled ruefully. "Thought I was being clever."

"I wonder, did the outlaws have any way of knowing that?"

"No. No one knew about my plans. Come on in and dry out, Ben."

"You don't have to tell me twice."

"Anyone get hurt?"

Riles was grim. "Yeah. Stanton. The damned fool."

Ethan knew Stanton to be a shotgunner, but he didn't know the man all that well. He was relieved that Riles was unharmed. Ben Riles was one of the Overland's best drivers. As a whole, Holladay's drivers were a proud bunch, famous for their grit, not to mention their talent for carousing when off duty. They were well paid, too—a reins man of Riles's caliber earned a hundred dollars a month, which was nearly what Ethan got paid. As a rule, they were intensely loyal to Holladay and the Overland.

Once Riles was at the table with a steaming cup of coffee cradled in his hands, the water dripping off him already forming a puddle under the bench, he told his story.

"They took the mail sack, and the passengers' valuables. One man said he was carrying over a thousand dollars, and he was holding the Overland responsible for every last cent. Now me, I've never seen a thousand dollars all at once, so I wouldn't know, but if you ask me he didn't have that much on him."

"If he did that's his bad luck," said Ethan. "The Overland isn't responsible. They ride at their own risk."

"We were coming up out of Arroyo Rojo when they stopped us. Got the drop on us something fierce. Before I could tell Stanton not to, the danged fool fired one barrel of his scattergun. He winged one of the owl-hoots but didn't kill him, though if he don't die of lead poisoning before sundown I'll be right surprised. Natcherly, Stanton got plugged for his trouble. Gutshot. He wasn't dead when I left, but he is now, I guarantee it. The outlaws run off the team, but one of the nags didn't run far, so I managed to catch her up and rode here."

Ethan nodded. He didn't fault Riles for leaving Stanton. There was nothing he could have done for the dying man.

"Until now, these road agents hadn't killed anybody," said Julie.

"They're not a bunch to be trifled with, I can tell you. Even after he saw Stanton get shot, one of the passengers didn't want to part with his wallet and pocket watch. He was actually dumb enough to put up a fight when one of the outlaws took 'em from him. He got pistol-whipped plenty for his trouble. Not to worry, though. I took a look at him, and he'll survive." Riles shook his head. "I tell you one thing. Holladay ain't going to like this, not one bit."

True enough, thought Ethan. Holladay would be furious. The Stagecoach King hated to lose an employee like this. And he took it personally when one of his coaches was robbed. That was just plain bad for business. Ethan could hear him now. *Payne, if you can't get the job done I'll fire you and find somebody who can.* And he would likely be hearing that, too, since the division agent had informed him that Holladay had come to Salt Lake City precisely because of the recent rash of robberies. It was bad enough to get a telegram from an irate Holladay. But to get raked over the coals face-to-face was something that no one who had survived it would ever want to endure again.

Riles knew Ethan's fat was in the fire—it was a troubleshooter's responsibility, and no one else's, to deal with situations such as these. The driver didn't much care that Ethan was in trouble. Ethan had no friends among the Overland's employees; he'd never made an effort to cultivate a friendship. Riles, being an amiable sort most days, had done his level best to make friends with Ethan when the latter first signed on, but Ethan had wanted nothing to do with him. Quite apart from this, Riles—like just about everyone else in the division—suspected that there was something going on between Ethan and Julie Cathcott. And that made Riles—again, like nearly everyone else in the division—pretty envious.

"You'd best get out of those wet clothes, Ben," said Julie, solicitous as always. "You can borrow some of Joe's things. And I've got some biscuits and bacon on the stove."

"I'm so hungry my belt buckle is scrapin' up against my backbone, Julie," declared Riles. "But I'll have to take the biscuits with me. I got to get a team back to the coach. I can't leave those folks out there too long. They're all greenhorns, and if I don't get back soon the desert'll kill 'em, sure as shootin'."

"Bring Stanton here," said Julie. "I'll see to it that he gets a decent burial."

"Yes, ma'am. Thank you."

Ethan turned to Manolo. "Saddle my horse, and get Ben a fresh mount."

Without a word, the mestizo departed the common room. Ethan produced a scrolled silver hip flask and touched up the driver's coffee with a generous dollop of "Oh Be Joyful."

"Obliged," said Riles, surprised. He hadn't thought that generosity was one of the troubleshooter's virtues.

"How many of them were there, Ben?"

"Five that I saw. Didn't get a good look at any of 'em. Like I said, day was just breaking and they had the sun behind them. They were wearing masks, too."

Ethan didn't waste breath asking which way the outlaws had been heading after the holdup. Their leader was a smart one, and by now the gang would be moving in an entirely different direction than the one Riles must have seen them taking.

"You're going after them, ain't you," said Riles. "You got to. Thing is, this frog-strangler will wipe out their sign. And five to one are pretty steep odds. Make that four to one, 'cause one of them snakes is probably in too much pain to put up much of a fight. But the odds don't matter, on account you won't catch them."

"I'll catch them this time," said Ethan. He hadn't before, when he'd tried to track the gang from a previous holdup site. He was a better tracker than most, but he'd lost that trail after two days. The gang had just kept moving south, and moving fast, and he'd entertained the hope that they were Mexico-bound and would no longer pose a problem for the Overland. That was obviously not the case.

He was aware that Julie was looking at him with a worried expression on her face. She knew his last comment was not empty bravado, but rather a firm commitment on his part. Only a man who felt he had nothing to lose would make such a comment, she thought. Ethan avoided her gaze, moving to the stove to pour himself a cup of coffee. It was the general consensus that Julie made the best coffee between San Francisco and San Antonio.

A moment later Manolo reappeared in the common room and told Ethan that the horses were ready. Ethan knew the mestizo was eager to see him go, as usual. Julie busied

herself mopping the rainwater off the floor as the troubleshooter and Ben Riles took their leave. Ethan paused at the
door.

" 'Bye, Julie."

"Good-bye."

This time she was the one who declined to look up.

Ethan felt a momentary regret. He wasn't sure if it was
because he knew Julie loved him and would worry about
him while he was gone, or because he was sorry he had
ever gotten involved with her, thereby placing her in the
position where she *would* worry about such things. One
thing was certain. She was a good woman, and deserved
better than to fall in love with a man who, brave in all other
matters, was too afraid to open up his heart to someone
again.

In two hours he and Ben Riles arrived at the site of the
holdup, having been slowed down by the fresh team of
horses they were taking back with them to replace the one
scattered by the road agents. Along the way, Riles told
Ethan about his passengers. Aside from the man who'd
been pistol-whipped whose name was Leverett, there was
a gambler from Mobile named Clooney and a lawyer, John
Morgan, traveling with his new bride, Margaret, to Sacramento.

The rain had slowed to a drizzle by the time they arrived.
The shotgunner, Stanton, was laid out on one of the
benches inside the coach. He was dead, and someone had
covered him with the blanket that Riles kept in the box.
Sitting on the other bench was a man with blood on his
bruised and swollen face. This, Ethan assumed, was Leverett, the man foolish enough to argue with an armed desperado. Margaret Morgan sat beside him because the coach
was the only shelter from the rain; she clearly would have
preferred not sharing it with a corpse. Her husband and the
gambler, Clooney, stood outside watching Ethan and Riles
as they rode up. As he dismounted, Ethan took Clooney's

measure—a tall, narrow man with dark eyes in a sallow face and a sardonic curl to his bloodless lips. He wore a black broad-brimmed hat and frock coat, both soaking wet. Morgan was a man of medium height, in his thirties, and paunchy.

"This here's Ethan Payne," said Riles. "He's the troubleshooter for this division of the Overland."

"You're a little late," said Morgan bitterly. "The trouble's been here and gone."

Ethan spared him only a glance, then turned his attention to Clooney. "You're not riding the line, are you?" Holladay strictly forbade cardsharps from plying their trade on the Overland, fleecing other passengers at the stations or enroute between them.

"Not me," said Clooney. "That's against the rules, isn't it? No, I'm just heading for California. A change of scenery."

"Are you wanted by the law where you come from?"

Clooney smirked. "No, I'm not. But even if I were, do you think I would tell you?"

"Most men in your line of work are," commented Ethan.

"Those highwaymen made off with a thousand dollars that belong to me," said Morgan curtly. "I want to know what you intend to do about that, Mr. Payne."

"I intend to hunt them down," replied Ethan calmly, "and kill them like the vermin they are. That suit you?"

Morgan stared at him, unsure whether Ethan was serious or not. "There were five of them."

"Yeah, I know. Ben told me."

"I would have put up a fight, except that I had Margaret—my wife—to consider. Besides, I was unarmed."

Ethan nodded. Morgan was just talking. He didn't look like a fighter at all. "I'm glad you didn't resist. You might be lying there next to Stanton."

"Mr. Leverett was also unarmed. But, since the robbery occurred, it has come to my attention that the gambler had a gun. What I believe they call a hideout. However, he did not see fit to use it."

Ethan turned to Clooney. The gambler produced a .22 caliber pocket pistol.

"They didn't search you?" asked Ethan.

"No. I handed everything over to them. Wallet, watch, ring." Clooney shrugged. "Easy come, easy go. Mr. Morgan apparently thinks I should have shot it out with the outlaws. But I don't play against five-to-one odds, not when the stakes are that high." He glanced wryly at the lawyer. "I suppose I could say that I didn't start any gunplay out of concern for the lady. But that would be a lie. I didn't do it because I didn't want to get killed, as I surely would have. Besides, sounds like engaging in gunplay with those bandits is your job, isn't it, Mr. Payne?"

"That's what I get paid to do. How much did they take from you?"

"About two hundred dollars," said Clooney. He seemed indifferent to the loss.

"They also subjected my wife to the indignity of taking all her jewelry," said Morgan.

Ethan peered at him. "You've never been out west before, have you, Mr. Morgan?"

"No, I have not. I don't see what that—"

"Take some free advice. When you travel, keep your money and valuables locked up in your baggage. Half the time these road agents are in too big of a hurry to search the top rack."

Morgan glanced up at the top of the coach, where a number of trunks and valises, covered by a lashed-down oilskin, were stowed. It was apparent to Ethan that the outlaws who had robbed this stage hadn't bothered going through the luggage.

"It's not really the money that's important," said Morgan, engaging in an abrupt about-face. "But look at what this has done to Margaret. She's terrified! She didn't want to come out here with me in the first place. It was all I could do to persuade her to come to Sacramento with me. And this had to happen. I would have thought the Overland would protect its customers."

"There's a man lying dead in that coach who tried to do just that," said Ethan coldly. "Maybe you and your wife would have done better to stay back east."

Morgan glared at him. "I can assure you that your employer will hear about how I've been treated here today."

"I'm sure he will," said Ethan.

"If you're a troubleshooter, then it's your responsibility to make this route safe to travel. Isn't that so? From the evidence, I must conclude that you are not very good at your job."

"Well, if I don't catch the men who robbed you, Mr. Morgan," said Ethan with a faint smile, "I'm fairly sure Ben Holladay will fire me. That make you feel any better?"

Riles had been hitching the team to the coach. Done, he stepped over to Ethan to report as much.

"Mr. Leverett looks to be in a bad way," Ethan told him. "I think you should leave him at Wolftrap, let Julie tend to him, and then go on to Jacobsville. Send a doctor back to Wolftrap."

Riles nodded. "I guess we'd better put Stanton on the rack and tie him down so that these gentlemen"—he nodded at Clooney and Morgan—"have a place to sit."

"Good Lord," exclaimed Morgan. "Must we travel the rest of the way with a dead man?"

"What do you suggest?" asked Ethan. "Leave him here for the buzzards?"

"I don't think I like your tone, Mr. Payne."

"And I don't like anything about you, Mr. Morgan. So keep your mouth shut."

Morgan fumed—but he took Ethan's advice, and said not another word.

With Clooney's help, Ethan and Riles moved Stanton's body to the top rack and tied it down. Then Riles climbed into the box and got the stage moving. Ethan swung aboard his horse, a leggy coyote dun, and bleakly watched the coach disappear down the road. The storm had passed, and the clouds were breaking up. But it had rained enough to make his task difficult. He rode a tight circle around the site of the holdup. Any sign that the outlaws' horses had left on the hard ground had been obliterated by the recent downpour. He had been thinking things over all the way from Wolftrap, and he had an idea where he might find the men he was seeking, or at the very least a clue to which direction they had taken. It was a long shot, but it was really the only thing he had.

Kicking the dun into a canter, he rode due south.

# CHAPTER SEVENTEEN

Ethan had heard a lot in recent months about the trouble brewing back east between the southern states and the northern, and it seemed clear to him that there was going to be bloodshed before long. Even seven years ago, back in Illinois, there had been some talk about slavery, that "peculiar institution" that many in the North considered a stain upon the fabric of the nation. It was a moral issue that just would not go away. There were those in the North who thought the southern states should be forced to do away with slavery, and there were many in the South who thought the northern antipathy for that institution was just a guise to mask a Yankee attempt to destroy the southern economy. Any way you cut it, there was trouble brewing back east. More and more these days, people were coming west not just for a new beginning, or to pursue a dream, but to put as much distance as possible between themselves and the sectional strife. One of those men was Wesley Grome.

Grome was a loner who hailed from Missouri, and who had for some years now made a living—though not much of one—as a mustanger. He was also a drunkard, a braggart, and a wife-beater. Ethan suspected that he also dealt in stolen Overland stock; the man had connections south of the border, and a year ago Ethan had suspected him of serving as a middleman between a pack of stock stealers and a Mexican rancher. The stock thieves had been caught and hanged for their crimes, but Ethan hadn't been able to pin anything on Grome.

The Overland troubleshooter thought it very appropriate that Grome lived near a place called Rattlesnake Springs, about twenty-five miles south of the spot where the stage had been robbed. Grome's adobe stood about a hundred yards away from the sweetwater spring, a waterhole located at the mouth of an arroyo and marked by the presence of a rock outcropping. There wasn't much water available in the badlands, and the spring was known to all who lived here. That included Apache Indians and bandits and the occasional Mexican bandolero who had to come north of the border because the Federales were making things too hot for him. Ethan figured it was possible that the road agents he was looking for were heading for the border, where they would lay low for a while before making their next strike—and where they could spend their ill-gotten gains in some bucket-of-blood border town on cheap whiskey and cheaper women. If so, they would need water to make the journey across the desert, and Rattlesnake Springs was one of the few places they would find it.

Grome didn't do much mustanging anymore—there weren't that many mustangs left in these parts—and while he had no visible means of support, he always seemed to have plenty of hard money for his Taos Lightning and shag tobacco, both of which he consumed in astonishing quantities. Ethan was convinced that Grome got that money from his long-rider friends, who used Grome's place when they needed a hot meal or a fresh horse. That was another commodity Grome always seemed to have in good supply—unbranded horses. Ethan figured Grome had an arrangement with horse thieves from Mexico who drove their stolen ponies across the border. Of course, this was a suspicion Ethan had no way of proving.

There was one other factor to consider. Ben Riles had told him that, thanks to Stanton, one of the road agents had been wounded. If the outlaws cared at all about their injured compadre they would want to take him someplace where he could be tended to. The nearest place where no one would ask questions was Grome's. Or, they might want to find a place to leave the man, who had to be slowing them down. On the other hand, there was a fair chance that wounded man would be left on the trail with a bullet in his head. There was that old saying about the want of honor among thieves. It all depended on how seriously the man was wounded. But Ethan was confident that Grome would take care of a wounded desperado—for a price, of course.

So he rode hard for Rattlesnake Springs, arriving in mid-afternoon on the rim of a hogback from which he could see the adobe in the distance. Leaving the dun tethered to an ironwood tree stubbornly asserting itself among the jumbled rocks at the base of the ridge, he took his .50 caliber Sharps Leadslinger, canteen, and a long glass from his saddle and began to approach the adobe—located about three hundred yards away—on foot.

Finding a jumble of rocks where he could get an unobstructed view of the adobe, Ethan settled down to observe, employing the long glass. Woodsmoke rose in gray wisps from the stone chimney of the hut, and he counted nine horses in the cedar post corral nearby. Some of the horses looked like they had recently been ridden hard and put up wet, which he took to be a promising sign, though this in no way guaranteed that the men he was hunting were guests of Wesley Grome's.

As he sat there among the rocks, Ethan had a strong sense of déjà vu. It all came back to him, then, in a rush— that night he had tracked Gil Stark and his bandit friends to an adobe, not that much different from this one, in an attempt to recover the Eldorado gold shipment Gil had taken from him. There had been horses in the corral in that instance, as was the case now. And, just like today, he had not seen anyone outside the adobe as he hid among the trees that marked a year-round spring. It gave him an uncomfortable feeling, and he could only hope—fervently—

that this situation did not take as many unexpected and unpleasant turns as that one had.

He made up his mind to stay put until dark, hoping to see something that would either dash his hopes or prove him the luckiest pilgrim south of the Absaroka. If he didn't see anything he would move in closer under the cover of darkness. Trying to get comfortable among the rocks, he longed for a drink, but refrained from taking a swig from the silver hip flask he carried. Now was not the time to indulge.

The last of the storm clouds had long since passed—Ethan could see them still, far to the east, just a thin line of gray above the horizon—and the sun blazed in a sky as blue as a robin's egg. Ethan reflected that in his youth he had been short on patience, but he'd acquired a lot of it in his years on the frontier, so the long hours that crawled by had little effect on him. The only problem he had was trying to keep his mind off Julie Cathcott. For some reason his instincts were telling him that the situation with her was about to change, fundamentally—and irrevocably. And it had been his experience that when situations changed—or, more precisely, when relationships changed—they changed for the worse. He reminded himself that from the start he had known it would end, and probably badly. It didn't take a genius to figure out that no one, not even Julie, who could tolerate a great deal, would tolerate a relationship in which the man she cared for refused to make a commitment. At times he'd tried to talk himself into doing just that, but those had been times of weakness, or so he told himself. It was just better not to make promises, no matter how earnestly they were made, or how determined one was to keep them. Because all too often, once a promise was made, circumstances conspired to make a person break it, and a broken promise usually equaled a broken heart. He often tried to convince himself that though she didn't realize it, Julie was much better off without a commitment from him. And he could only hope that in time she *would* realize it.

The sun crept lazily down the western sky, and the purple shadows of dusk began to stretch and deepen across the badlands. Then, just as the setting sun seemed to melt into a pool of shimmering fire on the far horizon, someone finally emerged from the adobe. Ethan snatched up the long glass to have a closer look.

It turned out to be Grome's wife, the Mexican girl, the ones folks said he had found in a border town brothel. What other kind of woman, said they, would tolerate such a man, except a fallen angel who had so disgraced herself, and so ruined her life, that she had no other prospects? Everyone knew that Wesley Grome abused her on a regular basis. A worthless drunk who cared only about his own pleasures—that was Grome in a nutshell. The Mexican girl had been pretty once, mused Ethan as he watched her, and not all that long ago. Then he forgot about Mrs. Grome's tragic existence, as he realized that she was carrying a plate in one hand and a tin cup in another as she headed for—where? Her course took her down a steep ravine, and for a few moments the contours of the desert hid her from view. Ethan waited patiently, knowing that the ravine emptied into the arroyo that marked the location of the spring. And sure enough, he spotted her again, emerging from the mouth of the arroyo not two hundred yards away, in plain view, right where the rock outcrop and some brush—an unexpected dash of greenery in the brownness of the desert—marked the spring. A man suddenly appeared atop the pile of boulders. He had seen Mrs. Grome, and he came down out of the rocks to take the plate and the cup from her. Ethan allowed himself a taut smile as he saw the man.

There was the lookout. The Mexican girl was bringing him his supper.

The woman turned to go, but the man said something and Mrs. Grome touched her hair, the gesture of a woman who has just received a compliment that has made her self-conscious. The lookout, Ethan suspected, wanted her to stay. Just for some company, maybe. Or maybe for something more. And stay she did. That was a shame, thought Ethan. He had hoped she would be clear of any trouble that might erupt. Desperate men did not ordinarily give up without a fight. And Ethan knew that he had to take the lookout before he could get any closer to the adobe. His instincts had been right; he'd been wise to linger here and keep an eye on things from a distance. Had he moved in closer the man in the rocks would likely have seen him. Might even have picked him off with the rifle he had just set aside to accept the meal from Mrs. Grome.

Gathering up his rifle, canteen, and long glass, Ethan made his way back to the ridge. He left his horse and made a wide circle around the adobe and the spring. It took him the better part of an hour, but he had to move cautiously, using the contours of the land to conceal his presence from the lookout. As he made the circle the sun dipped below the western skyline and the darkness, his ally, deepened. The lookout and Mrs. Grome were not in his line of sight for more than half an hour, but he didn't need to see them; he figured the lookout wasn't going anywhere. And as for the Mexican girl, he hoped she would return to the adobe. He made his approach on the rock outcropping from behind, and as he drew near he could hear the man's voice, which led him to believe that Mrs. Grome was still with the lookout. He wondered how she thought she could explain such a long absence from the adobe to Wesley Grome.

Neither the lookout nor the Mexican girl had an inkling of his presence—until he stepped out of the rocks with the Sharps Leadslinger held at hip level.

"Don't make any sudden moves," he advised.

The lookout's features registered surprise, then a stony resentment. He dropped the plate and groped for the pistol at his side, ignoring the rifle he had leaned against a nearby boulder. Mrs. Grome cried out in Spanish and turned to run as the lookout, rising, drew the pistol. He never got the barrel clear of the holster. Ethan took two quick strides forward and smashed the butt of the Sharps into the young man's face. The lookout dropped like a poleaxed steer.

Mrs. Grome froze in her tracks as she saw the man go down in a spray of blood—and stared in terror at Ethan as he aimed the Leadslinger in her direction. She was too afraid to think it through, to understand that Ethan couldn't fire the rifle for fear of alerting the men who were up in the adobe, and that this was why he had dropped the lookout with the butt of the rifle. But she just stood there, trembling, and Ethan felt sorry for her. He didn't let his sympathy show, however.

"How many up at the house?" he asked.

She didn't answer and he thought, *She's going to act like she doesn't understand English*, so he asked her again, this time in her native tongue. In five years he had learned to speak Spanish fluently.

This time she responded, feeling she had no choice. "Five, counting my husband."

"Is one of them wounded?"

She nodded.

Ethan felt a surge of elation. He had guessed right. His hunch had paid off. There could be no doubt about it—this was the same bunch that had held up the stage, shot Stanton to pieces, and pistol-whipped Leverett. Not to mention making off with Mr. Morgan's money and terrorizing Mrs. Morgan.

"*Mujer!* Woman!"

It was Grome. He was standing up at the head of the ravine, and Ethan could not see him in the deepening darkness, but reckoned he was probably seventy yards away.

The Mexican girl spun around like a puppet on a string at the sound of her husband's voice—and Ethan moved like lightning, grabbing her by the hair and wrenching her head back.

"Don't make a sound," he rasped.

"Dammit, woman. Get up here now!" Liquor slurred Grome's angry words. "What you doin' down there, anyhow?"

"If I do not go he will be suspicious," she said. "He will come down here to find me."

Ethan hesitated, knowing that she was probably right, and calculating the odds of taking Wesley Grome out without making noise, without alerting the four outlaws in the adobe.

"I will not betray you," she said, looking up at him with her eyes wide and shining in the darkness.

"Sure you will," he said, and let her go. She looked at him, wondering if it was okay for her to walk away, and that was when he hit her, his fist striking at the point of her chin, a carefully measured blow that knocked her out cold, but would do no permanent damage. She sagged, and he let her down to the ground gently.

When Grome came back inside the adobe, red-faced and scowling, Gil Stark said, "Did you lose something, Wes?"

Eakins and Lane, seated at the rickety table playing a desultory game of draw poker, chuckled at Gil's little joke. They all knew that Grome was very possessive where his wife was concerned. They were also aware of the fact that their compadre, Williams, the lookout, had his eye on Mrs. Grome. So they thought they had a pretty good idea what was happening down at the spring.

"I'll skin the bitch alive," growled Wesley Grome. "And if that friend of yours is messin' with her, I'll cut his *cajones* off. Just wait and see if I don't."

"Well," drawled Lane, "maybe then Willie would stay out of trouble."

"You treat your wife like a stray dog," Gil told Grome, his contempt for the man poorly concealed. "Wouldn't surprise me at all if she runs off with the first man who shows her the smallest kindness."

"Maybe you got something like that in mind, huh, Stark?" asked Grome truculently.

The two outlaws at the table forgot their card game and looked at Gil. They knew their leader had a volatile temper.

But Stark fastened a cool, steely gaze on their host, and his mouth curled into a crooked smile. "No, Wes, I don't. She isn't my type. I'm not one to muddy up another man's water. And none of my boys will, either, or they'll answer to me. And they don't want to do that."

Eakins and Lane exchanged knowing glances. They were aware of Stark's low opinion of Wesley Grome, but personal feelings played second fiddle to necessity. They needed Grome, so Stark was bound to tolerate him. Grome was a big bear of a man with a mean streak a mile wide, yet they knew Stark wasn't afraid of him. If he took a notion to do so, Stark could make hash of Grome, and do it quickly.

Somewhat mollified, and fooling himself into believing that he'd made Gil Stark back down, Grome snatched a bottle of Taos Lightning from the table and sank into a wooden rocking chair that stood near the fireplace. Laid out on a bunk on the other side of the room, Ed Hervey uttered a feverish moan and writhed beneath the blanket that covered him. Gil Stark walked over to the bunk and frowned down at the unconscious man.

"Is he gonna pull through, you think, Gil?" asked Eakins.

Gil shook his head. "Can't honestly say." His gut hunch was that Hervey would cross the river before daybreak. He'd dug a load of double-ought buckshot out of the man's arm. At first he hadn't thought the wound was that serious. But an artery had been severed, and Hervey had lost a lot of blood, and the long day's journey across the badlands, while unavoidable, had taken a lot out of him. Hervey had lost a lot of blood and there was still some lead in him, and even if he survived the massive blood loss, Gil thought it highly likely that infection would set in, and at best Hervey would lose the arm.

"He can't ride another mile," observed Lane. "What do we do about that? Let's say he's still alive come morning.

Do we leave him? We sure can't stick around here until he recovers."

Gil looked across at Grome, who wasn't paying attention to anything except the bottle of whiskey in his hand. "How much to leave him here?"

"How much did y'all get off that stage?"

"A few hundred dollars out of the mail sacks," said Gil. "A few hundred more from the passengers."

Grom chuckled. "You boys sure are small time, aren't ya? You'd do better robbin' that new bank they got up in Salt Lake City."

"That's what I've said," said Lane.

Gil glowered at Lane. "I've told you before. We aren't going to do the bank." He turned his attention back to Grome. "So how much?"

Grome shrugged, pursed his lips, made a production of mulling it over just to keep Gil on a hook. "Let's say two hunnerd. Hard money. And when he dies I'll even give him a decent burial."

"How do we know you'll wait until he's dead?" asked Lane sourly.

"He won't," said Eakins. "Soon as we're gone he'll cut poor Ed's throat from ear to ear and toss him out back for the coyotes to carry off."

Grome chuckled. "You know, I hadn't thought of that."

"Well," said Gil, glancing at Hervey's colorless, pain-etched face. "If he gets much worse, that might be doing him a favor."

"Should've just put a bullet in his brainpan a long time ago," remarked Grome. "Would have saved everybody a lot of trouble. I had to do that once, to a friend of mine. He was a *mestenero*. Tried to catch up this stallion, got tangled up in a rope and dragged a good mile across the desert. When I finally found him just about every bone in his body was broke. He couldn't talk—he'd had all his teeth knocked out, and he'd bitten off most of his tongue.

But I could see it in his eyes. He wanted me to put him down. And I did."

"That's a bunch of bull," said Lane. "You never had a friend in your life, Wes."

"Gil ain't like that," said Eakins. "He'll stick by you to the bitter end. That's why I ride with him. Remember when I got thrown in the hoosegow down in that border town? You all could have left me there to rot, but not Gil—he marched right in there like he owned the place, got the drop on both the deputies, and broke me right out of there."

"I remember that," said Lane, nodding. "I wanted to leave you there." He laughed at the expression on Eakins's face.

"Now ain't that touching," said Grome sarcastically. He took another long pull on the bottle of nerve medicine and belched loudly. "That bitch of mine better get back soon. She's got some explainin' to do."

"Just hold your horses, Wes," drawled Lane. "They're probably done by now. She's just got to get her dress back on."

Grome scowled at the outlaw, opened his mouth to say something—and then toppled backward in his chair, startled, when the adobe's door cracked back on its hinges.

Whirling, Gil Stark caught a glimpse of a man in a long black duster filling the doorway, a rifle held at hip level. Then he realized that Eakins was going for his gun, overturning his chair as he jumped up and reached for the pistol at his hip, and Gil yelled at him not to do it, but Eakins didn't hear him, and the Sharps Leadslinger roared, a deafening explosion in the confines of the adobe, a yellow blossom of flame at the end of the long barrel. The .50 caliber bullet hit Eakins squarely in the chest, at point-blank range. The impact picked him cleanly off his feet and slammed him down on the floor. His corpse overturned the table, and pasteboards went flying. The man in the black duster dropped the Sharps and drew his pistol—Gil identified it as a .44 caliber Walker Colt, the kind that the Texas Rangers carried—swinging it in Lane's direction. But Lane was in no hurry to follow Eakins to hell. As usual, he kept his wits about him, and slowly raised his hands high. The Walker Colt swung next in Gil's direction.

"Anybody else tired of living?" asked the man in the black duster.

The voice jolted Gil and he took a closer look at the face of the man as he stepped across the threshold and lamplight fell across his features.

"Hello, Ethan," he drawled, as he followed Lane's example and raised his hands. "Long time, no see."

Ethan Payne stared at Gil, and a flood of memories swept over him.

# CHAPTER EIGHTEEN

"What are you doing here, Gil?"

"Robbing stages."

"Damn your hide," said Ethan, shaking his head in amazement. "This is my section. Don't tell me you didn't know that. Least you could do would be to play the highwayman somewhere else. Or rob a bank."

Gil chuckled. "That's what Grome just said. But banks are too hard. A man could get killed robbing banks. You're only one man, Ethan, and you've got over four hundred miles of line to cover. That's a tall job, even for you."

"A man did get killed," said Ethan grimly.

"I—*Look out!*"

Ethan whirled, ducking as Grome came off the floor and hurled a chunk of firewood at the troubleshooter. He missed, but Lane saw his chance, and slapped leather. Ethan's pistol spoke. The bullet shattered the bones in Lane's arm, and his sidegun skittered across the floor as he fell, writhing in agony and cursing a blue streak. Grome had an idea about going for Lane's gun, but when Ethan swung the Walker Colt in his direction he decided against such a foolhardy play.

"Better shed that charcoal burner," advised the troubleshooter.

Using his left hand, Gil unbuckled his gun rig and let it drop. Then he went to Lane and used his bandanna as a tourniquet on the man's arm.

"You're a damned fool, Lane," chided Gil.

"I'd rather he killed me," hissed Lane through clenched teeth. "I don't care to have my neck stretched."

"Well, we all got to die sometime."

Lane glowered at Gil. "You should have made a play, Gil. One of us would have got him, for sure. He couldn't have stopped us both."

Gil smiled faintly. "I can't do that, though. He's an old friend of mine."

"We'll hang for sure."

Gil rose and glanced at Ethan. Ethan just stared at him. Lane was right—if Gil had gone for his artillery at the same time that Lane made his play, Ethan would have been beaten for sure. With a mounting sense of horror he realized that he was on the verge of being in a position—again—where he owed Gil Stark his life.

"I'm sorry about that shotgun guard," Gil told him. "It was the kid, Willie, who gunned him down. I told them all no shooting. But it was in self defense. That Overland man was bound and determined to put up a fight." He gestured at the wounded man laying the bunk. "He damn near blew Ed's arm off, first thing. That was after we asked him, all nice and polite, to throw down the greener. So, in a way you could say he brought it on himself."

"Willie?" asked Ethan. "You mean the one down by the spring?"

Gil nodded. "Did you kill him?"

"Not much of a lookout. He was too busy looking at Grome's wife."

Grome muttered an obscenity.

"I reckon you did him in, didn't you? I remember how it is. You don't take any prisoners."

"I didn't kill him."

"Doesn't matter if Willie was the one to pull the trigger or not. We're still all going to hang for the killing of that shotgun guard." Lane was trying to get up, and Gil helped him into a chair. Blood dripped from the elbow of his shattered arm and splattered on the floor planks. Lane glanced bleakly at Ethan. "I'm right, ain't I?"

"Reckon that's right," conceded Ethan, without enthusiasm. He was furious at Gil Stark for being here—but the idea of Gil playing host to a necktie party was not something that appealed to him.

There was a length of coiled rope hanging on a wall peg, and at Ethan's command Gil used the hard twist to tie up Lane and Grome. The Overland troubleshooter could tell at a glance that the outlaw laid up in the bunk would give him no trouble, but just in case he checked under the blanket that covered the man, looking for a concealed weapon. There was none. Collecting every pistol and rifle he could find, he walked outside with Stark and deposited the hardware in the rocks behind the cabin as they climbed down the ravine, then moved along the arroyo, single file, with Stark leading the way and Ethan holding the Walker Colt on him, until they reached the rock outcropping near the spring. The outlaw named Willie and Grome's Mexican wife lay there, both of them unconscious still. Gil looked at Willie's bloodied, ruined face, and shook his head.

"Never should have let him join up," said Gil. "Knew he was a no-account. And I always told him that a pretty girl would be the death of him. Looks like I could be right."

"You're hardly in a position to judge someone to be a no-account," snapped Ethan, crossly.

Gil smiled that crooked smile of his. "I kind of figured you'd be mad at me if you found out I was in your territory. But, if you'll recall, the last time we saw each other, you told me to get out of California and never come back. I did that. Just a coincidence, I guess, that we ended up in the same place."

"I don't believe in coincidence."

"After I left California I went to Colorado. And here's something you'll find amusing. I got a job as a station hand for a little scrapped-up stageline running out of Denver. I held on to that job for a few months, and then the company went belly up. They didn't pay me a red cent of my wages. So I took the best horse in the station corral and rode down to Texas. Found work as a drover. But that is no way to get ahead in the world, Ethan, I can tell you. And it's damned hard work, besides. You know how work and I don't mix. That's when I met up with Lane and Eakins. They were both Texas cowboys, and about as fond of honest labor as I was. We put our heads together and decided that we could make more money a lot quicker by rustling cattle and stealing horses. But then the Texas Rangers took an interest in our work. And you always come to a bad end once the Rangers get on your trail. So we decided it was time to leave Texas, and we came out here. You're right about me, Ethan. I'm really no better than this dumb kid. I'm not cut from the same cloth as you. You're willing to work and make an honest living. I've tried that. It just doesn't suit me. Another part of it is that I don't like taking orders."

"Get the kid up."

Gil tried shaking Willie, to no avail. He spotted the kid's canteen nearby, and emptied its contents on Willie's head. Willie came to, spluttering. Gil helped him sit up. Willie slowly got his bearings. When he saw Ethan standing nearby, he spat blood and glowered.

"You son of a bitch," he mumbled, his ruined mouth rendering him almost unintelligible. "The bastard snuck up on me, Gil. Snuck up like a stinkin' Injun, else I would have kilt him for sure."

Gil laughed. "A herd of buffalo could have snuck up on you, Willie, 'cause you were too busy trying to get under Mrs. Grome's skirt. You're just lucky. If anybody had killed anybody, it would have been him killing you. And, by the way—I wouldn't have shed any tears over your grave, either."

"I thought we were saddle partners, Gil," said Willie, hurt by Gil's cavalier indifference to his fate.

"When you killed that shotgun guard I should have

blown your head off. Now we'll all hang for sure."

"But he shot first. He hit Ed."

"You could have winged him. I've seen you shoot the wings off a bird in flight. You *wanted* to kill him, Willie, and now he's dead—and so are we."

Willie turned a malevolent gaze on the Overland troubleshooter. "You better hope they hang me, mister, 'cause if they don't I'll come looking for you someday, you bastard, and then we'll have our reckoning."

"You're not half man enough to handle him," said Gil. "So just shut up before he puts you out of your misery."

Ethan tossed Gil a length of hard twist he had carried from the adobe. "Tie up your young pup, Gil," said the troubleshooter. "That way I won't have to shoot him."

"But you're supposed to," said Gil. "You're supposed to shoot all of them, and then let me walk away. Don't you remember?"

Ethan couldn't tell if Gil was joking or not. He had this sudden crazy idea that Gil Stark had picked his division for the holdups on purpose—so that, just in case he and his gang got caught, he might survive, as he had survived the robbery of the Eldorado gold shipment five long years ago. Could that be possible? Ethan didn't want to think about it. But he couldn't deny that Gil Stark was devious enough to think along those lines.

Once Willie's hands were bound behind his back, Ethan checked the rope to make sure Gil had done a good job of it. Then he picked up the still unconscious Mrs. Grome and threw her over his shoulder. They returned to the adobe, Gil going first, Willie following him, and Ethan bringing up the rear, the Walker Colt aimed at the young robber's spine.

Back inside the adobe, Ethan tied Gil up and then put all four of them—Gil, Lane, Willie, and Grome—in the corner over near the fireplace, making them sit on the floor. Mrs. Grome was slow to come around, and just to be on the safe side, Ethan tied her up as well. He couldn't imagine that she would be willing to die for her husband's sake. And he wouldn't be surprised, he decided, if she thanked him for hauling Wesley Grome off to meet his just desserts. But there was no telling where women were concerned, and he wasn't in the mood to take any chances. Setting the overturned table to rights, he sat down at it and laid the reloaded Sharps Leadslinger within easy reach. Then he rolled a smoke. Finally he could relax a little.

"So what are we gonna do now?" growled Grome. "Just sit here and stare at each other?"

"We're going to wait until daylight," replied Ethan. "Then I'm taking you to Jacobsville, where I'll hand you over to Sheriff Evans."

"I ain't done a damned thing," said Grome. "I don't know these outlaws, or anything about what they done. You got nothing on me."

"No?" Ethan's smile was about as warm as the dead of winter. "Still, I'll bet you a dollar you hang right along with the rest of them."

"That surprises me," said Gil nonchalantly. "You never used to gamble, Ethan."

Grome stared at him. "Just how do you know this bastard, anyhow, Stark?"

Gil shook his head. "It's a long story. He and I go way back."

"What about my wife?" Grome asked Ethan. "What happens to her?"

"Like you give a hoot." Lane laughed. Ethan thought he was a pretty tough hombre—he could laugh even while bleeding from a gunshot wound.

"Shut your trap," snarled Grome. "Or I'll kick your teeth in."

"I'll cut her loose in the morning," said Ethan. "What happens to her after that is not my problem."

"You're a cold-blooded son of a bitch, aren't you?" sneered Grome.

"And Ed?" asked Gil, pointing with his chin at the wounded man on the bunk.

"He's not going anywhere," replied Ethan. "You know that as well as I do. If he dies before we leave, we'll bury him."

"And what if he's still alive come daybreak?"

"He stays here, dead or alive." Ethan knew he would have his hands full getting these four men to Jacobsville. He didn't need to burden himself further with someone like Ed Hervey, who was in such bad shape that he couldn't even ride. Once he had delivered Gil and the others he might swing back by and find out if Ed was alive or dead. But he already had a pretty good idea which one it would be.

"And what about him?" asked Grome, nodding at the corpse of the outlaw named Eakins. "Hell, this is my house. I don't leave dead bodies lyin' around."

"I'd rather not spend all night with a dead man, either," said Lane.

Ethan got up, dragged Eakins to the door by his legs, and rolled the body out onto the adobe's rickety porch.

"There," he said, closing the door. "You all feel better now?"

"You're a cold-blooded bastard," remarked Lane.

"So I've been told." Ethan resumed his seat at the table and scooped up the deck of grimy, dog-eared pasteboards Lane and Eakins had been playing with earlier. He started a game of solitaire, deciding that he might as well do something to pass the time. Getting some sleep was out of the question. With any luck he would have the robbers locked up in a jail by late tomorrow night. After that he could catch up on the shuteye.

"Hey, Ethan," said Gil, about thirty minutes later.

Ethan thought he sounded scared. It was beginning to sink in that the game was up.

"What do you want?"

"Just thought we could talk a bit."

"I don't want to talk anymore." He turned his attention back to the cards.

An hour prior to daybreak he shook Gil Stark awake. "Get up."

Using the wall at his back for support, Gil got to his feet. The cold in his bones made him shudder. A glance at the adobe's solitary window told him that it was still night outside. Grome and Willie were asleep. Lane looked to be half-conscious, moaning now and then in pain. Mrs. Grome sat cross-legged in a corner of the adobe, wide awake, watching everything with dark and expressionless eyes. Gil looked at the Overland troubleshooter, wondering why he had been awakened before it was time to head for Jacobsville. Then a thought occurred to him, and he looked across the room to the bunk where Ed Hervey lay.

"He died just a little while ago," said Ethan, without emotion. "Come on."

"Where are we going?"

"You're going to saddle some horses." Ethan glanced at Lane. "There's not a gun or knife in this house. I looked it over twice. So don't go getting any ideas. Try anything and I'll shoot you down. Long as you're alive you've got to figure there's a chance. But you'll have no chance with me. I would just as soon kill you here and now and go on home."

"He means it, Lane," said Gil.

Lane's eyes fluttered open and he looked up at the troubleshooter and gave a small nod to indicate that he had heard Ethan's words and understood their meaning. A night of suffering had taken all the vinegar out of him. Ethan was confident the man was in no condition to make trouble.

"You need to let me bind up his wounds," Gil told Ethan. "He's half bled to death."

Ethan nodded. "I'll let you, when we get back."

"If I didn't know better, I'd say you've let him bleed all

this time just so he'd be too weak to make any trouble for you."

Ethan nodded at the door, and Gil preceded him out onto the porch, where the gang's saddles had been deposited when they'd first arrived. Ethan took a storm lantern off the wall, shook it to confirm that it contained some oil, and lit it. Then he handed it to Gil, who held it aloft while Ethan thoroughly checked every saddlebag, pouch, and rolled-up blanket or slicker. He found two more pistols and a knife. These he tossed into the darkness, and stood there a moment, wondering if he had overlooked anything, failed to take some necessary precaution. If he made one mistake it would likely be fatal. The four heavy canvas mail bags were inside. They had already been ransacked. The Overland troubleshooter thought to check the pockets of the dead man, Eakins, whose stiff corpse lay face down on the porch. The effort netted him about eighty dollars in paper and hard money.

"Pretty slim pickings," he told Gil.

Gil nodded. "I guess you could say we were strictly small-time operators."

"That you were," concurred Ethan. "Until your saddle partner killed that shotgun guard. You got any of somebody else's money on you, Gil?"

"I've got about a hundred dollars that we took out of the mail."

"Is it worth hanging for?"

Gil gave him a funny look, one that Ethan couldn't quite fathom.

"You really think I'll hang for this?"

"I'd be surprised if you didn't."

"Guess I figured you'd look the other way again. But looks like times have changed, and so have we, huh, Ethan?"

Ethan took the bowie knife out of the sheath that rested in the small of his back, and cut Gil's bonds. He shook his head at the glimmer of hope in his friend's eyes.

"I'm not letting you go. You can't saddle horses with your hands tied behind your back."

"Oh. Right." Gil tried to mask his disappointment with a wry smile. "I see you've still got that big pigsticker. I still remember the day your mother gave it to you. I don't think I've ever seen anyone as excited as you were that day."

"That was another world, Gil," said Ethan gruffly. He thought he knew what Gil was doing, and he didn't like it. "Lot of water under the bridge since then. Now grab a couple of those saddles. It will be daylight in an hour and I want to be on the trail by then."

Gil reached into a pants pocket and pulled out the money—his share of the last haul—and handed it to Ethan.

"You're sure that's it," said the Overland troubleshooter.

"Yeah. That's all I took."

He bent down and picked up two of the saddles, and Ethan stepped back out of range, just in case Gil was desperate enough to try to swing one of the hulls into him and then make a break for it. It wasn't so much that he was afraid Gil would get away, but rather that Gil would force him to shoot. But Gil didn't try anything. He carried the saddles over to the corral, and Ethan followed him. As Gil saddled two of the horses, Ethan kept one eye on him and another on the adobe. Neither man said a word until Gil had finished strapping four hen-skins on four cayuses.

"What about your horse?" asked Gil.

"He's nearby. Either you or Grome will have to walk until we get to him."

"Make Grome walk," said Gil, grinning. He seemed to be his old self again. "I saddled the horses."

Gil leaned on a horse for a moment and peered at the gray threads of daylight that were beginning to streak the sky above the eastern horizon.

"I guess I've really messed things up this time, haven't I?" he asked.

"You could've done better."

"Too bad this isn't Texas. There's a five-hundred-dollar reward on my head in Texas. If anyone was going to collect it, I'd want it to be you."

"The last thing I'd want is the bounty on your head."

"Can I ask you one thing?"

"Sure," said Ethan, reluctantly.

"How come you never went back? To Illinois, I mean. To Lilah."

"You never did learn to mind your own business, Gil."

"Just curious. And whatever happened with that English girl out in California?"

Ethan grimaced. "Her father left the Eldorado Company, and she went with him."

"Sorry to hear that. So you haven't heard from Lilah lately, I take it."

"No, not for a couple of years. She stopped writing back, so after a while I stopped sending letters."

Gil nodded. "Guess you stayed away too long." He took a deep breath, then shook his head. "I wish I knew whether this was the right thing to do."

"What are you talking about?"

Gil reached under his shirt and pulled out a letter. "The first robbery we pulled—I was going through one of the mailbags, looking for letters and such that might have money in them. And found this." He looked at the letter, obviously reluctant to hand it over. "It's addressed to you, Ethan, care of the Overland office in Salt Lake City. It's from Lilah."

Mind racing, Ethan muttered a curse. "That was over three months ago when you pulled the first job. Damn it, Gil, you're always interfering with my life in one way or another."

"Before you get any madder than you already are, you should read the letter. But you won't like what it says."

"So you read Lilah's letter to me," said Ethan coldly, the anger building inside him.

"Yeah, after a while, I did. At first I didn't, though. At

first I thought I ought to try to get it to you somehow. But then curiosity got the best of me, and I opened it. After I read it I thought about burning it. On the assumption that you'd be better off not ever seeing it."

Ethan felt the blood in his veins run cold. Gil was as serious as he'd ever seen him, and it was obvious that he was genuinely concerned.

"Give me the letter," said Ethan, extending a hand.

Gil handed it over. Ethan hesitated, afraid to open it, afraid of its contents. But he steeled himself, and read:

*Dear Ethan:*

*I have not heard from you in a while, but I trust that you are well. Though I find it very difficult to do so, I must tell you of a strange turn of events. My father has had bad luck with the farm these past couple of years. First there was all the rain and the flooding, and then, last year, there was no rain at all. He became discouraged, and one day told my mother that he wanted nothing more to do with farming. She agreed that he should go to Chicago and try to find work there if that was what he wanted to do. He did find work, at a stockyard. A month later he sold the farm. I wrote to you then, but as I have not received any reply from you since then, I am assuming that you never received that letter. If this is so you must be very surprised to know that a country girl like me has been living in the city for more than half a year now. But you will be even more surprised to learn that I am getting married. His name is Stephen, and he is the son of the man for whom my father works. He loves me madly, and I love him. He treats me like a princess, in fact I sometimes think he treats me better than I deserve. Both my mother and father like him very much. I should add that my mother had often encouraged me to find someone else. She insisted that you were not coming back. I would always defend you, and some-*

*times we would get into these horrible rows. Please don't be angry with her. She is concerned only with my welfare, and carries no ill will toward you. And, as it happens, she was right and I was wrong.*

*Oh, Ethan, I wish things had turned out differently for us. I still think of you often, and care for you, and I hope you know that you will always be in my heart. I don't know when, exactly, I came to the realization that things were just not going to work out for us. I hope, as well, that you are happy wherever you are. I like to think that you have found someone to share your life with, someone who makes you happy, and I mean that, even though I feel a twinge of jealousy when I think of you with someone else. I firmly believe that things happen for a reason. When you left I was convinced that we were meant to be together always, but obviously that wasn't the case. God had other plans for us, and we must trust in His judgment, and be confident that His plans are superior to our own, and will lead to complete fulfillment.*

*This doesn't mean you can't write to me at the address below. I have told Stephen all about you, and he has been very understanding, and it was he that urged me to ask you to write so that I may know that all is well with you. I can only hope that if and when you do write it will be to congratulate me, and to sincerely wish me all the best, as I wish for you from the bottom of my heart.*

*Your devoted friend always,*
*Lilah*

Stunned, Ethan slowly folded the letter and returned it to the envelope.

"I really am sorry," said Gil softly. "You never should have listened to me about going to California."

"You didn't make me go. Fact is, I didn't want to be a

farmer. I wanted to be anything *but* a farmer. And if I had stayed and been one, I would have failed. Just like my father did. Just like *her* father did."

"Well, Lilah is the best person I ever knew. I hope she *is* happy."

"Yeah," said Ethan, feeling as empty as he had ever felt, like the mere husk of a man that the cold night wind could blow right through. "Me, too. Mount up."

Gil was confused. "It's not dawn, yet. Sorry if I'm in no big hurry to get to Jacobsville and the hangman." He smiled, but it was forced.

"Mount up and ride."

Gil stared at him, not sure he had heard right.

"Damn it," growled Ethan. "Make dust before I change my mind."

"What are you doing, Ethan?"

"Saving your worthless hide again. But this is the last time, you hear? Get going, and don't stop until you're one step beyond as far away from me as you can get."

Gil opened his mouth to say something, but had second thoughts, and turned to his horse. As he climbed into the saddle, Ethan removed the gate pole.

"I owe you," said Gil.

"I won't collect, because I don't plan to ever see your face again."

"You'll catch hell for this."

"I'm used to catching hell. You'll come to a bad end, Gil. But it won't be at my hand."

Gil Stark nodded and kicked his horse into a gallop. He was quickly swallowed up by the pre-dawn gloom. Watching him go, Ethan slid Lilah's letter under his shirt. And that immediately brought back strong memories of Ellen Addison—particularly that night at the creek not far from the Eldorado Number One mine, when Ellen had discovered the letter under his shirt. He shook his head. Everything he had ever wanted was gone now. Nothing ever seemed to work out as he had planned for it to. And he didn't know if letting Gil go was the right or wrong thing to do. But he didn't care. He certainly didn't care about any consequences. It didn't matter anymore.

When he returned to the adobe without Gil, Lane was the first one to question Stark's absence.

"Where is he?" asked the outlaw. "Did you cut his throat? I didn't hear a gunshot. Maybe you're saving up on your ammunition."

"He got away," said Ethan flatly.

"Got away hell," scoffed Lane. "You let him go, on account of he was your friend."

Ethan just stared at him, his voice as emotionless as his expression. "Like I told you—he got away."

"I bet Sheriff Fuller will be mighty interested to hear about how he managed that," said Grome.

"Go ahead," said Ethan. "Muddy up my water. But I'll still see you hang. That is, unless something happens to you between here and Jacobsville."

"You heard him, Lane," said Grome. "He's threatening to murder me unless I keep my trap shut."

"Then keep it shut," advised Lane.

"You're not as dumb as you look," Ethan told him.

"Just because I'm going to hang doesn't mean I have to have Gil hangin' right alongside me to make me feel better," said Lane dryly. "So he got lucky and I didn't. That's how it goes. Some people always get a break, and some people never do."

"Yeah, I know," said Ethan, feeling sorry for himself— and then shaking it off. "Grome, get up. You've got a couple of graves to dig before we leave."

"I'm not digging no damned graves."

Ethan nodded. He gathered up a handful of Grome's shirt and pulled the man to his feet—before slamming his head against the adobe wall several times. A quick glance in the direction of the Mexican girl revealed that Mrs. Grome was still just watching, without emotion. Ethan couldn't read her, and it was beginning to make him a little nervous that he couldn't.

"You can dig two graves," Ethan told Grome, "or I'll dig three. Your choice."

Grome nodded. The hate was brimming in his eyes, but he wisely kept his mouth shut.

# CHAPTER NINETEEN

After depositing Grome, Lane, and Willie at the Jacobsville jail, Ethan went directly to the barbershop for a bath and a shave, swung by the Alhambra Saloon to buy a bottle of whiskey, then rented a room at the Grand Hotel. He had stayed there many times before, and the clerk knew to give him a room at the back, away from the hustle and bustle of the town's main street. As he entered the room, it struck Ethan—the way it always did—that in the five years that he'd been in Ben Holladay's employ he had never had a place to really call his own. The closest thing to a home he had was the Wolftrap Station, and of course that was Julie's home, not his. He was just a guest there, even though she would have preferred it to be otherwise. In fact, Ethan decided, he hadn't really had a place to call home since leaving Roan's Prairie. The bunkhouse at the Eldorado Number One mine was an accommodation that few would categorize as a home. Such musings did not make him feel much better about things.

There was nothing grand about Jacobsville's only hostelry, but at least the sheets were clean. Ethan took a couple of swigs from the bottle, hit the bed, and fell instantly to sleep and didn't wake up until morning. That was the one good thing about going several days without any shuteye—no matter how grim the thoughts in your head, you *would* sleep when given the chance.

Surprised to find he had an appetite, Ethan visited the

hash counter at the Alhambra Saloon and consumed enough eggs, ham, biscuits, and good strong coffee to fill two men. He was just finishing up when Jacobsville's sheriff found him.

Frank Fuller had seen about fifty winters, but though he was gray and grizzled there was still plenty of hard bark on him. He was a good, solid, reliable man who did his job well, having been a peace officer all his life, starting out as a deputy in Arkansas, which for several decades had been about as lawless a place as any to be found. The mere fact that Fuller had survived that experience said a lot about his resourcefulness.

"John Tattersall came over to get those mail bags this morning," said Walker.

Ethan nodded. Tattersall was the Overland division agent. "I thought he'd be in Salt Lake City. I've heard Holladay is there."

"He came in on the stage this morning. Said he'd gotten word of the robbery. He's looking for you now, and he's plenty hot under the collar. One of those road agents told him that you cut a member of the gang loose."

Ethan looked Fuller in the eye and said, "What if I did?"

Fuller shrugged. "What you do on the Overland is none of my business. But Tattersall never has liked you, as you well know, and he's willing to believe anything bad about you."

"Who told him?"

"Wesley Grome."

"That figures. Where is he?"

"I told him to check the hotel, that he'd probably find you there. Then I came over here to warn you."

"I'm obliged, Frank."

Fuller nodded and left the saloon. Ethan was grateful for the fact that the sheriff hadn't asked him if Grome's accusation was true. Fuller wasn't one to judge another, and he minded his own business. Unless it had something to do with law and order in Jacobsville, he just plain wasn't interested.

Ethan paid his bill and started to leave. Then, abruptly, he changed his mind and angled over to the bar.

"Whiskey," he said.

"Little early for you, isn't it?" asked the barkeep, pleasantly.

"Are you a bartender, or a nursemaid?"

Stung, the apron shrugged and poured Ethan a shot glass full of amber nerve medicine, then moved off to the other end of the mahogany to continue his perusal of the Jacobsville newspaper.

Ethan regretted barking at the bartender, but just the thought of Tattersall raised his hackles. The division agent was a self-important little martinet who resented the scope of Ethan's authority, and he would milk this situation for all it was worth if he thought he could undermine Ethan's standing with Ben Holladay.

A few minutes later Tattersall showed up. As usual he was dressed to the nines in broadcloth, with a derby hat on his head and high-polished half-boots on his feet. Spotting Ethan belly up to the bar, he marched over.

"Payne, I want to have a word with you," he said officiously.

"Well, I don't want to have a word with you, so get the hell away from me."

At the other end of the bar, the apron glanced up, apprehensively. The tone of Ethan's voice alerted him to the possibility of trouble.

Tattersall fumed. "I think Mr. Holladay will be very interested to hear that you let one of those outlaws go free."

"You know what I think? I think Mr. Holladay will take my word over that of a man like Wesley Grome any day."

"Are you denying that you let a criminal by the name of Gil Stark just ride away?" queried Tattersall incredulously. "I've got Ben Riles's report on the holdup. There were five men in the gang, according to the report. You brought in two of them, and Gromes for giving them aid. Grome says that two more are buried at his place. Do you deny that?"

"Nope."

"Then that accounts for four outlaws. Where is the fifth man, Payne?"

"Wesley Grome is the fifth man."

Tattersall was stunned. "Grome didn't hold up that stage and we both know it."

Ethan shrugged and sipped the whiskey, letting the warmth that flooded through his body smooth out his nerves. But it didn't take the bad taste out of his mouth. He could scarcely believe it, but here he was covering for Gil Stark again, just as he had always done. It had nothing to do with his job. He didn't care about that anymore. But if he admitted to letting Gil go free, then the Overland would put a large bounty on his head. And there were plenty of bounty hunters in this part of the country who would not rest until they brought Gil in—more than likely draped dead over his saddle. As long as Ethan stuck to his story, and Lane kept his mouth shut, he thought he could pull it off. It would be his word against Wesley Grome's, and there weren't very many people in and around Jacobsville who had a good opinion of that man.

"You would let Grome hang for something he wasn't even a part of?" Tattersall shook his head. "You're a cold-blooded and unscrupulous man, Payne. I never took you to be a liar, but I guess I was overestimating you."

Ethan fastened a dark gaze on the division agent. "If you're going to go around calling a man a liar in this country, John, you had better start carrying a gun."

Tattersall cocked his head to one side, eyes narrowing. "Was that a veiled threat?"

"Grome's no saint, so why are you trying to protect him? He's done plenty of things he could hang for in his life-time."

Tattersall was astonished. "Last time I checked that's not

how it works, Payne." He was furious, and Ethan knew it was because Tattersall was beginning to realize that Holladay *would* take his troubleshooter's word over that of someone like Grome, and so Grome *would* become the fifth man in the holdup gang, and in all likelihood he *would* hang, because a jury of twelve good men from anywhere in the territory would believe it, too. And that meant Ethan Payne would get off the hook, would get away with letting an outlaw go. Worse still, he would get credit for bringing down the road agents.

"You won't get away with this," vowed Tattersall grimly. "Somehow I will nail your hide to the door on this. You've ridden roughshod over me long enough and I won't stand for it any longer. You think you're a law unto yourself, that you can do anything you're of a mind to. But I won't stand for it any longer. And one other thing. I don't know how you can live with yourself."

Ethan knocked back the rest of his whiskey and gently put the empty shot glass down on the bar.

Then he lashed out with a backhand blow that struck Tattersall across the face and knocked him on his butt.

"I live with myself because I have to," said Ethan softly, looming over the division agent, whose eyes were round with shock and fear as he dabbed with the back of his hand at the blood leaking from a cut lip. "But I don't have to live with you, John, so get out of my face."

The Alhambra's doors swung open, creaking on their hinges, as Sheriff Fuller strolled in.

"I saw you come in here, Mr. Tattersall," said the Jacobsville lawman. "Thought maybe I should linger outside for a spell, just in case there was any trouble." Fuller looked at Ethan. There was a faint and friendly smile on his lips, but his eyes were like steel. "Are you done, Ethan?"

"Yeah," said Ethan. "I'm done." He stepped over Tattersall and headed for the door.

"You should arrest him, Sheriff," said Tattersall. "He's a dangerous man."

"There are a lot of dangerous men in these parts," observed Fuller.

"He assaulted me. For no good reason."

"I can tell he assaulted you. I don't know about the no good reason." Fuller glanced at Ethan. "Did you have a reason?"

"He was annoying me," said Ethan, and without breaking stride went right past Fuller and through the doors. He was off the Alhambra's boardwalk and in the dusty ruts of the street when Fuller, emerging from the saloon, called to him to hold up. Ethan stopped and turned, expecting trouble.

"I'll walk with you," said Fuller, and bent his steps for the Grand Hotel. Ethan fell in alongside. "You know," drawled the sheriff, "I've always thought of you as a fellow lawman, even though you don't wear a tin star."

"Your point being?"

"A lawman has got to keep his feelings out of his work. If he doesn't, he's bound to make a mistake sooner or later. I think you know what I mean. It's happened to you."

Ethan didn't say anything.

"Back in Arkansas," said Fuller, "my cousin killed a man in cold blood. A dispute over a cow. Folks around there were poor. A cow is an important piece of property, so I could understand how an argument could get started over one. My cousin was a decent man, for the most part. He was struggling to keep his head above water, to provide for his family, and he was having a hard go of it. We were pretty close, him and me. We grew up together. But he broke the law. I had to hunt him down and bring him in. He was found guilty of murder, and he was hanged. That was the hardest thing I've ever had to do. But it was also the right thing. The right thing and the hardest thing are usually the *same* thing, in case you haven't noticed by now."

"I've noticed."

"Now, I'm wondering, had you been in my shoes back

there in Arkansas—could you have done the right thing?"

They were in front of the hotel, and Ethan stopped walking. He didn't mind walking with the sheriff, but he would be offended if Fuller walked him all the way to his room. "No," he said flatly.

"I reckon that's because it's not justice that you're really interested in. To you, this is just a job. Now, you take your responsibilities very seriously. And if somebody robs a stage on your line you take it personally. There's nothing wrong with that. But for a lawman to last, he's got to want more than just to do a job well."

"Like what?"

"What I said—justice. When a wrong's been done, you have to want to set it right. And you can't step over the line and do wrong yourself, no matter what the stakes. That old saying about how two wrongs don't make a right? Well, that's something every man who wears a badge has to keep in the front of his mind all the time."

Ethan just looked at him and didn't respond.

Fuller smiled. "Okay, here endeth the lesson. If you wanted to be preached at you'd go to Sunday service and get a good dose of fire and brimstone. But I will say this. If I were you, Ethan, I'd come clean right now. You like being top dog on the Overland. It's all you've got. It's your home. Without it you'd just be another yonder man. A drifter. But no job is worth selling your honor cheap."

"Thanks for the advice." Ethan went inside. Upstairs in his room, he slammed the door shut behind him and muttered a curse at the four walls. He knew Fuller was right. Part of him wanted to head straight to the telegraph office and send a wire to Ben Holladay in Salt Lake City, admitting that he had in fact cut Gil Stark loose. But he didn't. He couldn't give John Tattersall the satisfaction, for one thing. And he realized that he *did* care about his job, after all. The news from Lilah had thrown him off stride. There for a while he hadn't cared about anything, hadn't seen any reason to. But Fuller had hit the nail on the head—the

Overland *was* his home. More than ever now, it was all he had.

He rode out of Jacobsville after writing a terse report about the capture of the holdup hang and leaving it at the Overland station there. He made no mention of Wesley Grome in terms of the man having taken an active part in the robbery. Fuller caught him before he left and told him that the circuit judge would not arrive for another fortnight, at which time Ethan could expect to be called upon to testify at the trials of the three men currently residing in the jail. Ethan understood. He didn't know what he was going to do about testimony at a trial. He had lied to Fuller and Tattersall about Grome's participation in the robbery. He didn't want to lie under oath, though. Bringing Grome in had been a mistake, he realized that now. But he wasn't sure how to set things right. And what if a jury concluded, even without his testimony, that Grome had been the fifth road agent, and condemned him to die for his part in the murder of the shotgun guard? The man's blood would still be on his hands, whether he testified or not.

His destination was Salt Lake City, and ordinarily he would have taken an Overland stage straight through, but that would take him into Wolftrap Station, and he didn't want to see Julie Cathcott right now. He missed being with her, of course. He always did. When he lay in her arms the memories left him alone, at least for a little while. But that longing in her eyes was what he had to stay away from, that desire for permanence that he could not satisfy.

To avoid Julie he had to take a circuitous route through the Gila Range, and that took him all of one day and part of the next. Salt Lake City was the closest thing to a bonafide metropolis to be found between Denver and San Francisco. It marked the western terminus of the division that was his responsibility, and his job had often brought him here. It never ceased to amaze Ethan how quickly the town had grown. Just in the five years since he'd first set eyes on the place, it had tripled in size. Once a small but thriving Mormon community, Salt Lake City was the biggest boom-town in the territory. And there was no indication that the growth was going to slow down. The Mormons and the "gentiles" who had come by the hundreds in the past few years lived in a kind of wary harmony.

Assuming that by now John Tattersall had conveyed, by telegram, his suspicions to Holladay, Ethan expected to find a note from the Stagecoach King awaiting his arrival at the Palace Hotel, the hostelry located at the corner of Main and Fillmore Streets while he customarily stayed while in Salt Lake City. But there was no message. He spent the day roaming the streets, stopping in a few saloons for a drink or two. There seemed to be a watering hole or gambling den on every street corner, so he didn't want for a place to cool his heels and wet his whistle. He didn't see anyone he knew until he reached the Gilded Lily. That was where Clooney, the gambler, came up to him as he stood at the bar nursing a shot glass full of good whiskey.

"I hear you caught the road agents," said Clooney. "Congratulations."

"What are you doing here?"

"I've got a job here."

"You work for Ike Spoon?"

"I do now. I run a table for him. Poker. Care to sit in? I'm betting the Overland pays you pretty well for what you do. I wouldn't mind relieving you of some of that money." He grinned.

"No thanks. I don't gamble."

"You gamble all the time," said Clooney. "But, whatever you say. It's a shame, if you ask me."

"What is?"

"That you don't play. You'd be good at it. You've got to have nerves of steel to win at poker. And you've got to have a lot of stamina. It's when the game's been going for three or four hours that the nerves start to wear thin, and you're tired and prone to make a mistake. You can't start to worry when the cards are running against you. You've just got to keep playing, keep your losses at a minimum, and wait for the tide to turn. And you also have to be a real good judge of the odds in every situation. I think you fit that bill."

Ethan shook his head. "No, thanks. Not interested."

Clooney shrugged. "Well, there is no shortage of victims in this town." He chuckled. "Ike takes ten percent off the top of everything I make, money and gold dust both. But that doesn't matter. I'll make more in a month here than I would all year back east. We've got prospectors and miners, soldier boys and cowboys, and they all take one look at me and want to buy into my game. Already had a couple of gold hunters throw their claim titles into the pot. They both lost, too. But they seemed to take it pretty well."

"Long as you run an honest game, most of them will."

"I don't need to cheat to win," said Clooney. He didn't take offense. It was just a simple statement of fact.

"I'm glad to hear it."

Clooney said he had to get back to work, and left Ethan's side just as the Overland troubleshooter saw Ben Riles stroll into the saloon. The jehu paused just inside the doors and scanned the crowd. He spotted Ethan and gave him a nod, then worked his way over to the bar. The reins man ordered a beer and downed half the brew before taking a breath. He smacked his lips and wiped the foam off his dusty mustache.

"You just get in?" asked Ethan.

"Yeah. And guess who I brought with me."

"Who might that be?"

"Your friend Tattersall. I hear you and he had sort of a falling out in Jacobsville."

"Tattersall can go to hell."

"Well, he said he was going to make it plain to Mr. Holladay the kind of man you are."

"I'm sure he's given Holladay an earful."

Riles nodded. "Not too much of one. Holladay was at

the station when we rolled in. They talked for a few
minutes, and then parted company. Mr. Holladay left on
the next stage."

"Holladay is gone?'

"Yep."

Ethan was surprised. He'd felt sure that the Stagecoach
King would want a word or two with him before departing
Salt Lake City, and he wasn't sure if Holladay's abrupt
departure was a good sign or a bad one.

"Just between you and me," said Riles. "Did you let one
of them road agents ride?"

"Were you held up today, Ben?"

"Nope."

"Then what are you worried about?"

"Tomorrow," Riles continued. "Talk in Jacobsville is
that Wesley Grome will hang. Some folks don't think he'd
have the nerve to ride with robbers and risk getting shot at.
Not to say that he has any friends there, because he doesn't.
And most of them won't lose any sleep if he does swing."

"Will you lose any sleep over it?"

Riles thought about that for a moment, then shook his
head. "No, I guess not. What about you?"

Ethan finished his drink. He wanted another one, but he
didn't want to linger if Ben Riles was going to keep talking
about Wesley Grome and the hangman. When the barkeep
wandered down the mahogany, Ethan shook his head. Riles
knew this meant the Overland troubleshooter was preparing
to take his leave.

"Hold on," said the reins man. "Before you go, I've got
some news from Wolftrap."

"Is Julie okay?"

"Well, that's a good question. Joe Cathcott showed up
at her doorstep yesterday."

"What?"

Riles nodded. "I'm not pulling your leg, Ethan. Lord
knows that ain't something I would joke about. No, this is
the gospel truth. He asked her to forgive him. Or so she

told me when I rolled through early this morning. Said he would walk the straight and narrow from now on if she took him back in."

Ethan scoffed at that. "She's too smart for that." He studied Ben's expression—and experienced a sinking sensation. "She didn't."

"Yeah, she did. She took him back."

"That can't be. You've got it wrong somehow."

"I saw him with my own two eyes, Ethan. He's moved back in, acting like nothing ever happened, like he didn't just ride off and leave her there alone all this time."

Ethan was hit by waves of disbelief, anger, and then a profound melancholy as the full realization of what he had lost came to him. He knew Julie loved him, and that she couldn't love Joe. In fact, she'd told him that she never had loved her husband; not really. But love didn't have anything to do with her decision. She could have Joe Cathcott. She couldn't have Ethan Payne. And above all, she was lonely. God only knew how many times she had told him how lonely she was. . . .

Riles was sipping his beer now, and watching him like a hawk over the rim of the glass, so Ethan tried to keep his composure, hoping he could fool the jehu into believing that this news was of no real consequence to him. He didn't want Riles or anyone else to know how much this hurt.

"Well," he said, and his voice sounded hollow to his own ears, "I hope he sticks this time. And that he treats her better than he has in the past."

"She asked me to tell you when I saw you," said Riles. "And she said she didn't want any trouble."

"No," said Ethan flatly, pushing wearily away from the bar. "There won't be any trouble."

"I don't think she was worried that you'd be the one to start any. But Joe. Well, you know how he is. Hair-trigger temper. And as we all know, he can be a violent man. First time you ride into Wolftrap and he sees the way Julie looks at you, or how you look at her, that's when the fur may fly."

"He'll just have to get used to me being around," said Ethan curtly. "I am still the troubleshooter for this division. I can't just ride around Wolftrap all the time." He didn't think he needed to mention that yesterday he had done just that. Now he was doubly glad that he had. Because there was no telling what might have happened if he'd shown up and found Cathcott sitting there like he owned the place.

He took his leave of Ben Riles and the Gilded Lily. On the boardwalk he built a smoke with unsteady hands, cupping the sulfur match against a drift of dust from a passing wagon. It was getting late in the day, and the respectable businesses were beginning to sweep out and shut down. But the saloons and gambling dens and dancehalls would go until late into the night. He could hear drunken laughter and the clangor of an out-of-tune piano from the Blue Wing across Main Street. It was a lonely sound, he thought. Now, suddenly, he knew how Julie had felt all this time. Loneliness was like a heavy weight on his shoulders—and on his heart. Yellow light was spilling out of doors and windows as the blue shadows of evening lengthened across the wide, rutted street. The light gave him no comfort, nor did the frosty stars spangling the night sky, or the cold, probing fingers of the wind that was whispering a lonesome lament in his ears. Keeping to the shadows, he wearily bent his steps for the Palace Hotel.

# CHAPTER TWENTY

Julie Cathcott dreaded the day when Ethan Payne would show up at the Wolftrap Station. She knew that day would come. It was inevitable. Ethan couldn't do his job and completely avoid the station for very long. As the days turned into weeks, and there was still no sign of him, the apprehension she experienced became almost unbearable.

The way Joe was acting just made the waiting worse. She had wanted to believe him when he swore to her that he was a changed man who had seen the error of his ways and only needed a second chance to put everything right between them. At first he was on his best behavior, and she almost dared hope. But in the end he proved that her suspicions were correct—that it was all just an act, that he was just pretending to be changed, and that Joe Cathcott was the same man he had always been: crude, brutish, and overbearing. Of course, Julie began having second thoughts about her decision to take him back in. She had cured the problem of being alone, yes. But was the cure worse than the ailment, in this case? At times she thought so.

Joe refused to tell her where he had been all these months, and he could never give her a straight answer when she asked him why he had left her in the first place. Julie thought he owed her that much, at least. Hadn't she done everything he'd asked of her? She had let him walk all over her, abuse her mentally and physically, and not once had she given him any indication that she was leaving, when she had every right to—when, in her opinion, any other woman with even a shred of self-respect would have left. She kept after him until, finally, he lost his temper and hit her a backhanded blow. He was the same old Joe, sure enough.

The second time he hit her was when he found out about Ethan. That was inevitable, too. Julie had toyed with the idea of telling him about it, straight out, working on the theory that since just about everyone in this division of the Overland had long suspected that there had been something going on between her and the troubleshooter, Joe would hear the rumor sooner or later, and it would be better if it came from her. But then she realized that it wouldn't be better. Joe wasn't the kind of man who would give her credit for being honest. She would suffer to the same degree whether she told him or someone else did. So she decided to keep it to herself, and in that way bought a few more days without being hit.

When he hit her this time, Julie hit back. She was as surprised as he was by her reaction. But she was mad, as mad as she had ever been. How dare he take offense at what she had done. He was the one who had run out, leaving her alone and lonely in this Godforsaken place, not knowing whether he was alive or dead, whether he would ever return. And he was angry at her?

"Then why didn't you just let him move in here?" Joe asked her.

"I would have let him. But he didn't want to."

"So you were just his little whore."

She tried to hit him again then, but he caught her arm by the wrist. "I ought to kill you," he said. "I got every right to, after what you done."

"Go ahead," she snapped, defiantly. "Go ahead and kill me, and see what happens to you when Ethan finds out."

Joe acted like he didn't care what Ethan Payne found out, but there was a glimmer of fear in his eyes, and she saw it, and knew that her husband was afraid of the Overland troubleshooter. He didn't hit her again. In the days to follow he began to drink more heavily than usual. He spent most of the day sitting in the station drinking cheap liquor and brooding—and leaving Julie and Manolo to do all the work. Julie thought that her husband was brooding over her being with Ethan. It was gnawing at his guts day and night. She didn't mind seeing him suffer. It was just his pride, after all. She refused to believe that he actually loved her and was suffering for that reason. No man could treat a woman he loved the way Joe treated her.

"I'll kill the bastard," Joe told Ben Riles one day. "You see if I don't. He better walk wide around me or I'll shoot him down like a dog, so help me." His words were slurred by the liquor.

Riles just shook his head. "Don't be a fool, Joe. Ethan is not one to trifle with. And he's bound to show up eventually. He can't help that, and you can't stop it. He's the Overland troubleshooter for this stretch and this is an Overland station. And you're an Overland employee, don't forget that. Just let it go. What's done is done. Live and let live, that's my motto."

"Well it ain't my motto," growled Joe. "You tell him when you see him that him and me, we're due a reckoning."

"Okay," said Riles, with a wink at Julie that Joe was too drunk to see. "I'll tell him next time I see him."

Julie knew that Ben would do no such thing. But others would. Joe made sure that every driver that passed through Wolftrap knew he had an account to settle with the troubleshooter. In this way he threw down the gauntlet, and virtually guaranteed that word would get back to Ethan that a challenge had been made. The only question was whether Ethan would accept the challenge. Julie was afraid that he would. Ethan was a proud man, prouder than he himself realized. And he had a reputation to protect—one that stood him in good stead in his line of work. If he was seen to back down from Joe Cathcott, it would just make his job more perilous than it already was. These days, most road agents and horse thieves steered clear of the division because they didn't want to tangle with Ethan Payne. If rumors got out that the troubleshooter was a coward, that would change. It was something Ethan couldn't afford to let happen.

Two weeks passed, then a third, and still there was no sign of the troubleshooter. Joe started telling the drivers that Ethan was a yellow coward, knowing that would get back to Ethan, too.

And then, at the end of the third week, Manolo disappeared—and one of the Overland horses disappeared with him. The word went down the line, and a couple of days later, Ethan Payne showed up at the station.

Fortunately, Joe wasn't at Wolftrap that particular morning. He was gone to Jacobsville to get some supplies—which meant as many bottles of liquor as he could buy and just the bare necessities where everything else was concerned. He would be gone all day, and perhaps well into the night. Occasionally he stayed over in Jacobsville, if he got too drunk to make the trip back, or if one of the dancehall girls or calico queens caught his eye. As she watched Ethan ride up on his dun gelding, Julie could only pray such would be the case on this trip.

"Hello, Julie," said Ethan, sitting his horse in front of the station, waiting for an invitation to step down. "Been a long time."

She gazed up at him, and realized just how much she had missed this man.

"Too long," she replied softly, confused by the array of emotions that the sight of him awoke in her. Almost two months had passed since that stormy day when he had left Wolftrap with Ben Riles, on the trail of those road agents who had held up the stage and killed the shotgun guard who was now buried out behind the station. "Come inside," she said, with a sigh. "Joe's gone to Jacobsville. I have some coffee brewed."

He stepped down out of the saddle and followed her into

the common room, removing his hat and black duster while she poured him a cup of java.

"I don't know when Joe will be back," she said as she placed the cup on the table in front of him. It was a veiled warning. But she could look at Ethan and tell that it didn't matter to him if Joe Cathcott showed up or not. He wasn't worried. And the fact that he wasn't worried her even more. This was not a man who would back down from a fight, and she could only hope that Joe would.

"Is he treating you well?" he asked.

"As well as can be expected." Thank God, she thought, that the bruises from the last time Joe had struck her had faded.

Sipping the coffee, Ethan said, "So Manolo stole a horse and made dust. I can't say that I was surprised by the news."

"You never liked him." Julie sat down at the table across from the troubleshooter. "But you don't know the whole truth. Joe hated Manolo. Tried to drive him away. But Manolo wouldn't go. I think he was . . . was worried about me."

"So why did he leave, and steal a horse in the leaving?"

Julie sighed again and looked out through the open door at the distant horizon. "I think he did that because he knew it would bring you here."

"I see. So that I would have to kill Joe."

"Which, where Manolo is concerned, would be a good thing. Especially for me."

"That would mean Manolo cares a lot about you, Julie, if he's willing to be branded a horse thief, and face a hangman's noose, just to free you from your husband."

"Yes," she said, in a small voice.

Ethan sipped his coffee for a moment, thinking things over, and a moment passed before he spoke again. "So did Manolo have reason to worry?"

Julie kept looking out through the doorway.

"I guess what I'm asking is if Joe has changed at all."

"Not much," she confessed.

Ethan drank the rest of his coffee. Before he could get up to get himself some more, Julie took his cup and went to the stove. As she poured, she said, "The day before Manolo left, Joe got up and started drinking even earlier than he usually does. By mid-morning he was as drunk as I've ever seen him. He was sitting right there where you are when he suddenly jumped up and said somebody was outside. I told him it was only Manolo, but he said no, it was you. And he grabbed his rifle and went outside on the porch and took a shot at Manolo, who was over by the corral. Luckily, he was so drunk that he didn't hit Manolo or any of the stock. I think Manolo wanted to kill him right then and there. He had that look in his eye when I went out to make sure he was okay, and he was handling that big knife of his like he wanted to use it on Joe. I begged him not to. The next morning he was gone." She brought the fresh cup back to the table. "I'll reimburse the company for the loss of the horse, Ethan."

"How? You don't have any money, do you? Holladay buys the best stock he can find. That's why we used to have so much trouble with horse thieves. That horse would cost you a hundred, maybe a hundred and fifty dollars."

She shook her head. "No, of course I don't have that kind of money."

"No," he said dryly. "I thought not. It all goes for Joe's whiskey, right?"

"So what will you do? Hunt Manolo down? Kill him?"

Ethan smiled. "I think I'll just save myself the trouble and reimburse the company myself."

Julie's face lit up. "Oh, Ethan! I—I don't know how to thank you."

"I didn't really come because of Manolo. I figured he'd had enough of Joe and that was why he left. I came to see you, Julie. To see how you were doing. Ben Riles told me the other day that as far as he could tell, Joe was up to his old tricks. Now Ben wouldn't even tell me that much if he wasn't concerned about you. You know how he is. He doesn't want to start anything."

"Ben's a good man," said Julie. It was all she could think to say.

"Yes, he is. So—are you happy?"

"Yes."

"You're not a very good liar," said Ethan, smiling at her.

She walked to the doorway, putting her back to him, and he watched how the wind that always seemed to be blowing across the desert flats whipped her long brown skirt and the tendrils of yellow hair that had escaped the bun she'd tied it all up in that morning. "I wish you hadn't come, Ethan. Joe swears he's going to kill you."

"So I've heard." There was more than a trace of contempt in his voice. "Julie . . ."

"Don't. Please don't say it, Ethan. I've made my choice. Maybe it was a mistake. But there's no going back. He's my husband and I'm stuck with that."

"No going back," murmured Ethan. "I've often told myself that very thing." He drew a long breath. "Guess I'll be moving on, then. Thanks for the coffee."

He stood, gathered up his hat and coat, and stepped out into the shade of the dogtrot. It was all Julie could do to refrain from putting her arms around him and holding him tight. She so wanted to hold him, and to be held. But if she did that he might not leave. And he had to go, or someone would die. She remembered their last morning together, when she had awakened to find him standing out by the corral, oblivious to the cold-to-the-bone zephyr that was buffeting him. Ethan was a strong man, and brave. Gentle at times, too. He was everything in a man that she had always wanted. Except she could not have his whole heart and soul. He would not give them to her. He had given them to someone else in the past, and suffered for it. So she resolved to let him go. It was the only thing she could do.

She followed him out onto the dogtrot and wondered why he had stopped to stand at the top of the steps, and what he was looking at—until she moved and saw Joe standing out on the hardpack between the station and the corral, a sawed-off shotgun in his white-knuckled grasp.

"Prepare to meet your Maker, you son of a bitch," he sneered.

Julie recovered from her shock, realizing that Joe must have seen Ethan's dun gelding from a distance, and had left the wagon down the trace a ways to Indian-up on foot.

"Put that scattergun down, Joe," said Ethan quietly. "Julie's in the line of fire."

Julie brushed past the Overland troubleshooter and ran out to stand halfway between the two men.

"For God's sake, Joe," she whispered. "Don't do this!"

"Tryin' to protect your lover, eh?"

She could smell the liquor on him even at ten paces. "Yes," she said. "He was my lover. And I don't want to see him hurt."

"And what about me? I've got a right to kill the low-down snake what's been messin' with my wife. I kill him and there's not a jury in this country that would find me guilty."

"He'll kill you," she said. "Don't you understand?"

Joe advanced on her, menacingly, trying to cow her into moving, but Julie resolutely stood her ground. It was more defiance, and it infuriated him. He backhanded her, and took vicious pleasure in seeing her sprawled in the yellow dust, a trickle of blood appearing at the corner of her mouth. He loomed over her, his stubbled features contorted with rage.

"I ought to kill you too, you whore."

"Cathcott."

Joe looked up and saw Ethan coming off the dogtrot, his hand resting on the Walker Colt that was still holstered at his side. The troubleshooter's eyes blazed with anger, and Joe felt a sudden surge of panic as he saw his own death reflected there.

With a strangled cry he swung the greener in Ethan's direction and fired, full bore. He squeezed the triggers too soon, though, before the scattergun was leveled, and only some of the buckshot hit the mark. Enough, though, to cut Ethan's left leg out from under him. The troubleshooter fell, but when he did, it was to the side, and Joe's elation at seeing him go down was short-lived. The next thing Joe saw was the Walker Colt coming out of the holster, swinging up toward him—and he realized, with a sinking feeling in the pit of his stomach, that he'd made a fatal mistake by firing both barrels of the shotgun at the same time, and not reserving one to make sure Ethan Payne was dead. That was his last thought an instant before the bullet drilled him in the midsection. He doubled over with a low, animal sound escaping his lips. Then the Walker Colt spoke again. Joe didn't hear the second gunshot, because the bullet entered his skull and killed him instantly.

Stunned, Julie sat there in the dust and stared at her husband's corpse.

Feeling cold clean through, Ethan managed to get to his feet. Blood was filling his left boot. He hobbled over to the dun gelding and found he could not lift his leg to fit foot into stirrup. That perturbed him. It also slowed him down long enough for Julie to reach him.

"You're hurt bad, Ethan," she said, her voice remarkably calm and composed. "Come, let me help you inside."

"No."

"Don't be so stubborn! How far do you think you'll get?"

"Far as I'm meant to."

She balled up a fist and hit him in the chest.

"Damn you, Ethan Payne! Get in that station this instant!"

"Sorry, Julie."

"It's my fault, not yours."

"No. It's nobody's fault. Things just happen. And all we can do is learn to live through them."

"You were just defending yourself, I know that."

"In a way, though, he was within his rights to do what he did."

"That kind of talk won't help anyone now."

"It'll be better if I go."

"It would be better if you *stayed*."

He looked at her, wanting to stay, but knowing he wouldn't. Not for as long as she was hoping he would. Because now that he had killed her husband right in front of her eyes, more than ever before, there were too many memories coming between them.

"Julie . . ."

She put her finger to his lips, and a single tear coursed her dusty cheek. He said no more, but let her help him into the station.


Julie dug eight double-ought pellets out of his left leg, then cleaned and dressed the wounds. He spoke of leaving Wolf-trap on the next day's stage, but she wouldn't hear of it. The trauma of the wounds left him weak and a little feverish for a day or two. He stayed in bed all the next day, and she brought him food and changed the dressings. The reins man and shotgun guard on the stage that rolled in that morning buried Joe Cathcott. The driver came in to see for himself how Ethan was doing.

"You want me to tell Tattersall anything when I get to Salt Lake City?" asked the jehu.

"Yeah," said Ethan flatly. "Tell him I shot and killed Joe Cathcott." It wasn't the message he wanted to give Tattersall, but it would have to do.

The driver lingered, expecting there to be more. "That's it?" he asked.

"That's all."

"Well, you want me to tell him it was a fair fight?"

"It won't matter to him whether it was or not."

The driver nodded and left the room without another word.

Julie slept in the common room, on blankets laid out on the floor by the fireplace, for the first two nights. On the third day Ethan was feeling better, and that afternoon he got up and tested his leg. It hurt like hell, but she assured him there was no infection, that the leg would be fine. He would not allow her to sleep on the floor for the third night in a row, and changed places with her. Few words passed between them, otherwise. Ethan didn't know what to say about killing Joe, and small talk seemed ludicrous at this point. One thing was certain: he and Julie were finished. He hadn't actually been sure of that even when he'd learned of Joe's return. But now he was certain. He had killed Julie's husband and no matter how she really felt about Joe—that part of it would always remain something of a mystery to him—the killing was a chasm between them that neither would be able to cross. It saddened him to think of it, but this chapter of his life was closed. They seemed to be closing pretty quickly.

That first jehu through Wolftrap after the killing took word of it back to Jacobsville, and from there it went to Salt Lake City by wire, and Ethan figured in a matter of days Ben Holladay would know what had happened. Tattersall would make certain of that. A few days later, Ben Riles rolled in on a stage, bearing the telegram Ethan had been expecting. It was from the Stagecoach King.

KILLING CATHCOTT NOT IN MY BEST INTERESTS STOP
SURE YOU AGREE STOP YOUR SERVICES NO LONGER RE
QUIRED STOP GOOD LUCK STOP

"I have to admit," said Riles, "that I never have been sure about you, Ethan. Sure about what kind of man you really are, I mean. Guess you know that by now. But if it's any consolation, I think Mr. Holladay is wrong to hogleg you for this. Julie told me it was in self defense. But she really didn't need to tell me something I already knew. That Joe was just hellbent on trying you, and that was his mistake."

"Doesn't matter," said Ethan, sitting at the table in the station, drinking coffee. "I was going to quit anyway."

Riles cocked his head to one side. "How come?"

"I lied about Grome. He wasn't part of the robbery. I did let one of the road agents go."

"Why did you do a thing like that?"

"He was an old friend. We grew up together. Came out west together, thinking we'd find fame and fortune." Ethan smiled faintly. "Neither one of us found either. He took a wrong turn, ended up an outlaw. But he saved my life once, back in California. I couldn't let him swing."

Riles nodded. "So you let him go. You think he'll rob any more Overland stages?"

Ethan shook his head. "I think he's about as far from here as a man can get, by now."

"Then you did your job, which was to prevent that gang from committing any more robberies. And you didn't have to sign your friend's death warrant to do it. I'd say that was probably the right thing to do, under the circumstances."

"Is that what you would have done?"

Riles smiled. "We just never know what we're gonna do, until we're faced with a situation, now do we? But we're bound to make mistakes when it's like that. And when we do make one, we have to do two things right after. We have to learn our lesson. And, just as important, we have to forgive ourselves. Seems to me that's the only way to live with yourself."

"I think you might just be right."

"Well, that happens every now and then." Riles thought about it, then stuck out a hand. "Good luck, Ethan. Try to keep the wind at your back and your powder dry."

"I'll try."

Riles turned away, but when he got to the door that

opened onto the dogtrot he saw Julie standing out at the stage, talking to a woman passenger while the shotgun guard switched out the teams.

"What about Julie?" asked Riles. "She know you're leaving?"

"She's known it for a while."

"Good woman."

"She deserves better," said Ethan. "I'm sure you'd agree."

Riles nodded. He didn't look around, so Ethan couldn't see his expression. "Yeah, I reckon so." He paused, then stepped across the threshold, and said, in parting, "But she could do worse, too."

# *Author's Notes*

Prior to the gold rush, the central event of this novel, California was a thinly populated frontier colony with just a few sleepy coastal hamlets serving a sea trade that consisted of whalers putting in for wood or water and merchantmen arriving to carry off cargos of hides and tallow. Inland, there were some cattle ranches and a few Franciscan missions. That was about it.

This all changed rather quickly. John Augustus Sutter, a German-born Swiss, fled creditors after his business in Germany went bankrupt and then wrangled a grant of 50,000 acres of land from the Mexican governor of California, Juan Bautista Alvarado, in 1839. Sutter built a stockade and called his place, located in the central valley east of San Francisco, New Helvetia. Within ten years he was producing 40,000 bushels of wheat a year and owned 12,000 head of cattle, 10,000 sheep, 2,000 horses and mules, and 1,000 hogs. He had so many Indians working as field hands that four or five steers had to be slaughtered daily just to feed them all. But Sutter wasn't content with this success. He had grandiose dreams, and started many projects. For some of them he required lumber, and lumber required a sawmill. So he entered into a partnership with James Wilson Marshall, a carpenter from New Jersey. Marshall picked a spot on the south fork of the American River, 50 miles northeast of Sutter's Fort, for the sawmill. His crew consisted of ten Indians who had previously worked for Sutter, and ten

Americans (the majority of them veterans of the Mormon
Battalion). They built cabins and dug a millrace. On Mon-
day, January 24, 1848, Marshall was making his morning
inspection of the work when he spotted several gold nuggets in the water. He took the nuggets to Sutter, who was
not happy that gold had been discovered. "Of course I knew
nothing of the extent of the discovery," he later wrote, "but
I was satisfied, whether it amounted to much or little, that
it would greatly interfere with my plans." A gold rush
would lure away his workers. And gold seekers would in-
vade his property and run off his stock.

Sutter thought initially that he could keep the discovery
quiet, which was quite naïve. Within a month the news of
the gold find had spread throughout California. By May
there were a few hundred gold seekers in the field. By the
middle of the summer there were 4,000. By the end of the
year there was between 8,000 and 10,000. In the year 1848,
an estimated quarter of a million dollars of gold was taken
out of the ground. This was only the beginning. Colonel
R. B. Mason, the new military governor of California
(which had just passed into American hands), sent a tea
caddy filled with about $3,900 worth of gold samples to
Washington. President James K. Polk was pleased that gold
had been found, since he wanted the nation's new territorial
acquisitions to be populated as quickly as possible. There
was nothing like talk of gold to spur a mass migration. The
gold from Colonel Mason's tea caddy was placed on display in the War Department, and Polk mentioned the gold
find in his message to the second session of the 30th Con-
gress. The news of the gold strike was reported in newspapers around the world. "We are on the brink of the Age
of Gold!" declared news editor Horace Greeley in the *New
York Daily Tribune* on December 9, 1848. "We don't see
any links of probability missing in the golden chain by
which Hope is drawing her thousands of disciples to the
new El Dorado, where fortune lies abroad upon the surface
of the earth as plentiful as the mud in our streets."

The "thousands of disciples" began to flock to California. Many of them joined "associations" like the New York Overland Mutual Protection Association for California—or the Buckeye Rovers. They pitched in to buy supplies for the long journey, and made their traveling arrangements, deciding whether to go overland or by sea or a combination of the two. There were three major routes: overland by one of several trails, clear across the continent; down the Atlantic coasts of both North and South America, around Cape Horn, and up the Pacific coasts of the western hemisphere's continents; and by sea as far as Panama or Nicaragua or Mexico, then by land to the Pacific, and by boat again up the coast to California. And then there was Rufus Porter's "aerial locomotive," which, claimed Porter, would carry passengers over mountain and prairie to California in just three days. Unfortunately, Mr. Porter's aerial locomotive never got off the ground. The overland route was shorter—about 10,000 miles shorter than going 'round the Horn—and it was cheaper, too. An estimated 30,000 Argonauts chose this route in 1849. There were a good many perils along the way, and hundreds never reached their destination. Those who went by sea were faced with the prospect of a rough and perilous voyage that took anywhere from four to eight months, unless one caught a ride on a clipper ship, which could make the journey in 100 days or less. Of those who chose the third option—crossing Central America and taking passage on a ship along the Pacific coast—most went by way of the isthmus at Panama (as do Ethan Payne and Gil Stark in this story). A treaty signed in 1846 had given U.S. citizens free transit across the Republic of New Granada (Grenada). The journey across the isthmus usually began at Chagres, where the ruins of the fortress of San Lorenzo, raided in 1670 by the pirate Morgan, loomed out of the jungle. A reporter named Bayard Taylor made this trip in the summer of 1849, on assignment for the *New York Tribune*. His boatmen were "Ambrosio

Mendez, of mixed Indian and Spanish race" and "Juan Crispen Bega, almost entirely of Negro blood."

Once they reached California, the prospectors flocked to the foothills of the Sierra Nevada and gold camps with names like Hangtown and Grizzly Flats and Rich Bar. Some did indeed strike it rich. One young New Yorker spent six weeks on the middle fork of the American River and gathered up over $20,000 in gold, including a nugget that weighed fourteen pounds. A couple of Frenchmen found $5,000 in gold in a hole made by an uprooted tree. In three months John Sullivan, formerly an ox-team driver, took $26,000 out of a gulley on the Stanislaus River, and used this stake to found a banking concern in San Francisco. But generally, panning for gold was extremely hard work. Taylor wrote: "Those who ... return home disappointed say they have been humbugged about the gold, when in fact they have humbugged themselves about the work."

Within a few years large mining companies had moved into the area. Shafts were dug into the earth, sometimes 700 feet deep. Entire rivers, like the American, were diverted from their original course. Hydraulic mining tore thousands of tons of gravel and dirt off the sides of mountains with high-velocity streams of water—millions of gallons a day—shot through eight-inch nozzles.

In seven years the gold rush produced $350 million worth of gold. It seems like a lot, but was in fact considerably less than would be taken in later strikes in Nevada and the Dakotas. In 1853 there were an estimated 100,000 Argonauts in the California gold fields. But the gold rush, for all practical purposes, was over within a year or two. Of the 400,000 gold seekers who had participated, the vast majority were no better or worse off than they had been before striking out for California. Some returned home, but many remained in California and settled down. Perhaps the most important product of the gold rush was the quick entry of California into the Union; only two years after John Marshall made his find at Sutter's Mill, California became the thirty-first state.

The opening of the west in the decade prior to the Civil War required men of vision, and one of these was most certainly Ben Holladay. In 1846, Holladay—born in 1819 as one of seven children on a poor Kentucky farm—mortgaged what little he had, bought fourteen wagons and sixty mules, and took a cargo of trade goods to Santa Fe. A few years later he started up a trade business with the Mormons, who had not too long before relocated to Utah to escape persecution back East. He also drove a herd of cattle to California during the gold rush heyday, and made a killing; the Pacific Mail Steamship Company paid him thirty cents a pound on the hoof for beef that had cost him less than a penny a pound to deliver.

Holladay was wealthy enough even then to have retired and lived the rest of his life in the lap of luxury. Instead, he went into partnership with William Russell, senior partner of the freighting firm of Russell, Majors & Waddell, which operated both the Central Overland stage line and the Pony Express. In league with Russell and Secretary of War John Floyd, Holladay entered into a scheme of his own making. Contracting to deliver Missouri flour purchased by the Army at seven dollars a hundredweight to outposts in Utah, Holladay took the cargo to Denver instead, and sold it for forty dollars a hundredweight. Then he bought Mormon flour at a dollar a hundredweight and delivered it to the Army posts. Secretary Floyd went along—for a share of the illicit profits. Thanks to Floyd, Holladay was also able to buy Army wagons and livestock at auction as "surplus," which they were not, for pennies on the dollar. As always, it paid to have friends in high places.

Not long after that, Holladay bought out Russell, Majors & Waddell, to whom he had loaned large sums of money with the Central Overland stage line as collateral. He paid $100,000 for the struggling line—lock, stock and barrel. The Overland extended 1,200 miles from Atchison to Salt

Lake City. (From that point to the Pacific coast was handled by the Overland Mail Company, an entirely different entity, and one not owned by Holladay.) Holladay was determined to make the Central Overland (hereafter called simply the Overland) into the best stage line in the world. He expected his drivers to maintain an average speed of five miles an hour. This required good drivers and even better stock; Holladay went to great lengths to acquire the best men and teams. Before long stages were making the run from Atchison to Salt Lake City in eleven days. These were Concord coaches—also the best money could buy—and Holladay painted them red and had "Holladay Overland Mail & Express" in gilt plastered on the sides. Charging fares of $150 for the whole Atchison to Salt Lake run, Holladay's passenger revenues soared to $60,000 a month. The company generally made twice that much hauling valuable cargo, like bullion—and more still thanks to a subsidy from the United States Mail. In its heyday, the Overland consisted of 20,000 vehicles, 15,000 employees, and 150,000 head of stock.

Holladay was a ruthless businessman. When Denver merchant David Butterfield decided to challenge Holladay with the Butterfield Overland Despatch, Holladay sent spies to infiltrate the competition. Some said he also hired gunmen to dress up like Indians in warpaint to raid the Butterfield stages. Before long, Ben Holladay owned the Butterfield Overland Despatch. He knew, however, that the next challenge would be one he could not meet. The railroads threatened his empire, and the railroads were more powerful than even the Stagecoach King. In 1866, Holladay sold his company to Wells, Fargo for $1.5 million in cash and another $300,000 in stocks.

Holladay owned more—much more—than the Overland. He ran a fleet of sixteen steamers, as well as slaughterhouses, packing plants, and gold and silver mines. He had an opulent home in Washington, D.C., at 1131 K Street, within walking distance of the White House. In New

York City he owned a mansion on Fifth Avenue and north of the city he had a 200-room palace on the 1,000-acre Ophir Farm. He was one of the most astute, influential, and ruthless businessmen of his time. He had many enemies, and did some underhanded things, but Ben Holladay was the kind of hard-driving visionary needed to tame the West.

# JASON MANNING

## THE OUTLAW TRAIL

Young Sam Bass lit out for Texas with visions of a cowboy's life dancing in his head. Honest hard work got the Midwestern farm boy on a real life cattle drive to Dodge City. But soon Sam made a fatal choice, and found himself in Deadwood, South Dakota, a place that could turn even the best men bad. Once Sam Bass picked up a gun and robbed a stagecoach, there was no turning back. The law wanted him dead, fate wanted him in Texas, and the outlaw trail waited in between.

# READ THESE MASTERFUL WESTERNS BY MATT BRAUN

*"Matt Braun is a master storyteller of frontier history."*
—Elmer Kelton

### THE KINCAIDS

Golden Spur Award-winner THE KINCAIDS tells the classic saga of America at its most adventurous through the eyes of three generations who made laws, broke laws, and became legends in their time.

### GENTLEMAN ROGUE

Hell's Half Acre is Fort Worth's violent ghetto of whorehouses, gaming dives and whisky wells. And for shootist and gambler Luke Short, it's a place to make a stand. But he'll have to stake his claim from behind the barrel of a loaded gun . . .

### RIO GRANDE

Tom Stuart, a hard-drinking, fast-talking steamboat captain, has a dream of building a shipping empire that will span the Gulf of Mexico to New Orleans. Now, Stuart is plunged into the fight of a lifetime—and to the winner will go the mighty Rio Grande . . .

### THE BRANNOCKS

The three Brannock brothers were reunited in a boomtown called Denver. And on a frontier brimming with opportunity and exploding with danger, vicious enemies would test their courage—and three beautiful women would claim their love . . .